M S O M I

R.L. Gunn

VANTAGE PRESS
New York

This is a work of fiction. Any similarity between the names,
characters, and places in this book and any persons,
living or dead, is purely coincidental.

Cover design by Susan Thomas

FIRST EDITION

Copyright © 2004 by R.L.Gunn

Published by Vantage Press, Inc.
419 Park Ave. South, New York, NY 10016

Manufactured in the United States of America
ISBN: 0-533-14738-7

Library of Congress Catalog Card No.: 2003096164

0 9 8 7 6 5 4 3 2 1

MSOMI

Contents

Preface

It is never a simple matter to give credit to all who contribute to a novel such as *Msomi*. Even the name came out of my distant past. It was the name of a gentle, soft-spoken, very black African who sat in the stands in back of me as I bowled in the league each week, and applauded my efforts. The end of the season ended my contacts with him—still the name lingered in my memory.

A change of lifestyles, which included retirement from employment as a psychologist for the Veterans Administration, and a move to Del Webb's Sun City, Roseville, California, provided an opportunity to put many of my thoughts into words. I became a member of the Scribes Club of Sun City, Roseville, California.

The novel, *Msomi*, was critiqued from the beginning to the end by a small group of fellow writers, spearheaded by Jacklyn Brown. She brought experience, patience, and interest to our efforts and kept us flowing to completion.

1

Mbondu's Prophecy

Brilliant flashes of lightning lit the African night, and rolling thunder shook the house like a leopard shakes a monkey. The storm increased in fury. Trees bent to the ground as they gave way to the driving rain and the gusting winds, which howled like some creature from the fires of hell.

"It will be a long night," sighed Ibanga. The tall, black, skinny woman of the village was present to once again perform her midwifery duties in the prosperous city home of a former villager, Daniel Msomi. She glanced across the room at the grizzled, nearly toothless elder of the village tribe.

Mbondu's attention was so intent upon the approaching storm that he did not acknowledge her comment. He was a tribal doctor, from a village on the outskirts of the city, brought in to assist in the impending birth. Clearly apprehensive about the raging storm, he paced back and forth from one window to another.

Low moans came with increasing frequency from the room where a birth was imminent. All was in readiness, but the son was not quite ready to leave the world of his ancestors and enter the world of man.

Daniel Msomi, the soon-to-be father, came from a long line of tribal doctors; his father expected him to follow in their path. In mission school, he proved to be a quick learner and, in time, finished his education at one of the best universities in England. His experiences in England had widened his view of the world and of the wonderful things one could buy or do with money. Because he only returned to his village for brief visits, his father predicted dire happenings. Daniel, with some misgivings, accepted his ancestors' displeasure at his decision to turn his back on the village. More than once he had sacrificed a goat or chicken to his ancestors in a vain hope of appeasing their anger. Nothing he did could relieve his guilty feelings for rejecting the role he was expected to play in his village. Although his visits to his village became less and less frequent, he could never completely put it out of his thoughts.

Shrewd as well as intelligent, Daniel Msomi quickly established himself as an authority in matters of finance and politics and was recognized throughout the Third World. The discovery of oil on his property hastened his progress toward wealth and a position of importance in Niberia, his native country. His marriage to the daughter of the prime minister clearly helped. Niberia was just beginning to emerge from being a backward African nation to being one gaining recognition among the leading nations of the world. Leaders from many countries beat a path to Daniel's office in the tallest building in Abakuta, the largest city in the country.

If there was one thing Daniel longed for to make his life complete, it was a son to carry on the work he had carved out of his society. Five times before, Ibanga had assured him a son would be born to his wife—five times before, she had been wrong. Once again, she pointed out that all the signs were favorable. He would have the son he so desperately wanted. His need for a son was so great that he convinced himself that indeed a son would be his lot this time.

Suddenly an exceedingly bright flash of lightning bathed the room from corner to corner. The thunderbolt that followed felt as if it would knock the house off its foundation. Mbondu, was near one of the windows.

"Come quickly. Look!" he called loudly.

Ibanga, whose days of doing anything in a hurry were over, nevertheless moved to the window as fast as she could. Her eyes followed Mbondu's outstretched arm as he pointed to the sky. For a brief moment, the clouds parted and the sky was flooded with moonlight. "Can you not see the ancestors on horseback rushing across the sky?" exclaimed Mbondu. "This is no ordinary birth. The ancestors are angry, very angry. See how they rush back and forth, how they whip the horses for more speed!"

As Ibanga looked at the sky, a blanket of darkness drifted across the moon.

"You are right, Mbondu, This is no ordinary birth. You are wrong if you think the ancestors are angry. Never have I seen so many ancestors welcoming one into the world," she whispered softly.

At that moment, a loud moan came from down the hall, barely heard above the furious sounds of the raging storm. Ibanga walked to the door and listened. "It is time. I must go and see what the ancestors have in store for us," she murmured and hurried from the room.

Mbondu looked silently out the window, as if trying to contact those who spoke so loudly. Slowly he began to unroll a bark cloth and sat it on the floor beside a sack that held the ancestral bones. They would tell him what to expect from this new addition to humanity.

Not being able to sit still, Daniel paced back and forth in the hallway. The storm that had been roaring and shaking the house abruptly became silent as the grave. A

3

full moon sent streaks of light down the hallway and into the rooms. Soon, he heard a sharp slap and the lusty cry of a newborn. Daniel Msomi could hardly contain himself. Was the son he had waited for finally a reality? Shortly, the door opened and Ibanga came out carrying an infant whose face was only barely seen amid the folds of the cloth.

"Is it—" Daniel began.

Before he could finish Ibanga replied.

"Yes, the son you have wanted so long is in my arms." Daniel pulled back the cloth and looked on the wrinkled face of his son.

A loud shriek came from the room across the hall. Ibanga quickly returned the baby to his mother. In a moment she joined Daniel, who was standing in the doorway of the small room, eyes fixed upon Mbondu, who was shaking violently and looking intently at the ancestral bones lying on his bark cloth. Ignoring Daniel and Ibanga, he looked up and slowly examined the room as if expecting to find some revered figure present. His whole attitude bespoke a respectful awareness of the invisible forces surrounding them.

"What is it, Mbondu?" Ibanga cried, hurrying into the room.

Engrossed in the ancestral bone, Mbondu made no effort to reply or even indicate that he heard the question. After a long pause, he collected the bones and once again tossed them on the cloth in such a way that they rolled off his fingers.

"*Aaiiee!*" he exclaimed excitedly.

Daniel Msomi was convinced that his son's birth was more than an ordinary birth. He thoughtfully stroked a lion's tooth that hung from his belt. When he was very young, it had been given to him by his father. It was to ward off all evil and clear his path of those who would try to prevent him from reaching his goals. Over the years, it had worn smooth. He would never be seen without it.

"What is it, Mbondu?" asked Daniel uneasily.

Mbondu turned around as if only then aware of Daniel and Ibanga. Without saying a word, he turned back to the bones and pointed.

"See," he replied softly. Following his arm with their eyes, they waited for him to continue. Lacking the many years of training and involvement as a tribal doctor, Daniel's knowledge of the ancestral bones was inadequate, to say the least.

"The ancestors have spoken, your son will be a leader of men in far places, many miles removed from his place of birth. He will be a credit to his ancestors, and the name of Msomi will be on the lips of people of all kinds."

"Go on, go on!" urged Daniel somewhat relieved. "Is there more?"

Mbondu looked long and carefully at the bones lying scattered on the cloth at his feet before replying. Ibanga, hearing the newborn's cry, left to attend to mother and child.

"The ancestors have spoken in a way never have I seen before." Mbondu's voice was restrained. "Yes, there is more."

Daniel gripped the old man's shoulders.

"Go on, go on" he fairly shouted. "What is it? What do the bones tell us?"

"There is trouble, much trouble, and your son will be in the forefront of it. There are many deaths, much conflict. The ancestors will call your son back to them at an early age."

Superstitious old fool, thought Daniel. *What gives him the right to speak of the future? How can he tell what is to come by looking at a bunch of old bones? Still, it is best to be on the safe side where such matters are concerned.*

Loosening his hold, Daniel looked closely at Mbondu.

"Throw the bones again. Perhaps you have not read them carefully," Daniel began.

"I have thrown them twice," retorted Mbondu. "The ancestors do not take kindly to being questioned. Besides, there was no difference between the first throw, and the last throw."

"All right, all right," sighed Daniel. Reaching into his pocket he pulled forth a few coins and handed them to Mbondu. With a wave of his hand, he indicated the session was over and that Mbondu could gather up his belongings and return to his village.

"We will sacrifice to our ancestors that he-goat tied to the back fence," declared Daniel. "Perhaps they may see fit to reconsider their early recall of my son." He watched thoughtfully as Mbondu performed a ritual of selecting each bone and placing it in the sack in a certain manner. He then rolled up his bark cloth.

"It is destiny," reflected Mbondu as he paused at the doorway leading into the hall. "Your son will have unheard of powers. Not only will he be able to understand the past and the present, he will be able to unravel what is tomorrow."

"And what is destiny, old man?" asked Daniel.

"Destiny," pondered Mbondu. "It is being provided with the means and opportunity to outwit one's enemies. It is having needed rain to make our gardens grow. It is taking the left fork when a hungry leopard lies in wait on the right fork. Destiny is all of life. It controls what we are, what we will become, and . . . how we will end."

"Can we not escape from this destiny?" countered Daniel.

"Some try, some fight against it, some accept it, none can escape."

"But can destiny be as powerful as our ancestors?" Daniel persisted.

Mbondu paused, mulling over Daniel's question.

"It is different, yet it is the same in many ways. It is true there is no force more powerful than the force of one's ancestors, nor can there be anything more gentle. They are the fire that flashes from the sky, the wind that blows down the strongest tree, the soft breeze that floats over the land bringing with it life-giving rains. Destiny is only one of the ways the ancestors make their presence known." Mbondu looked sharply at Daniel as if waiting for some response. Since none was forthcoming, he turned and slowly drifted away.

Even after Mbondu's footsteps were no longer heard, Daniel stood leaning on the doorway, contemplating all that had happened that night and all that had been said. A baby's cry broke through his musing. He hurried to his wife and son. As he entered the room, Ibanga was bending over the bed, watching the baby suckle at his mother's breast. Ibanga straightened up as Daniel came over to the bed.

"Is everything all right?" he asked, bending over the bed. His wife, Naomi, looked up with a wan smile and nodded. "I must prepare a proper ceremony to welcome my son to his new home," remarked Daniel.

"And what will the name of your son be?" asked Ibanga.

A slight smile broke over Daniel's face as he replied.

"This time, your prediction of a son has come to pass. My father's name, Joseph, will be carried on in my son."

"It is taken care of," said Ibanga.

"What?" asked Daniel.

"The proper welcome for Joseph to the house of Msomi," responded Ibanga. "Already the goat from the back lot is being prepared for sacrifice to the ancestors. Everyone in the village knows of the birth and should be on their way now. The news is spreading across the city. Joseph will be properly welcomed."

"In this storm?" murmured Daniel.

"It is no more. Look for yourself. The moon is shining brightly. The air is clean and fresh."

So passed the entry of Joseph Ngemi Msomi from the world of his ancestors to the world of the living. Those who came had long memories of food and drink, the songs, the dances, the drums, all marking the birth of Joseph Msomi. The celebration welcomed the sun the next morning and lasted until no scrap of food or drop of drink was left.

Daniel Msomi's delight with having a son to follow in his footsteps knew no bounds. He gave frequent thanks to his ancestors for their kindness. The parting premonition of Mbondu was all but forgotten in the merrymaking.

During a quiet moment, Daniel sat and reflected on his life. It seemed that everything he touched came out for the best, and now, a son. He had entered the oil business at a time when much money could be made in that industry. Soon his wealth far surpassed anything he could have imagined. With increasing wealth came power and prestige. Those who relied upon him for their well-being multiplied, but he never complained. He had more than he could ever use in his lifetime.

The years passed uneventfully for Daniel and his family. While enjoying a measure of prosperity well above the average person in this society, the Msomis did not face any more of the sadness or disagreeable aspects of life most people did. Life was good to them.

At the proper time, Daniel enrolled his son, Joseph, in a mission school. More and more, it became clear to all who knew Daniel that Joseph and his well-being was the most important thing in his life. He began to make plans very early for Joseph to follow in his footsteps. Joseph could often be found wandering around his father's office after school, poking his nose into one thing or another. He was an inquisitive youngster, one full of questions. Even at an early age, his knowledge of the world many miles from his native land was a surprise to his elders. To say that he was a source of pride to his father was an understatement.

Although Daniel's life revolved around the affairs of his city, Abakuta, he could never entirely forget the village of his ancestors and his birth. The little village in the distance, where the plains merged with the forest and the hills beyond, was frequently in his thoughts. In the summer of Joseph's tenth birthday, shortly after the first meal of the day, Daniel called Joseph into his study.

"My son," he began. "I must tell you about a dream I had several nights ago." He motioned to Joseph to take a seat in a chair in front of his desk. Joseph fixed his eyes on his father as he complied. Daniel leaned back in his swivel chair, hands clasped in back of his head as he reflected upon his dream. "It is only now becoming obvious to me," he murmured.

Daniel got up from his chair, shuffled over and closed the door leading into the hall where the noise of his daughters at play rang in the hallway. He then closed the open window, where the sounds from the street indicated the activities of the day had begun for many of the citizens. After a few moments, he turned and walked back to his desk, pausing briefly to look down at Joseph, who was slowly rubbing a shrunken monkey head given to him by

Ibanga to ward off evil spirits. Daniel patted his son's head and then returned to his chair.

"Your dream, Father?" asked Joseph impatiently.

"Ah, yes, the dream. It was a hot day and the lion families were resting in the shade, their bellies full, panting and flicking their tails to chase away the insects. I was hidden behind a tree so they could not see me, but I observed everything that happened."

"What happened, Father?"

"Do not be impatient, my son. I am trying to remember everything from the dream. Ah, yes . . . from somewhere far off . . . it seemed from the bowels of the earth, there came a roar like none I had ever heard before. It kept getting louder and louder. All the lions, young and old, got to their feet, their eyes searching for the source of the sound. The roars were coming from an opening in the side of a hill. I watched as a cloud of dust came out of the opening followed by countless old lions. They had long chin whiskers that dragged the ground as they walked. Some of them leaned on a stick as they plodded along. Others had to be helped as they came into the open." Daniel paused as he tried to remember exactly what had happened in his dream.

"And then, Father?" questioned Joseph. "Go on."

"Now where was I?" mumbled Daniel.

"The old lions were coming out of a hole in the side of a hill."

"Yes, yes. The elders were given the choicest places to sit under the shade trees, provided with cool drink and food, and accorded the utmost respect. Into the clearing came a beautiful young lion, yet without a mane, dragging his first kill. He dropped his kill in front of the gathering and stood back in a most respectful manner with head low. He was immediately surrounded by the ancient ones, who praised him and admired his kill. They looked into his clear eyes, felt his powerful muscles, inspected his teeth and claws. Without a doubt, they were very satisfied with him."

"And then what happened? Who was the young lion?"

"Patience, patience, my son," reiterated Daniel. "The old ones turned and slowly entered the hole in the hill from whence they came. As I looked, the hole was no more—only a grassy hillside."

"What does it mean, Father?"

"You are the young lion, and it is time for you to begin to prepare yourself for your rightful place in our society. Our ancestors are very pleased with you. With their help, there is no limit to what you can accomplish. But you have much to learn."

"What can I do? How should I begin to learn what I must learn?"

Daniel looked thoughtfully at the window before replying, searching his mind for images that had not been brought to the surface for a long time.

"Many years ago," he began slowly, "when I was a boy about your age, my father had me spend some time with the little people of the forest. I did not want to go, but as I look back, it was one of the most profitable experiences of my life. You will follow in my footsteps. You will spend some time with the little people."

"When will I go to the home of the little people?" asked Joseph.

"Tomorrow, when the cock crows for the beginning of the day." Daniel rose from his chair and walked around to his son's chair, placed an affectionate hand on his shoulder, and whispered, "Your mother will not agree with this, but I know best." Shortly after, Daniel left his home and went to his office.

It did not take the concerted crowing of all the cocks in the neighborhood to awaken Joseph the next morning. When his father walked into his room, he was dressed in a loin cloth and a pair of sandals. He had been to the village before and was aware of the proper dress. Daniel, too, was dressed for the occasion. Years before, he would have gone without shoes of any kind, but the soft living of the city had, over the years, softened the soles of his feet to the point where it was painful to walk very long on the trails or dirt streets of the country. A pair of soft, imported moccasins graced his feet.

"Come, my son," said Daniel with a smile. "We must go to the kitchen and get a bite to eat before setting out on our journey."

"I am not hungry."

"But you must eat something. The journey to the land of the little people is a long one, and there will not be much to eat along the way." Daniel remembered the state of excitement that overwhelmed him as a child when his father told him of a trip to the home of the little people. He well knew the emotion that was glowing inside his son. He patted Joseph on the head to show he understood the feelings that were so near the surface. His arm wrapped around Joseph's shoulder, Daniel guided him toward the kitchen.

Father and son ate sparingly. Before they finished, soft rustle of bare feet signaled the approach of Naomi, the who seemed not at all surprised to find her husband and son awake at such an hour and prepared for a trip. She had not been enthusiastic about Joseph spending his summer in the forest, but Daniel had been persistent and persuasive. As they ate, Naomi went to a cabinet and brought forth a knapsack filled with fruit and other things to eat and drink, which she placed on the table.

"Be careful," she cautioned them, and as softly as she entered, left.

"Come, Joseph, my son, we must be on. The sun is up and on its way across the sky waiting for us."

Two men were sitting on the steps of the front porch. Lapido, the eldest of the two, was a thin, grizzled, very black man in a breech-cloth. Lying by his side was a long knife and a spear. His bare feet showed the wear of many years walking along the paths far removed from the city. His eyes, constantly on the move, met those of Joseph's for a few moments before shifting elsewhere. Daniel always felt that there was little that escaped Lapido. Lamba, a youngish, wiry man, was aimlessly drawing lines in the dirt with a stick.

As Daniel and Joseph approached, Lapido rose from the step.

"Come," he declared. "We must be on our way. We have a long way to go to the edge of the forest where the little people live. The sun is well past the beginning of the day."

Although Daniel's natural tendency was to lead, it was plain that on this occasion that role would be taken over by Lapido. Daniel, Joseph, and Lamba followed Lapido out of the yard and into the street. Even at this early hour, the streets were beginning to fill with activity. Since Daniel's home was near the outskirts of the city, soon the plains spread out before the small contingent. They followed a well-worn path among the trees and bushes that provided some shade from the sun.

"How far is the forest of the little people, Father?" asked Joseph as they walked briskly along.

"According to Lapido, it is some three days' distant."

"Where will we spend the night? Who will feed us?" continued Joseph.

13

"Lapido has taken care of all that. We will stay in the villages of relatives. All our needs will be met. Do not worry. It is enough for all of us to keep our wits as sharp as possible. Danger is all around us even though we may not be aware of it. Keep a close eye on the birds. They are our friends. Whenever you see them fly up in alarm, it is a sign that danger may be near, and one must proceed cautiously."

The sun reached a point directly overhead, when Lapido raised his hand to signal a rest stop beside a stream that flowed through a patch of acacia trees. It was a time to eat and drink, with all sharing whatever the knapsacks provided. When they finished, all four stretched out on the ground and relaxed.

Without saying a word, Lapido rose and resumed the journey. The others followed silently. The shimmering heat waves on the plain created wavy patterns of the animals grazing as far as the eye could see. The steady pace set by Lapido was reflected in the passing miles.

"Are you all right, my son? Are you becoming tired?" asked a concerned Daniel.

"I am fine, Father."

It was not long before the sun, in its path across the sky, began to cast longer and longer shadows, indicating night was nearing. Lapido quickened his pace, a move that met with silent approval. Roaming across the plain and among the sparse trees that bordered it during daylight hours was one thing, but it was something quite different during the darkness of night.

Years of living in the city had not eliminated Daniel's fear of strange, dark places. Having a protective fire and the company of others was more to his liking. Evil spirits, sorcerers, and witches of all kinds were the masters of darkness, and even though Daniel was less than convinced, he felt it was the better part of sound judgment not to press the issue.

"We are near," calmly declared Lapido as they were passing through a grove of acacia trees.

"How do you know?" asked Daniel.

"Can you not smell the smoke of the cooking fires in the village?" Soon they reached a curve in the path, and there, before them, was the village.

Daniel heaved a sigh of relief as he saw the smoke from cooking fires rising from a disorderly collection of huts. The weary travelers had hardly set foot in the village before the last rays of the sun disappeared into night. Anxiety that had begun to roll over Daniel was shed like an uncomfortable cloak. This tribe and Daniel's tribe traced their family tree back to a common ancestor—they were not entering as guests. They were among family and were welcome to share the lot of the villagers. Soon, Daniel and his fellow travelers were provided with refreshing drink as they sat around the fire and watched the women prepare the evening meal.

After eating, Daniel and his little band joined the villagers around a communal fire and listened to the elders talk about the exploits of ancestors, about successful hunts, strange happenings, evil spirits, and happy times, as well as sad times. Daniel explained all that was not clear to his son and looked on with pride as Joseph joined the dancers whirling to the steady beat of the drums. Afterwards, the fire was allowed to slowly drift into glowing embers. Soon the villagers began to wander to their respective huts. Joseph found a friend in Myanga, the eldest son of the village tribal doctor. The roar of a lion in the distance, as well as the dying rays of the last few embers of the fire that had postponed total darkness, finally drove them to Myanga's home, where Joseph

15

found a place in the corner near his friend. Soon he was fast asleep.

Shortly after the first cock crow of the morning, when only a gray tinge could be seen in the eastern sky, Daniel touched Joseph on the shoulder.

"Come, my son, we must be on our way."

Rubbing sleep from his eyes, Joseph quietly followed his father out of the hut.

To the west, night was reluctantly giving way to the relentless advance of the sun. Lapido and Lamba were already preparing a simple meal as well as putting scraps of food in their knapsacks. Lapido had filled a container with water.

"We must be careful with water today," he cautioned. "There are not many water holes or streams to be found along our way."

The orange rays of the sun began to spread in the east when Lapido led Daniel, Joseph, and Lamba out of the safe confines of the village and on to the trails that would lead them closer to the forest. The pace that Lapido set was again steady, not too fast, but not too slow either. Vultures created effortless patterns, greeting the morning with an aerial show as they went about their business of finding food. Countless animals were slowly feeding, constantly moving and occasionally pausing to check for predators. Daniel rejoiced watching Joseph's eyes dart from one thing to another. Everything that impinged upon him was so new and he seemed to delight in the sights.

On occasion, birds would fly up before them or monkeys scold the travelers from the safety of trees along the way. The path was a well-worn one and the travelers had little need to cut away the brush that reached out toward them as they passed by. Suddenly, Lapido stopped and raised his hand in warning. Daniel and the others came to a halt and peered ahead. In a few moments, he resumed walking but at a slower pace. As they rounded a curve, a herd of elephants crossed in front of them, only a few hundred paces ahead. In a few minutes the whole herd, young and old, had come and gone.

"Father," asked Joseph as they walked along, "did you not say that the little people were good elephant hunters?"

"Yes, they are among the best. They seldom miss."

"How can people so small, some not as large as I, kill an animal as large as those we just passed?"

Daniel pondered the question for a moment as they kept pace with Lapido. Finally he answered.

"My son, we have a saying that you should remember."

"Yes, Father."

"Joining together, the ants ate the elephant."

The close of the day found the exhausted travelers once again spending the night at the village of another related tribe, where they were fed and provided sleeping arrangements. Prior to going to sleep, Lapido told his fellow travelers they would arrive at their final destination the next evening as the sun was going down.

The next morning, at the first cock crow, Lapido woke the others.

"We must leave," he whispered to each of them.

"We have many miles to cover today to reach our destination before the sun fades from view."

As they filled their knapsacks with scraps of food, Daniel noticed Lapido was not his usual patient self. Several times, he snapped angrily at something one or the other did as they prepared for the journey.

"What is it, Lapido, my friend?" asked Daniel.

Squatting and fixing his eyes on a stick with which he was tracing figures in the dirt, Lapido murmured softly.

"Last night, I talked long with Lukumba, the tribal doctor, about our journey today. He looked into his jar of medicated water and was frightened by what he saw."

"And what was it he saw?" Daniel grumbled after a reasonable time, without getting any satisfaction.

"He saw trouble ahead for us this day, trouble and unusual happenings," whispered Lapido. "Perhaps we should consider spending one more day here and continue our trip tomorrow."

"No," Daniel replied without hesitation. "I have promised my friend Iyanga that we will arrive tonight, and he is to have his little people there to meet me. The little people are not the most dependable under the best of circumstances. Time does not mean the same thing to them as it does to many of us. I am afraid that if we are not there, the entire trip will be for naught. Could the learned doctor have made a mistake in reading the medicated water?"

"I do not think so," retorted Lapido, turning away from his aimless drawings to face Daniel. "Lukumba took the ancestral finger bones, stirred the water again, waited until it had settled, and looked again."

"And . . . ?"

Once again, Lapido was slow to answer. "And what did the ancestors tell him?" urged Daniel.

"The medicated water spoke the same message. It did not tell him what exactly to expect, but he did advise us to be alert."

Even though Daniel publicly ridiculed the tribal doctors, he still listened carefully to their sage advice. "I have no choice but to proceed to our destination. I have my trusted high-powered English rifle, which should be enough to protect us against any trouble we may chance to meet. All we need do is give proper respect to such as lions. The others will be glad to get out of our way."

Although still not convinced that leaving a safe haven was a good thing, Lapido soon led the tiny band out of the village and into the scrub bushes beyond. He set a faster than usual pace, as if to outdistance anything that might bring harm to them. Daniel, although indicating a calm outlook on the matter, was far from pleased by the new turn of affairs. Lamba showed fear in his total behavior, constantly looking around and clutching his spear tightly.

The steady pace set by the travelers covered much ground, and as the day went by and nothing untoward occurred, all began to feel better about the trip. Lapido even suggested that perhaps the ancestors might have been mistaken this time, although he was careful to couch his doubts in language judged acceptable to them. He called a halt under an acacia tree near a stream. They rested and finished the repast they brought from the village. When they continued their journey, they were more relaxed, pausing occasionally to observe the birds and animals as they passed along.

All went well until they heard the frightened squeals of some kind of animal rushing through the bush. Lapido raised his hands to signal a halt. Crossing their path some hundred paces ahead was a troop of wart hogs with tails high, pigs in front, and adults bringing up the rear.

"We must be careful," advised Lapido. "Their haste has been prompted by some fierce creature, like Chui, the leopard."

Daniel nodded as his eyes searched the bush ahead for any sign of danger. After a pause, he was apparently satisfied.

19

"I see nothing. Perhaps it was only a scent of some big cat that frightened them."

"We are not in such a hurry that we should be careless," cautioned Lapido. "Remember Lukumba and the ancestor's warning. These wart hogs are fierce fighters, quite capable of taking care of themselves against most animals. There is something near that is causing them to run so fast. We must be careful not to stumble upon it unawares."

The travelers stood still and scanned the trail and the surrounding bush for any sign of a predator. Seeing nothing out of the ordinary, they proceeded slowly, carefully examining all sides of the trail as they trudged along.

Then it happened. Lapido, who was slightly ahead of the others, rounded a bend in the path and came to an abrupt halt. Not more than fifty paces in front of them was the largest, most ferocious leopard any of them had ever seen. His yellow eyes glowed as his tail slowly rotated from side to side, every muscle twitching spasmodically as he prepared to spring upon them.

Something incredulous caught Daniel's eyes. His heart pounded out of control. Joseph, his precious jewel, had stepped in front of the group. What was this? Daniel's fear was so great that he could not utter a sound, not even of warning. In a flash, he realized that the big cat would be upon them before he could bring his gun to his shoulder and fire. More than that, Joseph was in a direct line between him and the leopard. He, like Lapido and Lamba, could only stand petrified and watch. Meanwhile, Joseph, hand held high, was standing perfectly still, his eyes fixed upon the glaring eyes of the crouching cat.

All of a sudden, the quietness of the bush was disturbed by violent winds that came out of nowhere, bending trees and bushes to the ground. Accompanying the winds were howls that raised cold shivers up and down Daniel's back. Yet, there was something vaguely familiar to him about that uncanny scene. It brought back memories of the stormy night of Joseph's birth. Meanwhile the big cat flattened himself on the ground as the wind surrounded him with flying debris. He, too, looked around as if trying to locate the source of the unearthly shrieks.

As suddenly as the winds arose, they subsided. Joseph remained as immobile as before, his eyes unblinking, his whole being as if in a trance. Chui, the leopard, who only a few moments before had given every indication of an imminent charge, was quiet. The growls that chilled the blood of Daniel, Lapido, and Lamba were no more than whimpers. Chui arose slowly and began to slink toward a grove of nearby trees, giving a last look back at the motionless humans. As he disappeared, Daniel rushed to his son.

"Joseph, my son, my son!" cried Daniel as he wrapped his sweaty arms around him. "You are—?"

"Do not move just yet," warned Lapido. "We must give Chui plenty of time to get out of the area. There is no need to try the protection of our ancestors any more than necessary."

Joseph still seemed to be completely detached from all that was going on around him, his eyes fixed upon the spot where the big cat had been.

"Your son is indeed a favorite of our ancestors," said Lapido, as he peered closely at Joseph. "He has been chosen to be a leader and protector."

"I heard the voices of our ancestors," chimed in Lamba. "They were telling Joseph to never fear, that they were with him and no harm would come to us."

Joseph looked around him as if suddenly aware of

21

where he was. His eyes looked questioningly at his father, Daniel held his son and spoke soothingly.

"It is all right. We are safe. The danger is past."

"Lukumba was right," mused Lapido.

"What is that?" asked Daniel, as he relinquished his hold on Joseph.

"If you remember, Lukumba spoke of strange happenings and trouble before us this day. This is what the medicated water foretold."

"The strange events of my son's birth are becoming clear to me now," said Daniel. "My son has been given unusual powers by our ancestors. He will be a credit to them and to me. I can hardly wait to turn my affairs over to him at the proper time."

Lapido noticed that the sun had begun to sink lower in the west. "We must be on our way. There is still plenty of ground to cover before we reach our destination. I hardly think our ancestors will favor us with any more surprises today." On second thought, he added, "That is not that I am so bold as to suggest what they would do or not do if they so minded."

Without any further remarks, Lapido settled into his mile-eating pace. The others fell in behind him; Joseph, Daniel, and lastly Lamba.

Before the sun drifted behind the distant hills, the footsore travelers began to smell the cooking fires in the village of their destination. Although the sun was beginning to cast long shadows, it was still a few hours from darkness as they walked out from a grove of trees to see a large collection of huts no more than a few hundred paces away.

Daniel and Joseph trudged down a path until they came to one of the largest huts in the compound. It was the home of Iyanga, an old friend. There they were to meet one of the little people who would take Joseph with him into the forest. Sitting in front on a log fashioned into a chair was a short, black, rotund man, whose age was a matter of guesswork.

"Welcome to my modest home, friend Daniel," Iyanga warmly greeted Daniel and Joseph and motioned to them to sit beside him. Daniel acknowledged the greeting, and they sat with him on the freshly swept ground.

"This fine looking boy must be the son you wish to send into the forest to live with my little people?" Iyanga gave Joseph a long, thoughtful look. "My friend Daniel," he murmured. "Can you be serious? My little people have no culture. They are only a step above a monkey. Otherwise, how could they exist in a forest that every thinking man knows is peopled by evil spirits and witches? What could they possibly teach a civilized human being?"

Daniel listened patiently to his friend. After a pause, he replied.

"Iyanga, my brother, you are right in many respects. Cannot you see that by beginning at the very lowest level of human existence, all the advantages possessed by those of us further up the ladder will soon become clearer. It will be a considerable benefit to my son to observe first-hand how creatures only a step above our domestic animals eat, live, create, and, in short, to exist in such a forbidding surrounding as the forest."

"Yes, I see what you are saying. My little people do have their use. They furnish me with hides, ivory, and certain herbs that have medicinal value."

"By the way, have you seen your little man, Edudo? He was to meet me here today."

"No, I have not seen the little monkey for many days, but the little rascals have no regard for time. If you must carry out this wild scheme of yours, I can see nothing better for you to do than to accept the hospitality of my home and wait until he does arrive."

"My son and I will be most favored to accept your kind offer." Daniel tried to put a good face upon his disappointment.

Daniel and Joseph wandered about the village as daylight began to change to dusk. They passed several white men who came to the village to trade in skins and crafts or goods made by the villagers. The smells of food cooking, together with the pangs of hunger caused Daniel and Joseph to retrace their steps. They arrived back at the home of their host just as they were preparing to eat. With a wave of his hand Iyanga bade them sit.

The incredible behavior of Joseph when confronted by the leopard Chui, was told in glowing words by Lapido and Lamba to all they chanced to meet. Soon the news spread throughout the village.

Shortly after, Iyanga, his family, and guests finished their meal, the muffled sounds of the tribal drums summoned all to a gathering. Daniel and his son joined Iyanga and his family as they wended their way toward the sounds.

The meeting place was a large, open area near the center of the village. When Daniel and his host arrived, they found a huge fire burning brightly. Sitting in a circle around the fire were the men, women, and children of the village, all eyes trying to get a good look at Joseph. A prominent place had been reserved for the four travelers from afar, where they could be seen by most of those present.

Amboku, the old village tribal doctor, was one of the last to arrive. His usual place was provided for him along with his favorite chair. Amboku was a highly respected member of the tribe. He was the link between the past,

24

present, and future. He was the one who maintained contact with tribal ancestors and could interpret their messages no matter what medium was used.

When Amboku raised his hand, the proceedings began. First Lamba, then Lapido, and lastly Daniel stood and related the remarkable happenings involving the leopard that took place that morning on the trail. All three could be excused for embellishing the event to some extent. Lamba recalled that huge boulders rolled between them and the leopard at the command of Joseph. Lapido remembered a black cloud that hung overhead with angry flashes of lightning darting back and forth. Daniel told the gathering he could never forget the iron grip of the ancestors as they prevented him from seizing his rifle and shooting the savage creature, pointing to the marks on his hands for all to see.

Everyone marveled at the tale of Joseph and his power over the leopard and agreed he was surely to be one of the great leaders of the tribe. Some even commented upon how closely Joseph resembled a famous ancestor of the distant past. Amboku was far from pleased with the attempt to compare anyone with an ancestor, especially a ten-year-old boy. The emotional tone of the drums and dance, along with frequent cups of kola water, overcame much of his reservations. There were no dissenters when Joseph was described as a young lion who would one day be a leader in a world far removed from the village, one who would bring fame and wealth to every member of the tribe.

Daniel sensed another presence in the gloom just outside the ring of fire. Standing motionless and quietly eyeing them were three very small, rounded figures—the little men from deep in the forest. Joseph would spend his next few months intimately involved in their daily lives.

Iyanga, too, sensed their presence, for without looking up he spoke in the tongue of the forest people.

"Come closer to the fire, Edudo."

In an effortless manner, Edudo came closer and squatted near the fire. His two companions remained standing where they were. Edudo was not quite as tall as Joseph. His alert eyes, like Lapido's, missed nothing.

Daniel gestured toward Joseph and spoke to Edudo.

"This is my son, Joseph. He will one day be a very important person in the outside world. Yet, he has much to learn about life. It is my wish that he obtain some of the wisdom you and your people possess. He is prepared to go with you when the sun next rises."

Suddenly a shiver enveloped Daniel. He looked toward the dark blotch that was the forest, as if expecting some unearthly creature to rush forth and seize him. But then he remembered. The ancestors were with Joseph. They would protect him from harm.

The next morning, Daniel bid farewell to his son, not without misgivings, leaving him in the care of Edudo. He told the man of the forest to return with Joseph at the end of the dry season, when he would be there to meet them. Iyanga presented Joseph with a bracelet made of lion and jackal teeth.

"One cannot be too careful," he reminded Daniel and Joseph. "There are many evil spirits in the forest. One must be a lion to terrify one's enemies and a jackal to uncover the snares that might be placed in one's path."

As the years passed by, Daniel's pride in Joseph and his accomplishments was boundless. There was only one thing that was difficult for him to accept. He had long planned for Joseph to follow in his footsteps and take over the family businesses. But Joseph had other plans. He would enter the political arena of life. He was adamant about it. Daniel exercised his influence and helped Joseph obtain the position of ambassador to the United States from the nation of Niberia. At the meeting celebrating Joseph's appointment, Daniel presented him with an attaché case made by his good friend Iyanga. According to Iyanga, there was none like it in the whole world.

Joseph's visits to his home and family became less and less frequent. During the brief occasions when he visited his family, he was extremely reticent to talk about his activities. He had resolutely placed his feet upon a path that made life meaningful to him, whatever it was.

2

An Illegal Matter

Sergeant Patrick O'Donovan entered the kitchen, slowly walked to a counter, and turned on the television to listen to the news.

"...and the police are still without clues as to the identity of the rapist murderer who has been terrorizing our city," droned the announcer. "We wonder how long the citizens will have to." O'Donovan abruptly switched to another channel.

"Isn't that the case you're working on?" asked his wife, Virginia, who was busily preparing breakfast for the family.

"Yes," replied Patrick as he gave his attention to the news coming from another station.

"Well, why did you turn away from the news about your case on the other station? Aren't you interested in what they have to say about it?"

"Not really. Why should I listen to something I'm working with every day. The news media simply hype up the sensational aspects, scaring the public unnecessarily."

At that moment, a loud cry came from the back of the house.

"Mama, Michael is hitting me," came the tearful voice of Kathleen, their daughter, age ten.

"Michael!" shouted Virginia. "Leave your sister alone

and come out here and get your breakfast, right now." Turning her attention to her husband apparently oblivious to the commotion in the back of the house, she said angrily, "I don't understand why you leave it up to me to discipline that boy."

"You're doing a good job," he calmly replied. They had discussed the matter of discipline many times, and Patrick was content to let her handle it while he took care of providing for their needs and wants.

"That's what you always say, leave it up to me. The children must think I'm the bad guy," Virginia complained.

Patrick knew where such discussions lead. He was in no mood for an argument, so he prudently remained silent.

"It's like what happened to Jim and Doris," muttered Virginia, not ready to let the matter rest.

"What is?" As soon as he had spoken, Patrick knew he was trapped in another of their unresolved sessions about child rearing.

"Jim and Doris have two children about the same ages as ours. They went to a psychologist because they were constantly punishing their son for hitting his younger sister. Do you want to know what he told them?"

"Who?" Patrick snapped as he gave up trying to hear the news.

"The psychologist! You never listen to what I'm saying," bristled Virginia as she continued. "He told them that punishment was one way for their son to get attention from his father and mother. Do you see what I mean?"

"Not exactly. Do you mean to say a kid would endure punishment just to get some kind of attention?"

"That's what the psychologist said, and I think he's

got something there. What time do you give to the children? When you come home, whenever it is, You're always so tired that all you do is eat and go to bed. That leaves me to be everything to the children, including disciplining them."

"What am I supposed to do? Stay at home and take care of the kids? Besides, they would have a lot more attention if you weren't gone all the time to those damned arms protest meetings. And now, you've got mother going to them, too."

"Well, at least I've got the future of the children in mind. You don't seem to care."

"Now, what is that supposed to mean?"

"Unless we do something about the threat of war hanging over our heads, the future of our children looks pretty bleak. We've got to do something about it, and now."

Patrick glared at his wife before responding.

"All you and that bunch of peacenicks will do is get in a lot of trouble, if not get hurt. You may not know it, but there's orders at the precinct to get tough on all demonstrators. If I were you, I would spend more time at home and less time raising hell in front of some arms factory. You're up against some pretty powerful people and a bunch of shouting do-gooders are not going to have much of an effect on them."

"You're right. If everyone thought like you, the world would continue down the road to the Apocalypse."

"The what?"

"See what I mean. You don't keep up with what's going on in the world. It's nothing but police work for you. Meanwhile—"

The discussion ended with the arrival of well-scrubbed and dressed for-school Michael and Kathleen.

"Breakfast is ready," said Virginia nodding toward the table.

Patrick responded to the "good morning, Dad" of his children with his own "good morning," before sitting and joining them in the morning meal. When O'Donovan finished, he went to his bedroom, unlocked a drawer, took out his pistol and holster, and fastened it around his shoulder. He got the usual kiss from Virginia and with his usual "bye, bye" to all, got his raincoat from the hall closet and was on his way to the 77th Precinct for another day of attending to the law-abiding business of the city.

A hodgepodge of thoughts competed for O'Donovan's attention as he drove into the city that morning. Scattered clouds meandered across an intense blue sky and gathering humidity bolstered the weather forecasters' prediction of rain. Virginia was right. He hadn't been giving much time to the children of late. But what could he do about it? The case he was working on had everybody jumpy. The latest rape-murder had the commissioner of police demanding long hours from everyone associated with the case. Since he was the senior officer assigned to it, there was little chance he could find more hours to be home with the family, at least for the present.

Near the corner of 17th Street and Constitution, his thoughts were jarred back to the present when he found himself stalled in traffic. Seeing two cars tangled in the intersection, he got out of his car and walked briskly toward the accident. A uniformed officer was there trying to untangle the mess and get traffic rolling again amid the din of impatient drivers honking their horns. O'Donovan recognized the officer, a young man from the traffic division of the precinct. He was having his hands full trying to keep traffic moving in the opposite direction, clear the intersection, and keep onlookers out of the way. There was a man and woman sitting on the curb, the man attempting to comfort the woman.

"How's it going?" asked Patrick as he approached the officer.

"The usual. A lot of impatient drivers, people getting in the way, not to mention the clowns who slow down to see what's happening."

O'Donovan moved to the center of the street and vigorously kept the traffic moving in the opposite direction.

"Anyone hurt, Dave?"

"That woman sitting over there on the curb said her head hit the windshield when the other car struck hers. I've got a call in for the paramedics. It didn't look too bad to me, but you never can tell."

"Who's the guy sitting next to her?"

"You got me. He came out of the crowd and struck up a conversation with her. I wouldn't be surprised if he wasn't some kind of shyster lawyer."

In a matter of minutes, the wail of an approaching ambulance became louder and louder. When it arrived, two men jumped out and hurried over to the uniformed officer. After a short discussion they went over to the woman sitting on the curb, who was moaning as if in great pain. They soon assisted her into the ambulance and, with lights flashing and siren shrieking, left the scene.

The arrival of two other officers from the traffic division gave O'Donovan an opportunity to leave. He hurried to his car, made a U-turn, and headed for the 77th Precinct. On driving into the parking lot, he hurried to the place he usually parked, only to find it occupied. "Damn," he muttered, "that sonofabitch Linsky's got my place again." He finally found an empty space in the back of the lot. Glancing at the gathering clouds rolling in from the south, O'Donovan threw his raincoat over his shoulder and walked swiftly toward the dark gray building. He reflected, with a cheerless smile, that it looked like one of those days—leaving home in a foul mood, getting stuck in traffic, missing his usual parking space, and most of all, late for his meeting with the chief. Just inside the door of the 77th Precinct, he was greeted by a slender man dressed in a sports coat, matching slacks, and an open-neck shirt.

"You're late, O'Donovan," said the man, with a snicker. "The captain's going to blow his top. We were supposed to be in his office thirty minutes ago."

"Couldn't be helped, Pete."

The two men walked briskly toward a large, open room where the usual state of affairs for a morning in a police precinct was taking place—officers interviewing men and women, telephones ringing, various employees rushing here and there. The two men threaded their way toward a small office at the far end of the room.

"Hey, Linsky, O'Donovan, what's up?" came the voice of a youngish, black, plainclothes officer. "Wait a minute."

"Make it quick, Jules," barked O'Donovan. "We've got a meeting with the captain, and we're already late."

"I know. The captain's been out here asking for you two a dozen times, Whatever it is, it sure must be something important. You know what it's all about?"

O'Donovan shrugged his shoulders as he replied.

"No idea. It must be that rapist murder case. Maybe they've got some late dope on it. We briefed him a day or so ago, and there was nothing new on the case then."

"Well, something's got the captain uptight. Better watch yourself. The big chief from downtown was in his office this morning. The last time I saw him out here was when there was a big shakeup in the precinct."

O'Donovan and Linsky turned and kept on toward the captain's office.

"I can't stand that Jules," commented Linsky. "Instead of dressing like an officer should, he's in some far-out outfit and telling some crummy joke. I wonder why the captain lets him get away with it. They should transfer him to the 23rd where the rest of the smart aleck blacks are."

Just as they got abreast of the captain's office, a slender neatly dressed man with a military bearing came out of the office.

"Where the hell have you guys been?" he demanded. "I've been waiting all morning for you two. I thought I told you to be in here by nine!"

"It was one of those—" began O'Donovan only to be interrupted by the captain.

"In, in," he snapped pointing to his office. The two men entered, followed by the captain.

Captain Levine was dressed in a conservative, pin-striped suit, bow tie, white shirt, and black shiny shoes. He had been a colonel in the army and brought with him into civilian life many of the habits he had absorbed in the military. Berating a subordinate in front of others was not his usual style and he hurried O'Donovan and Linsky into his office.

The captain's office was modestly furnished—a few well-worn pieces of furnishing and a file cabinet in a corner. He motioned to the officers to sit down. He picked a pipe from a rack on his desk, filled it with tobacco, lit it, and took a few puffs before sitting. He wafted a circle of smoke toward the ceiling and spoke quietly.

"O'Donovan, Linsky, I'm taking you off the rapist case."

O'Donovan, who was trying to determine what was

an the captain's mind, was astounded. He knew he and Linsky had been following up every lead that had come across his desk, and they surely could not be blamed if the case had not been resolved.

"But, Captain, we're right on this guy's ass. All we need is a few more days," responded O'Donovan heatedly. "We think this guy's a loony. He's bound to make a mistake, and soon."

"Okay, okay, so what is new?" countered the captain. "So far, the guy has raped I don't know how many women and killed at least two we know about. Just what do you expect me to tell the people downtown, not to mention the press, who have been hounding me ever since this case got started. Answer that for me?" Captain Levine paused and looked intently at the officers. Not getting any response, he continued. "And what happened to that so-called eye witness you told me about some time ago?"

O'Donovan pondered a moment before answering.

"It didn't work out. She's scared of retaliation, like most people. She just doesn't want to get involved. Everybody says let's get the criminals off the streets, but when you try to get them to stand up and be counted, it's a different story."

"She did give us a very good description of the sonofabitch," added Linsky. "It checks with other descriptions we've got. We're planning to run an artist's sketch in the paper to see if we can get some kind of lead."

Captain Levine got up from his desk and with pipe in hand sat on a corner of the desk, his eyes searching the eyes of the two men. He continued in a low voice.

"I've been given a special assignment, and I need a couple of men I can depend upon. I had a call from a well-known senator. I can't reveal the name. He tells me there is a drug action going to take place in our district tonight.

I want you two to handle it as a temporary assignment. I don't think there's much to it, and it should not take much time away from what you're doing on the rapist case."

O'Donovan exploded.

"What the hell are the narcotics guys doing? Why can't they handle it?"

The captain raised his hand as if to cut off all discussion on the matter.

"Look at this as if it is a special assignment from downtown. It is something that must be kept quiet between the three of us. There might even be someone in narcotics involved. Anyway, I want you two to handle it. Okay?" He then sat down, his eyes fixed upon the two men. O'Donovan saw nothing would be gained by further argument, so he waited for more details. Linsky sat quietly, saying nothing.

"These are the details," began the captain. "I understand the action will take place at Marcel's, over on L Street—you know where it is." After unlocking the bottom drawer of his desk, Captain Levine pulled out a folder and laid it on his desk. He opened it and pulled out a photograph of a very black man wearing a light-tan trench coat and carrying an attaché case apparently made of an animal skin.

"This is our man," said the captain. "My informant tells me he usually eats at Marcel's around eight o'clock. The deal is supposed to take place in the restaurant during that time tonight. Be there. Any questions?"

Dammit, thought O'Donovan. *Another night away from home.* A policeman's job is no job for a family man. His children were growing up without knowing much about their father.

Captain Levine dismissed O'Donovan and mentioned

to Linsky he wanted to talk to him about another matter. O'Donovan arranged to meet Linsky at the Old Post Office around seven o'clock.

O'Donovan walked quickly across the squad room, looking neither left nor right. The corridor was even more crowded than it was earlier. He breathed a sigh of relief when he reached the door of the building. Hurrying down the steps, he brushed against a young woman entering the building.

"What's the rush, sergeant?" complained an athletic-looking woman as she bent over to pick up some papers that had fallen.

"Sorry," apologized O'Donovan. "I guess my mind wasn't on what I was doing. What brings a member of the D.A.'s office out here so early in the morning?"

"Not sure myself. But a good guess would be about the drug problems in this area."

O'Donovan gave her a friendly pat on the back and continued down the steps and to his car. It looked like it was going to be one of those steady, rainy days that he thought made doing anything outdoors something to be tolerated at best. His twenty-two years on the force had taught him that a policeman's job did not include anything related to weather conditions.

It was five minutes before one P.M. when he parked in front of the Museum of Natural History, where he was to meet an informant. He placed a police decal on the dashboard and walked swiftly over to a small lunch stand under the trees.

"Hi, Jerry," greeted O'Donovan when the last customer had been served. "Seen anything of Jack Sprat?"

"Not lately," responded a burly man wiping his hands on a dirty apron. "He came by this morning just before the rain started, but he didn't stay long."

37

"Give me one of those chili dogs and a cup of coffee, too. Put it on my tab." This was a standing joke between the two of them, since Jerry refused to accept O'Donovan's money.

"Can't see how they do it," said Jerry as his eyes followed an obese, middle-aged man jogging toward the Capitol. "I'm always expecting one of them to drop dead right in front of my stand."

"People have to do something to occupy their time. I guess jogging is as good as anything else."

"Jack is not the most dependable kind of guy," reminded Jerry. "Whether he comes or not is anybody's guess."

Jerry had been the go-between for O'Donovan and his informants for many years. Finally, he remarked, "If Jack comes, tell him I'll be in the usual place in the museum until three."

"Okay."

O'Donovan walked briskly to the Museum of Natural History, past the huge bull elephant with trunk uplifted, and found a seat in a corner where he could watch the visitors come and go. He took out his note pad and reviewed the rapist's case. The only pattern that emerged was that his victims were young Caucasian women who lived in an area of fashionable apartments.

O'Donovan checked the clock in the foyer, and impatiently paced the room before leaving the building. He dodged between the cars and trucks and made his way across the street to Jerry's stand.

"Any signs of Jack?" asked O'Donovan as he evaded a puddle of water forming in front of the stand.

"Nope, no sign. He's probably holed up with some broad, I'm thinking about closing up and calling it a day and going home and giving the old lady a hard time."

Jerry's last comment set off another chain of thought in O'Donovan's mind. Those intimate touchings and embracings that were so much of his and Virginia's life so long ago, seemed few and far between these days. He mused that permitting a behavior pattern to slip away makes it doubly difficult to get the process started again.

"Watch yourself," cautioned Jerry. "Some bad mothers on the streets these days with all kinds of shit to blow a guy away."

Seeing nothing more could be accomplished, O'Donovan waved at Jerry and slowly walked to his car. It was still several hours before he was to meet Linsky. As he drove along, he pondered the new assignment. *Strange*, he thought, *the picture of the suspect did not fit the image of a drug pusher. It only proved that one had to be careful when deciding what kind of person would be involved in the drug racket. In a country where money talks, somebody will always take a chance, no matter how illegal the activity.*

After driving around without purpose, he found himself at the Lincoln Memorial, where he parked in front of the building. His eyes were casually looking over the men, women, and children bustling about, when he spotted a familiar figure. O'Donovan slammed the door of his car and quickly followed the man into the building. During a moment when he had taken his eyes off the person he was pursuing, he was startled by a voice at his elbow.

"Ah, inspector," came the voice. "Whatever brings you out in such dreadful weather? I always thought you police types holed up in some warm, out-of-the-way place, hidden from the eyes of your superiors on such days as this."

The voice belonged to the man O'Donovan had kept in his sights since he saw him going up the steps into the

Memorial. He was a smooth-faced Caucasian who looked to be in his late forties and was dressed in a dark suit, white shirt, blue tie, and black shoes. A tan raincoat hung over his arm.

"I could ask you the same question, Duke," shot back O'Donovan, as if he didn't know the reason. James Randolph Adams, better known as "Duke," was one of the most proficient pickpockets in the Washington area. It was no surprise to find him in an enclosed place with a large number of people milling around. The guys at the bunco squad had been trying for years to tie Duke in with some con game or pickpocket caper, to no avail. The only time they came near to putting a handle on him was an occasion when he had teamed up with a disreputable-looking black man in a lost-wallet scheme.

O'Donovan's involvement with Duke began when he rescued him from an attack by a band of young hoodlums bent on mugging him. He had found Duke to be well-read and capable of talking about a wide range of subjects in a knowledgeable manner. Duke's knowledge of what was happening on the street had been an important element in helping him solve some of his cases.

Duke remarked solemnly, "I find it uplifting and spiritually rewarding to occasionally come to this place to commune with the! thinking of one of our most distinguished presidents. Too bad his kind is no longer with us."

This string of words evoked a sly smile from Duke and a knowing smile from O'Donovan, who was well aware that the rewarding aspects of Duke's being in the Lincoln Memorial had nothing to do with anything spiritual. "What's new in the horse racing business?"

"Not much these days. There are so many gimmicks that it is hard for an honest man to make a living in the horse racing business." Shaking his head mournfully, he added, "There is a pick six, a pick nine, pick three, perfectas, trifectas, daily doubles, and so on. In addition, so many of the track officials, riders, and owners are competing with the lottery that you might find a horse that hasn't won in a year running around the track as if it was the only horse in the race. Those of us who check past performances, workouts, and the like are left holding the bag. I don't know what has happened to the old virtues— honesty, integrity, and the like. Nowadays you just can't trust anybody."

Among Duke's many activities was a handicap sheet called "Duke's Choices," purporting to give the buyer the benefit of Duke's vast knowledge of what horses were likely to do once they got on the track. He provided the buyer with three choices in each race and all but guaranteed one of them winning, or at least in the money. If this did not occur, he then allowed the buyer, for an additional fee, to purchase his weekly "Gold Star" selections.

During the racing season, Duke would rise early and go to the track, meandering around the stables, laughing and joking with trainers, stable boys, and exercise boys, all the while picking up valuable hints about what horses were ready, which ones were out for the exercise, which ones were being primed for a future race, and anything that would help him make his selections for Duke's Choices.

"Know anything about the guy who has been raping and killing young women in our district?"

"I've heard about it. The guy must be some kind of nut. No one on the street, as far as I know, has any good idea of who he is."

"Well, keep your ears open. We're getting a lot of heat from downtown about it. Until we catch this guy, we'll be

41

a big presence everywhere you look."

"Will do, Inspector." Duke turned and wandered off to mix with the crowd.

O'Donovan slowly wended his way toward the exit of the Memorial. He drove past the Mall, scanning the street for Jack before heading for the Old Post Office.

The blare of a rock band impinged upon his ears as he parked out in front of the building. Once inside, he meandered in and out of the various shops.

"O'Donovan," came a voice from within the ring of tables fronting the stage. It was Linsky. O'Donovan strode among the tables, which were rapidly filling up with screaming youths, grabbed a chair, and sat down.

"Anything to drink?" asked Linsky as he downed a beer.

"A beer sounds good to me."

Linsky stopped a waiter who was passing by and directed him to bring "another of the same." The waiter left and soon returned with a beer.

"Been here long?" asked O'Donovan.

"About fifteen minutes."

"Had anything to eat?"

"Nope."

"Any preferences?"

"Not particularly. I've been to a little place on the second floor. Not bad. Nothing fancy, but good food."

"Look at the ass on that little broad," pointed out Linsky as his eyes followed a teenager who flounced past their table. He had a reputation at the precinct for having a roving eye and not above having extramarital affairs.

"Did the captain tell you more about our detail?" O'Donovan asked while waiting for their orders. He remembered the captain had asked Linsky to wait a few minutes following their meeting.

"Naw. He wanted to talk to me about another matter that had nothing to do with tonight."

"Something doesn't fit," murmured O'Donovan more to himself than to Linsky.

"What? What doesn't fit? Go on, what bothers you?"

"Well, if the captain is so sure of all the details he tells us, a drug exchange, the suspect, the time, and the place, there ought to be someone in narcotics he could trust rather than send us. Drugs isn't my thing. I don't know about you, but it's not mine."

Linsky's eyes narrowed as he blew a cloud of smoke upwards.

"The captain must have had his reasons. Besides, I don't think there's going to be much to it anyway."

"Mmm. I hope you're right. But we had better keep our eyes open for any surprises."

"Don't worry about me. I'll be ready for anything that comes up. We still have time. Why not sit downstairs and watch these kids for a while? No need to get out in the rain any sooner than necessary."

O'Donovan nodded and followed Linsky to a table at the back of the room, away from the stage and the performers. They sat silently, Linsky giving his attention to the passing scene, O'Donovan deep in thoughts swirling around his brain in a constantly changing pattern.

Finally, Linsky looked around and spoke.

"Guess I'd better get rid of some of that beer before we start out. Be right back." He hurried off to the rest room. "Thought I'd better check my gun while in the john," he remarked upon his return.

O'Donovan gave a sharp look at his partner. The rumors about Linsky's aggressiveness with his pistol flashed across his mind. He had been involved in several shooting episodes where the officer with him thought the incident could have been settled without bloodshed.

"Looks like the rain has slackened," observed O'Donovan as the two men hurried out of the building. "Let's take my car. It's parked a few doors down the street." This elicited a nod and an "okay" from Linsky.

Unlocking the car, O'Donovan said, "I'd better let the station know where we're going." That accomplished, they headed for their assignment. The singing of tires on wet pavement mingled with the flip-flop of windshield wipers, accompanied them to L Street. Marcel's restaurant was just east of 20th. O'Donovan parked a few yards west of 20th. It was seven forty-five.

3

A Shooting on L Street

The intersection of L and 20th was well lit that rainy night in September. O'Donovan and Linsky sat in their unmarked police car, eyes fixed upon the front door of Marcel's restaurant.

"About five after eight," remarked O'Donovan. "Wonder if the sonofabitch is coming? According to the captain, he's a guy whose movements could be predicted to the minute."

"I don't know where he got his information," said Linsky. "My experiences with niggers is that they're never on time." He pulled a package of cigarettes out of his pocket, lit one, took a few puffs, and watched the smoke curl up to the top of the car. "Looks like our man," whispered Linsky, pointing at a black man wearing a tan raincoat and carrying an attaché case and who was about to enter the front door of the restaurant. Since the captain's instructions were that although the drug transfer was to take place in the restaurant, he wanted them to wait until he came out before approaching him.

"I'd better call the precinct and advise them that we've made visual contact with the suspect and were waiting for him to come out of the restaurant," said O'Donovan. "Think I'll go over and check out the place. We may want to find out if guy could give us the slip by going out a back door."

"Good idea. Want me to come along?" Getting a negative head shake, he cautioned, "Better watch yourself. These guys are pretty sharp."

When O'Donovan entered the restaurant, he found less than half the tables occupied. He paused beside a cloakroom just inside the foyer and looked around, noting a large open dining room and a cocktail bar on one side of the room. He was startled for a moment when he failed to see the suspect. Had he left the restaurant? flashed in his mind. Then he saw him. He was sitting alone at a table in a far corner of the room, leisurely eating and occasionally glancing at a paper on the table beside him. Satisfied, O'Donovan turned to face the cloakroom attendant, a youngish, Latin-looking man.

"Can I help you, sir?" asked the man.

"I need some information. Is there another way out of the restaurant?"

"Only the back door leading to the alley."

"Can anyone leave by that way if they wanted to?"

"I don't think so. It's kept locked all the time unless there's some kind of delivery. The manager is the only one who has the key to the door."

O'Donovan, before heading for the exit, gave a last look at the suspect, who did not appear to be in a hurry to finish his meal.

"Everything all right?" asked Linsky when O'Donovan entered the car. "The motherfucker must have eaten up everything in the place by this time."

"No problem. He's finishing his dinner and should be on his way out pretty soon. Keep your eyes open." Glancing at Linsky, he noticed he had his gun out and was inspecting it.

"No need for that," growled O'Donovan. "Our man

46

doesn't look all that dangerous. Let's keep it as cool as we can."

Linsky reluctantly put his gun away.

"You never can tell about these black boys. I want to be ready for any surprises."

A tinge of anxiety came over O'Donovan.

"Just follow my lead. It's okay if you want to be ready, but no heavy stuff. I think—"

"Looks like our boy's coming out of the restaurant," said Linsky. The suspect paused, looked at the sky and placed his attaché case on the sidewalk while he put on his raincoat.

"He sure in hell don't seem to be in much of a hurry," noted O'Donovan.

"Damn right. I'd think that if he had just made a drug contact, he would be in more of a hurry to be on his way." Then in an undertone he mumbled, "Come on, motherfucker, get the show on the road."

"Keep cool. We've got as much time as he has. Remember what I said about no gun play."

"Okay, okay. Let's hope the black sonofabitch doesn't surprise us."

The suspect walked to the corner of L and 20th and waited for the traffic light to change. Moments later, O'Donovan nudged Linsky and pointed.

"Get ready. It looks like he's about to cross over to our side of the street." Then, for some reason, the suspect stopped, set his case down beside him, and looked west on L Street. The traffic light changed in his favor and still he made no move to cross the street.

"Wonder what he's looking for?" questioned Linsky.

"Can't tell. I don't see much of anything—a few people on the street, only one or two cars. We'll see."

The traffic light changed, and this time the suspect

hurried across the street.

"Let's go," said O'Donovan as he slithered out of the car, followed by Linsky. The suspect walked briskly east on L Street. A late model Mercedes automobile traveling east on L pulled up to the curb just beyond 20th and stopped. The suspect walked quickly over to the car, set his case down beside him, and leaned into an open window. He was observed having an animated conversation with someone in the car.

"Hey, we'd better get going. Maybe that's the drop," said Linsky.

"Let's wait a minute or two and see what happens. According to the captain, the stuff should be in that case, and it's still on the ground. Besides, the exchange was supposed to take place in the restaurant."

Linsky nudged O'Donovan.

"Maybe they're setting up a place to meet and transfer the stuff."

"I doubt it, but we've got him in our sights. There's no way he's going to get away from us. Just follow my lead.

"Okay, we'll play it your way. Let's hope that nothing goes wrong. The captain's got a lot riding on this case, and I wouldn't want to go back to the station and tell him we botched it."

"Let's go," said O'Donovan sharply. They had barely crossed the street when the person in the car suddenly pulled away from the curb in great haste.

"Did you get a look at the one in the car?" asked O'Donovan.

"Looked young and blonde. That's about all I could tell.

The suspect picked up his case and continued on his way.

"Hold it!" called out O'Donovan to the man who kept walking.

"I said hold it, fellow. We're police officers!" repeated O'Donovan even louder. The suspect turned around, pointing his finger at his chest and placing his case on the sidewalk. When the officers were four or five paces from him, he reached toward an inside pocket. He never completed this movement.

In a split second, Linsky pushed O'Donovan aside and fired two shots point blank into the chest of the suspect, who then crumpled in a heap on the sidewalk.

Suddenly a gust of wind from out of nowhere whirled along the street, scattering papers and debris before it as it rolled along. As abruptly as it came up, it was gone. The moon broke through the clouds that had been shrouding it and cast an eerie light on what was happening below. Ghostly figures raced around the heavens in complete disarray.

Linsky looked silently at the man lying at his feet. Suddenly, several sharp cracks of a pistol were heard, followed by impacts on the nearby building. O'Donovan dropped to his knees and looked around trying to trace where the firing was coming from. Linsky, apparently confused, remained standing. A single shot rang out. He slowly sank to the sidewalk, a surprised look on his face.

Pandemonium broke loose. Screams filled the air. Some pedestrians hid behind available vehicles, lay down, or simply ran away from the area. Someone lying near O'Donovan said that the shots came from the other side of the street in back of Marcel's restaurant. O'Donovan looked but saw nothing.

Two officers in a cruising patrol car came by as O'Donovan was leaning over to check the extent of Linsky's injury.

"Call for ambulances," directed O'Donovan to one of the officers "We have an officer wounded as well as a suspect. And keep those people back."

"Hold on, Pete," whispered O'Donovan. "Help's on the way. You'll be all right."

"The captain told me . . ." mumbled Linsky in a weak voice that was barely heard by O'Donovan as he placed his ear close to the mouth of his partner.

"The captain told you what?" No answer came as Linsky lapsed into unconsciousness.

O'Donovan went over to the suspect whose unseeing eyes faced the sky. He felt for a pulse, but found none. Nor was a gun to be found on his person. Finding a passport and identification papers, he opened them and read, "Joseph Msomi—Ambassador, Niberia." Finding a set of keys in the man's raincoat pocket, O'Donovan grabbed the attaché case. The only key that went into the keyhole wouldn't open the case.

More police cars arrived on the scene. An officer approached O'Donovan as he was trying to open the case.

"What's up?"

"Drugs."

"How is he?" asked the officer who noticed Linsky lying nearby.

"Not good. Where's that damn ambulance? How about getting me a screwdriver. I can't seem to get this case open." The officer left and quickly returned with a screwdriver, which O'Donovan used to force open the case, revealing a number of packets containing a white substance. Breaking open one of them he sampled a small amount.

"Coke?" asked the officer.

O'Donovan nodded as he put the sack back into the case and closed the catches on the sides of the case.

"Check across the street in the alley," he told the officer. "Someone said the shots came from over there. Be careful."

Two ambulances arrived on the scene, sirens blaring. Several paramedics hurried over to O'Donovan.

"One for the hospital," he said pointing at Linsky. "The other for the coroner."

O'Donovan picked up the attaché case and made his way to his car. He locked the case in the trunk of the car and reviewed all that happened. Loose ends. Linsky was trying to say something, but what? While trying to find a pulse in the suspect, he noticed an unusual bracelet on his wrist, apparently made of animal teeth, some a little larger than others. Perhaps it was a fetish or a good luck charm.

O'Donovan ended his musing with a decision to hurry to the nearest hospital. That's where Linsky would be taken. At the hospital, he approached a uniformed officer in the emergency room and flashed his I.D. card.

"Too late," said the officer. "He died in the ambulance."

"Is he in the room over there in the corner?"

"Yeah. Go on in."

O'Donovan entered and walked over to a bed where Linsky was lying in the pale posture of death. It was all so senseless he thought. Such a young man, a man in the prime of life. And his wife. Someone had to tell her. It wasn't going to be easy. It never is. He knew that grim task was up to him. Shaking his head in anger and in sadness, he plodded along the corridor toward the exit.

O'Donovan drove with a heavy heart to the building where Linsky lived. How would he convey the awful truth to his wife? Still, he knew he would do what was necessary.

Linsky's wife, Sue, met him at the door of their apartment, wearing a light-colored robe.

"Come in, Patrick," she said. "What brings you out on such a night?"

"There's something I have to discuss with you."

"Something's wrong, isn't it? Is it about Pete. Is he all right? Is he hurt?" she blurted out as she looked into O'Donovan's face.

Sue went over to the television and turned it off, but stood with her hand on it, as if for support. O'Donovan walked to her side and placed his arm around her shoulder.

"We had this supposedly simple drug bust," he said. "But something went wrong. We had the guy dead to right. I think Pete thought the guy was going for a gun, so he pushed me out of the way and shot him. There must have been a back-up involved. Whoever it was shot Pete."

"Where is he now?"

"At a hospital near 17th and Connecticut. Put something on, and I'll take you there."

When they got outside, the city was bathed in moonlight. The drive to the hospital was done in silence. O'Donovan parked at the hospital and waited as Sue tried to erase the signs of turmoil from her tear-streaked face. Once inside, he and Sue hastened past Captain Levine and several officials gathered in the lobby.

"Linsky's wife," O'Donovan said to the officer on duty at the room where Linsky's body was lying. He motioned for them to go in. O'Donovan started to go in but stopped when Sue raised her hand. He stepped aside as she slowly entered the room and closed the door behind her.

O'Donovan looked at the closed door briefly then turned and meandered along the corridors. He was in no mood for interviews. Neither was he in the mood to go over the happenings with the captain. The next day would be soon enough. Shortly after he returned to the room, Sue came out, her eyes red from weeping and her body bent with grief.

"I'm sorry Mrs. Linsky," said the officer at the door. She flashed a distant smile at him and began walking away from the room.

The return to Sue's apartment building went swiftly, only the monotonous tune of tires on damp streets providing a backdrop for her occasional sobs. She gave O'Donovan the keys to her apartment. As soon as he opened the door, Sue flopped heavily into the nearest chair.

"Is there anything else I can do before I leave?" asked O'Donovan as he eyed her closely. It took Sue so long to answer that he was not sure she heard him. "Is there—"

"Not that I can think of. You've been so kind. It's up to me now. I'm going to call my mother and brothers. They will know what to do."

"Are you sure you're okay? What about some kind of sleeping pill?"

"No, no, I'm all right. I've got some stuff in the bathroom. You should get on home, I know Virginia is worrying about you. Don't worry. I'll be all right."

O'Donovan lingered a few minutes more before saying good night and "call me if you need anything or anything I can do."

When O'Donovan got home, he found Virginia lying in bed reading, her gown barely covering her breasts. For a moment, a warm feeling come over him, a need to find relaxation in the pleasure of her body. Quickly the mood faded away, overcome by fatigue. She looked up as he entered the room.

"It was a bad day?" said Virginia in a questioning voice.

"Yes, pretty bad."

Virginia waited for her husband to continue. He remained silent.

"I listened to the late news. They mentioned something about a drug bust up on L near 20th. The announcer said a suspected drug pusher was killed. A police officer was shot."

"I know, I was there."

"Who was the officer?"

"Pete Linsky."

"Was he—"

"Yes. Died in the ambulance on the way to the hospital. I just left his wife. You can imagine how torn up she is."

A lone tear rolled down her cheek and trickled to her pillow.

"How!"

"Not tonight. I'll tell you about it tomorrow."

O'Donovan woke early the next morning. He reached out and embraced Virginia. His searching hands and beseeching lips ended in fires of passion that burned fiercely before ending abruptly in an outburst of mutual satisfaction.

"I will call Sue and find out what I can do to help," Virginia said, the next morning after breakfast. "It is so sad. She is so young to have to face such a problem."

"I know."

". . . and have no doubt about it," droned a voice coming from the television, "the people of our fair city can be sure their police department will track the scum to their holes and bring to justice those who perpetrated this despicable deed."

The corpulent individual speaking into the microphone was the commissioner of police during an interview at the hospital the previous night. Virginia stopped what she was doing and joined Patrick in listening to the report.

"And we want to make it perfectly clear," continued the commissioner, "that all those who deal in drugs will find that their hellish trade in this city is coming to a close. I would advise them that if they know what is good for them, they would pack up their belongings and move elsewhere. We will—"

"Bullshit," spat out Patrick. "Something for the public. He knows, just like anyone else who thinks about it, that words will not stop the drug dealing. As long as there is as much demand for the stuff as there is, someone will supply it. Sure, we catch a few of the little guys every now and then, but when have you heard of anyone catching any of the big fish, the ones who make the big money? We catch the little pushers, throw them in jail for a while, and the next thing you know, they're back on the street again. There's talk about going after those who use the stuff."

"I know. I hear that the users are not only in the black and Mexican communities, but have spread to some of the well-to-do sections as well."

"That's part of the problem," grumbled Patrick. "Can you imagine what would happen if we went into the better neighborhoods trying to bust those rich kids who are on drugs?" Virginia started to speak, but was stopped by Patrick. "They have Captain Levine on the tube. Let's hear what he has to say."

" . . . although we don't know who the back-up man is, we, the men and women of the 77th Precinct, will not leave any stone unturned until we bring him to justice."

"More bullshit for the public," retorted Patrick. "The public—"

The telephone rang ending his thought. It was Captain Levine.

"O'Donovan. I want to see you as soon as you come in," said the captain. "By the way, where in hell is the evidence? And where were you last night?"

O'Donovan thought quickly before answering.

"I've got the stuff in a safe place," he said firmly. "I went over to Linsky's to tell his wife the sad news." He had forgotten about the attaché case. What if the case was not in the trunk of his car?

"Good, but bring that case directly to my office when you get here."

"Will do." O'Donovan hung up the phone and hurried to his car and breathed a sigh of relief when he found the case in the trunk.

When O'Donovan drove into the parking lot at the 77th Precinct, the thought struck him that he no longer need be concerned about Linsky's parking in his space. Funny, he brooded, how such an unimportant thing as a parking space came to mind at such a time. The police business of the day was in full progress when he opened the door to the squad room and strode toward the captain's office with the case under his arm.

Captain Levine was sitting at his desk, puffing on his pipe, when the phone rang. It was the commissioner of police.

"Levine here. Good morning, Commissioner. What can I do for you this morning?"

"I hope you're underway on that drug bust in your district last night. I'm calling from my home. I'm not sure whether or not I'll go to my office this morning. I can expect the media will be waiting for me like a bunch of hungry wolves. It's always that way when something like this happens. Let me know as soon as you come up with something."

"I certainly will, Commissioner. I'll put my best men on it right away."

"I guess you know the man you killed was an ambassador, from one of those small African countries that hardly anybody knows."

"An ambassador?"

"Yes. I found out last night. The coroner's office found his passport found among his possessions. I need not tell you this adds another dimension to the problem. Because of the international aspect, you can bet your last dollar the FBI will be in our hair right away."

Captain Levine was quiet for a few moments.

"Are you there, Levine?" asked the commissioner.

"Yes, sir. I was trying to think of the best man to put on the case."

"What about that lieutenant, what's his name? You know, the one who cracked that kidnap and ransom case a year ago. I was very much impressed by his professional handling of a pretty ticklish situation."

"You mean Sergeant O'Donovan?"

"Yes. Yes. That's the one. What do you think of him?"

"I guess you don't know. He was one of the officers in the drug bust. His partner, Officer Linsky, was the one killed by the back-up man."

"All the more reason for putting O'Donovan on the case."

"But I've got him on another case, a rape-murder case."

"Well, pull him off! Put someone else on the rape case. With all the heat I'm going to get about the killing of an ambassador, we need to get the very best men we've got to make sure everything done will be able to withstand the public scrutiny we're bound to get. What about

O'Reilly over in the 75th? I hear he's a sharp cookie. I can get him transferred, just for this case, to work with your man."

"No need. We'll take care of it. Just leave it to me."

"Well, keep me posted. I want a daily report on your progress."

"Yes, sir."

Captain Levine's conversation with the commissioner ended with that note. He sat at his desk for a few moments before unlocking the bottom drawer and staring at a telephone before removing it and dialing a number.

"Hello," was the response.

"Captain Levine, Senator. I'm sorry to call you so early, but I need to talk to you."

"Go ahead."

"That tip you gave me on a drug action wasn't as simple as you thought it would be."

"What happened?"

"You didn't tell me the suspect was an ambassador from one of those little African countries. There was—"

"What about the suspect? Is he—"

"Taken care of. He was killed in a shoot out, along with one of my best men."

"What was that?"

"Officer Linsky was killed by some unknown backup man. The commissioner of police has been on the phone this morning. He wants action, and quickly. To hear him talk, you would think we had an international incident on our hands. What do—?" A knock on the door interrupted him. "Hold it a moment," he whispered into the phone. Placing his hand across the speaker he asked, "Who is it?"

"O'Donovan, Captain."

"Hold it a moment." Returning to the conversation with the senator, he murmured, "I'll get back to you later." He hung up and placed the phone in the bottom drawer. Leaning back in his chair, he called out, "Come on in."

O'Donovan briskly entered the room and without delay placed the attaché case on the captain's desk. Captain Levine leisurely opened the case and inspected the contents.

"It's the real stuff," said O'Donovan quietly. "No key on the suspect worked, so I had to use a screw driver to force it open."

"All right. Tell me all about it. And where were you when I needed you last night? I thought you might show up when we were being interviewed by the media."

"I had my hands full with Linsky's wife. She was pretty broken up about what happened, as you can imagine."

"I know," grunted the captain. "What about the arrangements?"

"She's got family to help her over this period. I told her she could call upon the department for help."

O'Donovan gave a detailed account of the events of the previous evening. After listening to him, the captain sat, eyes riveted upon the open case.

"I don't understand it," murmured the captain.

"What was that, Captain?"

"Uh, what?"

"I think you said, you don't understand—what?"

Captain Levine did not immediately answer.

"You said there was a back-up man?"

"There must have been. Someone shot Linsky and got away during all the commotion."

"Do you think the woman in the Mercedes was the one who shot Linsky?"

"I don't think so. She took off when he and I

approached the car. It had to be someone across the street in the alley. One of the bystanders told me the shots came from that direction."

"I'm not sure where we're going with this, but for the time being, I'm going to keep you on it. I want you to keep me posted on everything you find out in your investigation. Everything. Is that clear?"

"Okay, Captain. I've got you."

"I'll put Jules on that rapist's case. Make sure you give him all the facts you've got on the case. You're going to need someone along with you. What about that female officer. What's her name?"

"You mean Lucy Panelli?"

"Yes. That's the one. She showed me she knows how to take care of herself. Lucy has been pushing me to let her into something more important than writing tickets or handling traffic. She's one of those women's lib type. All I need right now is to get mixed up in a hassle with her about discrimination in assignments."

"Hold off on that for a little while, if you don't mind, Captain. I'm not up to being responsible for another officer at this time."

"Okay, okay, if that's the way you feel about it."

O'Donovan, sensing the session was over, stood and prepared to leave.

"Anything else? I'll fill Jules in on the rape case and spend the rest of the day chasing down some of my contacts. I might pick up something on the drug bust."

"I can't think of anything. Refer all requests for information on that ambassador shooting to me."

"Coming through clearly Captain," said O'Donovan as he turned and quickly left the room.

4

Anguish

"Father! Father! wake up," cried Sheia, the youngest daughter of Daniel Msomi.

"Uh, uh, wha...wha." responded her father, not quite awake.

"Are you all right? You were moaning and threshing around in your chair. Tell me what was that all about." She placed cup of coffee on the table beside him and waited for an explanation.

"A dream, a very troubling dream. I am glad you woke me."

"What was it?"

"It was so clear. I'll try to see if I can remember it." Msomi took a sip of coffee then began.

"There was an eerie quietness in that gathering of lions, old and young, as they sat twitching their tails to scatter the flies. All eyes were fixed upon an opening in the hillside. Slowly coming out, rubbing their eyes in order to accustom them to the light, was a procession of very old lions, their manes silvery white. Without a sound, the old ones shuffled toward a figure lying motionless in the middle of the throng." Daniel took another sip of coffee, rose from his chair, and walked over to a window and stood, hands clasped behind his back, looking out on the street below. After a few minutes, he returned to his chair and sat down apparently lost in thought.

"Can you remember any more of the dream, Father?" asked Sheia.

"Yes. There is more. So many lions had gathered that it was difficult for those on the outer edges to see what was going on. One lion in particular paced back and forth nervously, trying to see over those in front of him. He could tell that the figure was not so young, or so old, what must have been a lion in his prime. After gazing at the figure lying so still, the old ones started pulling it toward the opening in hillside. A collective moan arose from the onlookers. The lion who had been pacing on the outer edges finally found an opening only to see the procession disappear in the hillside."

"Anything else?"

"No. You woke me at that point. Nothing to worry about. Just a dream."

"There is some juice and rolls in the refrigerator. You know where to find the instant coffee."

"Yes, thank you. I plan to stop at that little restaurant near the park for a cup of coffee and a sweet roll during my morning walk."

The images of the dream continued to annoy Daniel Msomi. It was at times like this that he missed the wise counsel of the village elders. His close friend and present tribal leader, Mavenbola, would have no difficulty finding a solution to his dream.

Daniel made his way to the door of the apartment and called out to his daughter, "I am on my way, I shall be back around noon."

"Do not forget. We have a dinner engagement with my friend from the agency."

In spite of his intent to push the dream from his thoughts, it came back with all its foreboding as soon as he closed the door of the apartment. Who was the lion in the middle of the throng? What happened to him? Why was there so much sadness? These thoughts flooded his mind.

"Good morning, Mr. Msomi," came the cheery greeting from the attendant as he opened the door to the outside for Daniel Msomi.

"Good morning, Andrew. Have a pleasant day."

It was indeed a good day, thought Msomi as he walked along. The sun was shining warmly, and the city had a clean look after the rain. He comforted himself with the thought that little of any real importance could go wrong on such a beautiful day.

Finding a seat in the park across the street from the White House, Msomi sat and listened to the outpourings of those present. Several groups were gathered, broadcasting to all who would listen, their impassioned tale of past or ongoing misdeeds by some group or institution.

He eyed the group immediately in front of him. They were complaining about the amount of attention man gives to increasingly deadlier weapons while whole populations were on the verge of starvation. There certainly was some truth to their complaint, he thought. Hunger had been a close companion of many tribes in Africa for untold years.

Daniel tried to get his son Joseph to give up being ambassador to the United States and accept a leadership role in his nation's affairs. On the few occasions when he was able to have a serious talk with him, the direction of their discussion turned to some never-explained higher level of responsibility for mankind. A shadow fell across him. He looked up to face a stout, black man carrying a placard that read, "No more for weapons of destruction."

"Are you with our protest against trillions for weapons while millions starve?" asked the protester.

Daniel shaded his eyes as he looked up at his questioner.

"No. Although I am in full accord with what you are doing, I am not a part of your group." Without another word, the visitor to his thoughts returned to his fellow protesters.

Tiring of the scene, Daniel left the park and made his way to the little café near H Street. When he entered the café, there was a heated discussion going on about drugs in "our" society.

"I hear there was an African involved in a shooting during a drug bust last night," said one of the participants. Some called warmly for direct action against those countries known as suppliers of drugs, which, if not halted, would be the ruination of the youth of America. Others, not so bloodthirsty, cautioned against too hasty an action, especially if it involved trampling upon the sovereignty of another country. Daniel had little interest in the whole issue of drugs, generally assigning it to one more problem of those countries wealthy enough to experiment with such foolishness. He felt that those who believed the problem could be solved without doing anything about the demand were setting themselves up to fail. Before leaving the café he made a call to his son, but got no response.

Msomi set a leisurely pace on his way back to the apartment, pausing occasionally to look into the windows of the shops he passed.

Once inside the apartment, he called for his daughter but received no answer. Lost in thought, he wandered around the room finally reaching the kitchen. On the table was a note. "Call the embassy as soon as you get home. They did not tell me what it was all about. Sheia." Daniel wondered what it was the embassy wanted, and in such a hurry. When he called Mr. Khumale at the embassy, he was told that something important had come up and he was to come there at once. Before he left the apartment, Daniel called security and requested a taxicab. A cab was waiting when he walked out of the building shortly before noon. He told the driver to take him to the Niberian Embassy on F Street.

Daniel's perplexing dream was forgotten in the rush of thoughts that engulfed his mind since he read the note left by his daughter. What could it be about? Had there been trouble in his native country? There had been predictions of troubles in the latest election, but such talk was common whenever an election was scheduled. Even his son Joseph had not escaped threats if he entertained thoughts of running for a higher office in the government.

The embassy was a plain, three-story building surrounded by a low wrought-iron fence. There were several men and women milling around on the sidewalk and in the front yard when Msomi got there. He was let into the building by one of the lesser officials.

"What is that all about?" asked Daniel, pointing to the throng outside.

"Mr. Khumale will tell you. Here he comes now." A slight built black man wearing a loose-fitting, colorful African garment was approaching, wringing his hands in obvious distress.

"Bad news! Very bad news, Mr. Msomi," exclaimed the distraught Mr. Khumale, the senior officer of the embassy.

"What news? What news?" snapped Daniel Msomi, inwardly dreading an answer. His eyes fixed anxiously on the face of the other, who was clearly groping to find the appropriate words to express himself.

"Then . . . you have not heard . . . ?"

"Heard what? Heard what? speak up. What is it you are trying to tell me?"

"Let us go into my office." Mr. Khumale turned and beckoned to Daniel to follow him. In the office, he closed the door and motioned to Daniel to have a seat.

"There has been some trouble—a shooting," said Mr. Khumale. "Early this morning, I was called by the coroner's office. I was told to notify you that you are to come down and identify your son Joseph."

"My son Joseph!" exclaimed Msomi, leaping to his feet. "What is this all about? What has happened to my son?"

"I do not know all the details. The officer I talked with said he could tell me no more."

"Could Joseph be hurt in some way?"

"Hurt people are not taken to the coroner's department. I am afraid it is a great deal more serious than that."

"You mean . . . ?"

"I am afraid so. If you prefer, we can go out the back door and miss those reporters in front. They have been here all morning, pestering us for interviews."

A few minutes later, Daniel and Mr. Khumale were out of the embassy and into an automobile on their way to the coroner's office. As he rode along images of his dream flashed before Daniel's eyes. It all became clear to him. Of course. The young lion in the center of the grieving throng was his son. The ancient lions coming out of the hillside, only to take that still figure back with them were his and his son's ancestors. The lion seeking the identity of the figure lying so quietly beyond his view was himself. Yes, it was so sadly clear. It was foretold many years before, at Joseph's birth. Mbondu was right, or was it the message of the ancestral bones, pondered Daniel as they rode along.

Mr. Khumale drove up and stopped in front of a gray, unattractive building that housed the coroner's department.

"Are you ready, sir?" he asked. "I know this is difficult for you, Mr. Msomi, but—"

"I know. We must go whether we wish to or not," replied Daniel as he reached out to grasp the hand extended to him. "It is such an ugly place, but come, let us get on with it."

Both men hurried into the building. On an inquiry at the information desk, they were directed to the office of the chief of the department. His secretary looked up as they entered and motioned to them to take a number and have a seat. When it became Daniel's turn, he followed Mr. Khumale into a small windowless office containing no more than the bare necessities required of an office—a couple of chairs, a file cabinet in the corner, and a desk behind which was seated a harried-looking individual of Asian ancestry.

"This is Mr. Msomi," began Mr. Khumale, nodding toward Daniel. "We are here because of a call you made to my office this morning. I am the senior officer of the Niberian Embassy. Mr. Msomi is my countryman."

The official, a Mr. Otono, began to shift through a pile of papers on his desk.

"Msomi, Msomi," he mumbled more to himself than to them. "Ah, here we are," he said, pulling an envelope from the pile. On opening the envelope he examined the contents briefly. He looked up, directing his remarks to Mr. Khumale.

"You can understand why it is necessary for me to handle this case rather than turn it over to one of the other employees. Because of the international nature of this affair, an ambassador, all kinds of people are involved, some at pretty high levels in our city and government. You understand..."

Daniel was becoming impatient with what he viewed as uncalled-for delay in getting at the bottom of a dreadful affair.

"What is this about my son? Why was he killed—assassinated?" demanded Msomi.

Mr. Otono raised a hand to stop the flow of words coming from the distraught Daniel

"Not so fast. We must first make the proper identification. That is the primary reason for your being here this morning." Rising from his chair, he motioned to the two men to follow him. They took an elevator to the basement and the morgue.

Mr. Khumale stood quietly at the door while Daniel followed Mr. Otono to a table in a far corner, where he pulled back a sheet to expose the face of a body lying there.

Daniel, with hardly any emotion showing, nodded.

"Yes. It is my son Joseph."

The three men retraced their steps to Mr. Otono's office, where he asked them to be seated.

"This matter has taken up most of my morning," he told them. "Even before I got here, the FBI was here waiting for me. I had no answers for them. I'm sure I will have no answers for you either."

"Well, who does know anything about this matter?" demanded Daniel.

"If I were you I would get in touch with Mr. Levine, the captain of the 77th Precinct. What happened, happened in his district."

Mr. Khumale nudged Daniel and spoke softly.

"It would be better if we leave. We can call Mr. Levine from my office. There is much we have to do. Arrangements have to be made. Many things must be taken care of." He rose from his chair, thanked the coroner, and turned to leave.

The ride back to the embassy was made in total silence. Daniel contemplated the workings of fate, although he stopped short of questioning the motives of his ancestors. Still, he could not hold back the bitter feelings that welled up inside him as he reflected upon the tragic turn of affairs that had robbed him of an eldest son, who was expected to follow in his footsteps. Perhaps the ancestors were angry because of his putting too much distance between himself and the traditions of the village and the tribe. He recalled he had felt more than a little uncomfortable when he named his first-born son Joseph. As a consequence, when fortune favored him with a second son, he gave him an African name, Ntombi. He was already a great help in the business, a rapid learner and highly motivated to make a success in the business world. Mr. Khumale's voice brought Daniel back from his musings.

"We are here, Mr. Msomi," said his companion in a soft voice. Mr. Khumale, noticing reporters still milling around, had driven to the back door of the embassy and had the car door open for Daniel to step out. "Let us hurry to my office. I must give some kind of statement to the press. If not, they will be here until I do. I will have one of the ladies bring you a cup of coffee." He then left to meet the press.

When Mr. Khumale returned, he found Daniel staring at a half-empty cup of coffee. "Well, we are rid of that collection of vultures. It did not matter if I kept telling them over and over again that, at this time, we did not have any more details than they had." A secretary quietly entered the room, bringing fresh cups of coffee for the two men.

Coffee in hand, Mr. Khumale took a sip and leaned back in his chair. He lit a cigarette and blew a cloud of smoke toward the ceiling. "We must put in a call for Captain Levine at the 77th Precinct," he remarked softly. "Do you prefer I talk to him?" Daniel nodded.

An associate placed a call for Captain Levine. She was told he was out and would not be back for the rest of the day.

"I just remember," said Daniel.

"Remember what?" asked Mr. Khumale.

"So many things were going on that I forgot to ask for Joseph's things when we were at the coroner's office. Do you think his things will be there?"

"It is not your fault. I should have thought of that myself. We must go back to the personal effects department. I will have one of my men drive you back. He will drive you home, or anywhere else you might like to go."

"I think I shall want to go home after we leave the coroner's. I have an unpleasant chore ahead of me. My daughter Sheia must be told. That will not be easy. She was very fond of Joseph. Yes. Yes. This will be quite a blow, quite a blow." Daniel murmured a deeply felt expression of gratitude as he passed by Mr. Khumale on his way out of the embassy.

Daniel had no trouble finding the personal effects section when Nhlanla, Mr. Khumale's assistant, let him out at the coroner's department. Again, he found himself in a line of men and women, all there for a common purpose, to get the belongings of a close relative, or someone dear. When it became his turn, Daniel rose with a heavy heart and approached the counter. After giving suitable identification, he waited, lonely in thought, while the clerk went to get his son's things. The clerk, upon his return, threw on the counter several articles of clothing wrapped in a raincoat: a hat, and a paper bag containing a number of loose articles, such as glasses, watch, passport, and a bracelet made of jackal and lion's teeth.

The memory of many years earlier rolled across Daniel's eyes as he saw the bracelet fall out of the bag. It was a small village on the edge of the forest. Iyanga had made this bracelet for Joseph to protect him from the evil spirits that patrol the forest. It seemed, thought Daniel, that while the bracelet did protect his son from evil spirits during the time he was in the forest with the little people, it failed utterly to protect him in the most civilized of countries.

"Please check each of the items and sign on the bottom of the form," directed the clerk, bringing Daniel back from his musing. He reviewed all of the items listed, signed the form, and left. Nhlanla met him at the front door of the building and directed him to the car.

"Where would you like to go now, Mr. Msomi?" asked Nhlanla.

"To my apartment. Thank you." Daniel took the bracelet out of the bag and turned it round and around, looking at it intently as they drove along. When they arrived at the building, Nhlanla helped him carry his son's things into the apartment, expressed a few words of sympathy, and left Daniel with his sorrow.

The sound of a key turning in the door of the apartment disturbed the macabre silence that pervaded the apartment. Joseph's things were in the same place Daniel had dropped them when he came home from the coroner's earlier in the day. No matter how hard he tried, he could not come up with an explanation of the events of the past hours that would lessen the blow on his daughter.

"Father, are you here?" cried Sheia anxiously.

"Yes, in here, the living room."

Sheia entered the room, lit only by a street light. She turned on a light to find Daniel huddled in his favorite chair near the window, his eyes fixed upon a pile of clothing lying on the sofa.

"Are you all right? What are all those things on the sofa? Whose are they?"

Daniel had no ready answer to any of her questions. His customary answer to her first question was "I am fine." Tonight he really was not feeling fine. As to the other questions, he watched Sheia walk over to the sofa to get a better look at the pile of clothing.

"They are your brother's things," he said softly.

"Joseph's? What are his things doing here?"

Daniel knew there was nothing left to do except tell her the whole story, at least what he knew about it. He stood and edged over to his daughter.

"Your brother . . . Joseph, has gone to join our ancestors. He—"

"What! What are you saying? Was it an automobile accident? Speak up, Father!"

"It was not an accident. He was shot, assassinated. No one seems to be able to give me any details about what really happened. I have been referred to a Captain Levine at the 77th Precinct police station. Mr. Khumale at the embassy called his office but was unable to contact him."

Uncontrollable tears streamed down Sheia's face. Daniel led her to a chair, placed an arm around her as she sat, shoulders heaving with every sob. They were aroused from their grief by the persistent ringing of a telephone. Sheia rose to answer it—a friend offering sympathy.

"Perhaps we should turn on the television," said Daniel. "There may be some news on this matter."

Sheia turned the television to their favorite channel and anchorman Don Nester. They tuned in as he was mentioning the shooting the previous evening.

"... an alleged drug bust on 20th Street and L at approximately eight o'clock last evening left two dead, one a police officer. Full details are not available at this time. It is believed that the man supposedly carrying the drugs was a member of the diplomatic corps of one of the Third-World countries. The police estimated the cocaine in his possession had a street value of twenty million dollars."

"It is a lie!" shouted Daniel at the television. "My son would never get involved in anything connected to drugs. Lies! Lies! Lies!—"

"Calm down, Father," interrupted Sheia. "Let us listen to the rest of the news."

Don Nester continued.

"... and the police are seeking the identity of the mystery woman in a black Mercedes who pulled up and talked to the suspect just before the officers arrived on the scene. A search is also on for a back-up man who shot the officer. Commissioner of police, Blake O'Sullivan stated at a news conference that all efforts would be given to find the culprit. Because of the nature of this case, the FBI has been brought into the matter." This ended Don Nester's account of the shooting, and he went on to other news.

Daniel watched the television for a few more minutes, hoping to hear more details about the shooting. None came. Finally, he spoke faintly.

"I have heard enough, let us turn the devilish thing off." The turmoil that raged inside Daniel pushed him to do something . . . to wander around the apartment, to the kitchen, to the bedroom, and to the window where he loved to look out and see the Capitol. "There is something fishy about this whole matter and I intend to get at the bottom of it. I know my son. He would never get involved in something as sordid as drugs. I know that! I know that!"

"Father, we must make arrangements to return to our country. Perhaps we should call Mr. Khumale to find out what we should do."

"Yes, yes, you are right. Please call him."

Sheia joined her father at the window after she made the call to Mr. Khumale.

"The only thing we have to do is to arrange our trip to our home. He will take care of all that needs to be done. It would be advisable for us to be there when the plane with Joseph's body arrives."

"What to tell your mother? We will have time enough to think about that during the next few hours."

Because of the emergency nature of their trip, and with the assistance of the FBI, reservations were made for an early flight the next morning.

5

Investigative Services Inc. (ISI)

It was a cloudless fall day with a cool dry breeze from the north when Daniel Msomi and his daughter Sheia returned to the city of painful memories, following the burial of Joseph among his ancestors in his native land.

Ntombi, Msomi's only remaining son, told him of a rumor about threats on Joseph's life made by a political aspirant for a high office in the government of Niberia. Daniel put the matter in the hands of a good friend, Leleti Nkombo, with instructions to follow up any lead and to keep him informed of his findings.

Toward evening, Sheia began seeking news about Joseph's death on the television. She tuned into the last part of Don Nestor's account of the news.

". . . the police are leaving no stone unturned in their search for the back-up man who shot officer Linsky and for the unknown blond woman in the late model Mercedes who stopped and talked with the suspect shortly before the shooting. The FBI has retired from the case, since it seemed a straightforward case. Further investigations would be up to the local authorities."

"There is something unmistakably fishy about this whole situation," grumbled Msomi as he rose and turned off the television set. "Instead of clearing my son of this absurd drug charge, the authorities have decided his guilt without a full investigation." Pounding his fist on the arm of the sofa, he thundered, "I know my son Joseph. There is some kind of cover-up going on here, and I intend to get to the bottom of it, I, Daniel Msomi, will let them know that no matter what they think, I am not a man to be trifled with. If they cannot find the truth, then I shall find it for them."

"What do you think you can do that the police are not doing, Father? Even the FBI has decided there is nothing more they can do." Sheia waited patiently for her father to answer.

Daniel pondered her questions for a moment.

"That is it, that is what I will do," he mused. "I will conduct my own investigation."

"What on earth are you talking about? What do you know about investigating anything? Besides, what do you think you could do that the FBI could not?"

"Very simple. I will hire my own investigator. Get Mr. Khumale on the telephone." A few minutes later, Sheia returned and handed Daniel the telephone.

"Mr. Khumale," said Daniel. "I have a need for your services. I am not at all satisfied with the job the authorities are doing regarding the murder of my son. I intend to do something about it, no matter what it costs me. Can you put me in touch with a reputable person, a private investigator, who could delve into this despicable affair and clear my son's good name?"

After a short pause, Mr. Khumale replied.

"I know just the right man for you, Mr. Msomi. His name is T.J. Fowler, a man whose services we have, on occasion, used for certain sensitive matters. We found him to be dependable, honest, and thorough in his investigations. The embassy was very pleased with his work. I have no qualms about referring him to you. When would you like to have him come and see you?"

"Just a moment. Let me check with my daughter." Learning she would be available that evening, he returned to Mr. Khumale. "The sooner the better. This evening if at all possible."

"I cannot promise this evening, but I will do all I can to get in touch with him and prevail upon him to come and see you this evening. I will make it clear it is urgent with international implications."

"It is in your hands. I look forward to hearing from you as soon as you have made the arrangements. My daughter and I will be home all evening. It is usually quite late before we go to bed." Hanging up the phone, Daniel turned to Sheia and murmured, "Perhaps we shall soon get to the bottom of this murder, this assassination. Mr. Khumale is impressed with this Mr. Fowler. Let us hope he is as good as he is described to us."

The evening passed slowly. Daniel reached for a book, opened it but found the words soon ran together without meaning. There was nothing on the television that elicited more than a momentary glance. Waiting for a call about the private investigator seemed interminable. Then it came—the call from Mr. Khumale. They could expect Mr. Fowler to arrive within the hour.

At a quarter to nine, security telephoned to tell them a Mr. Fowler was there to see them. A few minutes later, Sheia opened the door to admit a visitor. She led him into the living room and to her father.

"Mr. Fowler . . . my father, Daniel Msomi," said Sheia by way of introduction.

Msomi rose and extended his hand in acknowledgment. He judged the visitor to be in his mid-thirties, about six feet tall, and weighing around 180 pounds. He felt that something was out of place in that brown-skinned face. His eyes that seemed to take in everything

77

in the room were green.

"My card, Mr. Msomi," said Fowler.

Daniel motioned for him to take a seat in a chair facing the sofa.

"T.J. Fowler, Investigative Services Inc." he remarked. "What do the letters T.J. stand for?"

"I've been asked that many times," replied Fowler with a smile. "That's all there is. I've been called T.J. as far back as I can remember. An uncle thought it stood for Thomas Jefferson, but that was only a guess."

"Investigative Services. Is that the same as private investigator?"

"I suppose you could say so. I just didn't like the words and the images people have of private investigators."

Daniel took a hasty look at Fowler before he and his daughter sat down on the sofa facing him. Their visitor was casually dressed, light sweater over an open neck shirt, slacks, and a pair of athletic shoes. It seemed like a strange dress to initiate a business meeting, thought Daniel. But, Americans appear casual about many things that would be done differently in his country.

Sheia began the conversation.

"Thank you for coming, Mr. Fowler. I need not tell you that this unfortunate death of my brother has made life difficult for me and my father these past weeks. Given my father's status in this country, conducting a private investigation may not be looked upon with favor by those in authority."

"I understand that," said Fowler. "But you must be aware there are limits on just how quiet you can keep such an investigation. However, we can deal with that when it comes up. I think we should talk about some other things first."

"Your fee?" remarked Daniel. "You come well recommended by Mr. Khumale. We will pay whatever you charge."

"No. That is not what I mean. I've been following the news account of the shooting ever since it happened. Even the FBI has concluded there was nothing unusual about the case and have turned it over to the local police."

"See! Just like the others. He has decided my son is guilty," Daniel exclaimed, turning to his daughter.

"Be calm, Father. Let us hear what Mr. Fowler has to say. It seems to me that drinks are in order at this time. What would you like, Mr. Fowler?"

"Scotch and water is fine for me."

Sheia left and soon returned with drinks discussing the attaché case Daniel had given Joseph for his birthday.

"I must go down in the morning and have Captain Levine turn my son's case over to me."

Fowler, drink in hand, leaned back in his chair and waited for Sheia or her father to continue.

Sheia broke the silence.

"Go ahead, Mr. Fowler. You were about to tell us some things that have come to your attention in this case."

Fowler fixed his eyes upon Daniel.

"I didn't mean to I imply I think your son was guilty of anything. All I wanted to do was point out a few things that have been brought out in this case. First, I know the police officer, O'Donovan, who is involved in the shooting. I believe him to be an honest policeman. He stated, on television, your son had in his possession, in that case we've been discussing, cocaine worth a street value of five million dollars."

"Did you have any chance to actually see the case?" asked Sheia softly.

"They showed a picture of it on television a couple of nights ago. It was a pretty fancy case made out of zebra skin, or something like that."

"You may not be able to get the case when you go down to the captain's office. These things take time to work themselves out. When you add the international part to the situation, it makes it more difficult for the wheels of justice to move quicker."

"Could we go back to what you were talking about earlier?" asked Sheia. "You mentioned Officer O'Donovan. Was there anything else?"

"The other officer on the bust, Linsky, was killed during the shootout. I didn't know him too well. I need not tell you the police look at the killing of an officer a little differently than the killing of an ordinary citizen. It does not matter that the FBI have bowed out of it, the local police are looking into it very closely. They consider the shooting the work of a back-up man tied to your son."

A shroud of silence drifted over the room. Daniel got up, hands clasped behind his back, and slowly walked over to the window and looked out.

"There is one more thing that's got the police uptight and convinced they were dealing with a drug bust," declared Fowler.

"And that is what?" asked Daniel without turning around.

"They are seeking the identity of an unknown woman in a Mercedes who pulled up and had words with your son just before the officers arrived on the scene."

"Is there anything else we should know?" asked Sheia.

"Those are the main points I have picked up."

"Does that mean you are convinced my son is guilty of the charges made against him?" asked Daniel turning around and facing his visitor.

"Nope. I only wanted to point out certain things before you make up your mind to go ahead with an investigation on your own. I believe in leveling with my clients before I take on their case. If I think there is something they should keep in mind, I will tell them in advance. If they still wish to go ahead, I can promise them I will bring to light anything that has a bearing on their problem, and I do mean anything.

"I'm finishing up my latest case and I will be available in a day or two. Call my office and let my secretary know if you plan to go ahead with an investigation."

On his way out of the building, Fowler mulled over his evening with the Msomis. It never seemed to fail, he thought. Most people had no difficulty dealing with wrongdoing by someone else. The story was a lot different with their immediate family. No matter how he looked at the evidence as presented by the FBI and the police department, it looked like an open and shut case. There seemed to be too many things that tied Msomi's son to the usual drug bust. There was no doubt of some exaggeration in the account of the street value of the dope found in the case, but that wasn't unusual. Yep, plenty of problems.

He got into his car and sat there several minutes while images of Sheia flashed across his mind. The loose-fitting robe did little to hide the curves of her figure, and the grace of her walk as she moved around the room was something else. He had known a few African women, but none impressed him as much as Sheia. Funny about the Africans he had known. They all spoke with a British accent and were formal down to the letter.

The drive to his apartment was direct and hasty. He would find out in the morning whether or not Daniel

Msomi wanted to hire him. Somehow, he felt reluctant about taking on the Msomi problem. He wasn't sure whether he would find anything that would ease their pain and suffering.

Daniel and Sheia were lost in their thoughts following Fowler's visit. Neither was sure he had said anything positive about the shooting of a son and a brother. The somber silence that pervaded the room and its occupants finally faded away when Sheia spoke.

"What do you think of Mr. Fowler?"

"I think we have a man we can trust to get to the bottom of this mess. My first impression is that once he sets his teeth in a problem, he will never let go until he reaches a solution. I am sure he will find Joseph had nothing to do with this sordid drug affair. Someone has gone to a lot of trouble to destroy my son's good name. But mark my words, I will get to the bottom of it. Everything will become clear to us before long."

Sheia's thoughts shifted to Fowler. Could they trust him to do all he could to solve this mystery? Still, he came highly recommended by Mr. Khumale. But there was something unsettling about him. During the few times their eyes met, she had the feeling he was probing deep into her thoughts. In addition, she felt uncomfortably naked before his searching gaze. She was not sure she shared her father's confidence in Mr. Fowler, private investigator.

"We must make arrangements to meet with Captain Levine in the morning," said Daniel. "I am anxious to find out whether that really is Joseph's attaché case he has. I gave that case to him. I will know if it is his or not."

"What about Mr. Fowler? Should we call his office and instruct him that we wish to hire his services?"

"He is our man. More than that. I wish to have him accompany us to the police station to meet with the captain."

"As you wish. I will make the arrangements in the morning."

6

Many Questions—No Answers

The modest office of Investigative Services Inc. (ISI) was located on the second floor of an old office building on Florida Avenue near Howard University. When Fowler entered the office, he was greeted impatiently by Henrietta, a plump brown-skinned woman who looked to be in her late fifties.

"Where have you been?" she snapped. "That African, Mr. Msomi, or his daughter have been trying to reach you all morning. I can't get my work done for answering the phone and telling them you're not in. What's it all about?"

"I'll tell you later. Get Mr. Msomi on the phone and cool down. By the way, I closed the domestic case this morning on my way to the office." Thus said, he walked into the cubicle that served as his private space.

Henrietta had been with him from the beginning of his career. She managed the office, leaving him to take care of the outside work without having to deal with details. She took the place of his mother who died when he was a boy. Whether he accepted her tirades or concerns did not matter; he knew she meant well.

"Your party is on the line," shouted Henrietta from the outer office.

"Daniel Msomi here. My daughter has arranged an appointment with a Captain Levine of the 77th Precinct for two o'clock this afternoon, and we want you to attend the meeting with us."

"Let me see," Fowler said checking his calendar. "All right, I'll meet you at the entrance of the precinct building at two o'clock."

Henrietta stood in the doorway, eyeing Fowler at his desk.

"I can't see why you're thinking of taking a case like that," she cautioned. "From what I've read and heard on TV, it looks open and shut. They caught the man dead to right, and what about the policeman who was killed in the shootout?" She paused and rummaged through her notebook. "Besides, a Mr. Jackson called about you looking into a matter for him, if you remember."

"Another cheating wife case. I need a rest from racing around town and sitting across the street from some cheezy motel waiting to take a picture of a spouse coming out with a lover. Let's pass on that one."

"At least those cases pay our bills," reminded Henrietta. "Let's not turn up our noses on the work that keeps us going. Anyway, you know how hard it is to get along with you when things don't go just right, and my guess is all you're going to out of that Msomi situation is a lot of frustration."

"You might be right. But something about this case interests me. Call Jackson and tell him I'm tied up. Refer him to Bill Jones."

"Okay, if you wish, but my sixth sense tells me you're making a mistake. You know how—"

"I know all about your sixth sense. How about trusting mine for a change?" Giving her a wink, he headed for the door leading into the corridor. "I'll be out for the rest of the day. I might try to catch Alabama Slim and a couple of my homeboys or homechicks before meeting the Msomis. If anything important comes up, call me. Fowler looked at his watch. *Good*, he thought, *I have at least two hours before my meeting.*

Fowler walked to his car, peeling off his coat and loosening his tie. He tossed his coat into the back seat and slid beneath the steering wheel and entered the passing scene, headed for Lafayette Square. He parked, placed his coat in the trunk, and wandered into the square. Out of the corner of his eye, he saw a familiar figure. A thin, black man dressed in shabby clothes and a floppy hat was patiently working the visitors for any loose change that would help buy a meal for a veteran down on his luck.

Waiting while the man made a successful approach and stood with cup outstretched, Fowler mulled over the ways people satisfied their needs. Alabama Slim, the name he was known by, was one of the best at getting someone to part with his loose change. He was quick to appraise anyone who approached, varying his tone and appeal according to his assessment of what was likely to work. His manner was always pleasant, his gratitude cheerful, no matter how small the amount given.

"Hey, Slim," said Fowler, tapping him on the shoulder. "What's happening, m'man?"

Without looking around, Slim protested.

"Can't you see I'm busy! Things haven't gone so good these past few days. I've never seen such poor tourists as this year. It's been tough making ends meet." Turning around to give Fowler his full attention, Slim mumbled, "Okay. Okay, what is it you want this time? Tell me what kind of information you need, and I'll determine what it'll cost you. And bear in mind the cost of living has gone up quite a bit since I last saw you."

Fowler smiled. Things must have been pretty good for Slim. He was in a good mood. He was a reliable source of information. On rare occasions, he talked about his past life in various cities in the southeastern part of Alabama. He graduated from a little Negro college with a degree in education and taught elementary classes in an all-black school in his state. His degree opened no doors when he left Alabama and went north. Regardless of the city or state, he faced one barrier after another. After years of trying to find work that pleased him, he simply gave up and joined countless others making their living on the streets.

"I've got a client involved in the drug bust that went down the past week or so," began Fowler looking intently at slim.

"Which one? There's so many these days, you would think that's all the police have to do. One thing about it. It's given us poor honest working people a chance to earn a decent living without being hassled by the cops." He winked and smiled. "They can't spend their time on these drug dealers and chase after us at the same time." Pausing, he asked, "Which drug bust are you talking about?"

"That one up on L Street, about a week or so ago. An African ambassador was killed as well as a policeman. What do you hear about that one?"

Slim thought for a moment, looked toward an empty bench, and slowly walked over and sat down. Fowler followed and leaned on the back of the bench.

"Yeah, I heard about that one. The cops caught the dude red-handed with the stuff in some kind of a bag. A blonde in a Mercedes was involved. They think she was the contact. I—"

"Yeah. Yeah. I know all about that," said Fowler. "But what's being said on the street? Who's behind it?"

"It looks like you're going to strike out this time, Jimbo. I haven't heard anything more than what's in the newspapers and on TV. Nobody I've talked to knows anything else. Look at it this way my boy..."

"Go on, go on."

"Why shouldn't the Africans get some of that easy money? Why should they let those guys from South America get it all? Kind of surprising though."

"What?"

"Well, those African motherfuckers always struck me as being pretty smart, sort of better than the rest of us. Then to get caught with the coke on him like that. Even the kids come up with slicker ways of passing the stuff along."

"You mean you really haven't heard any more on the street than that?"

"There's nothing out there, Jimbo. What you've heard is what you've got. If there was more to it, I'd know about it. It's not there. Believe me."

"What about Rat? Do you think he has any information? He's got some pretty good contacts in the drug scene."

"No chance there. He's been off the street for the past month. Things got tough, so he pissed in front of a cop and got arrested for lewd and obscene behavior. At least he ate good for a month. But, they're about to throw his ass out, from what I hear. He might have picked up on something in jail though."

"What about Fat Susie?"

"She's hanging out behind the State Department. She's hoping some foreign diplomat will come to town so someone will give her money for a room and a meal just to keep her out of sight. You might try her, but I don't think you'll have much luck. If I haven't picked up on anything, the chances are good there's nothing out there."

"Keep your eyes open, and if you hear anything related to the case let me know." Fowler turned and hurried to his car. Although the clouds that floated lazily overhead had begun to darken, indicating a change of weather was in store, it was a sticky warmth. He got into his car, rolled the windows down, and was on his way.

There was no need to rush, the 77th Precinct was little more than ten minutes away. He found a space in front of the building and, still early, sat and watched those entering and leaving the building. He wondered how people would handle their problems if there were no police departments. There had to be some kind of agreed-upon procedure for managing deviant behavior if society was to function in an orderly manner. Everyone would have to give up some freedom for the good of the total society.

"Mr. Fowler."

Sheia's voice at the window on the passenger side of the car interrupted his thoughts. When he got out of the car to join them, he saw Sheia was wearing a tight-fitting pair of slacks that outlined every curve of her body topped by a colorful blouse and several well-manicured toes peeped out from a pair of comfortable-looking sandals. Her father was dressed in a business suit. Beads of perspiration had formed on his black face and trickled down on his white collar.

"We are glad to see you, Mr. Fowler," said Sheia as she walked beside him up the steps. "This is our first time in a police station in this country. We do not know our way around, so it is good to have you along. My father and I appreciate the adjusting of your schedule so you can be with us when we meet with Captain Levine."

They entered a large, gray room filled with officers conducting police business. Daniel Msomi and his daughter kept pace with Fowler as he made his way toward an office in a far corner, underneath a large round clock hanging on the wall.

"This is the captain's office." Fowler paused and gave several sharp knocks on the door.

A shuffling noise came from the room followed by an invitation to enter. It was a small room simply furnished, a few chairs fronting a plain desk, a couch on one side of the room, a file cabinet in a corner. In the window a little air conditioner whirred busily, keeping the room cool. Captain Levine, a short, slightly built man rose from behind the desk and greeted them.

"Come in," boomed the captain in a voice that Fowler always felt was out of place for a person of his stature. "Have a seat," he indicated to all of them and held a chair for Sheia to sit. Nodding toward Fowler, he said, "Well, good to see you again." With the formalities over, the captain took his seat.

Fowler leaned back in his chair, eyeing those present, not sure who would initiate the discussion. He did not feel it was his responsibility to get things moving.

"What can I do for you?" Captain Levine asked, directing his question to Daniel Msomi.

"I am Daniel Msomi. My son, Joseph Msomi, ambassador from Niberia was murdered by two of your men exactly two weeks ago. You have one of his possessions, an attaché case. I am here to obtain it."

"Murdered!" Captain Levine's voice rose in anger. "Because of your son, two of my best men were put in jeopardy—one, a fine young officer and family man was killed. Murdered, you say! You've got a nerve coming in here and accusing my men of murder. Right now I have one of my men spending all of his time trying to find your son's back-up man and his woman accomplice when he should be dealing with other problems of this city. Don't come into my office and tell me anything about a murder!" His eyes glared into the eyes of the other.

Fowler marveled at the composure of Daniel Msomi. Other than a tightening of his lips, one would never guess at the anger that flowed beneath the surface. For a moment, he felt Sheia was going to answer for her father. This was not to be. In a clear soft-spoken voice, dripping with venom, Daniel Msomi replied.

"I know my son Joseph. He would never, I mean never, get involved with anything as sordid as drugs. I intend to get to the bottom of this matter."

The last word barely escaped Msomi's lips before the captain leaped to his feet, face livid with anger.

"What do you mean? Are you suggesting this was some kind of put-up job? How dare you, especially after one of my men was killed in that bust?" Reaching down beside his desk he picked up an attaché case and placed it on his desk.

The look on Daniel Msomi's face was all Fowler needed to know the case belonged to his son.

Captain Levine deliberately pushed the case toward Msomi. He spoke in a calm voice.

"Take a look at this case. Can you identify it?" He sat down and watched him warily.

Msomi slowly reached for the case without replying. His eyes roved over it as his hands began to turn it from side to side. He paused for a moment to look closely at the initials, J.N.M. (Joseph Ngemi Msomi). He tenderly rubbed his hands back and forth across the case before turning to Sheia with a sad grimace.

"It is Joseph's case. It is the one I had made for him when he became ambassador. I would know this case—"

Sheia placed her hand on his, aware of the emotion that rolled over him and garbled his words. Without saying a word, Msomi took his other hand and patted hers. Fowler could see it was a difficult time for both of them.

Msomi watched intently as Captain Levine took the case and laid it flat on the desk. With a key from his inside pocket he unlocked it and exposed the contents—a number of clear plastic bags containing a whitish substance. He sat back in his chair and looked silently at the three of them. Msomi sat focused upon the bags without comprehension.

Fowler poked a finger into an open bag, under the steady gaze of the captain. He tasted the substance, paused, then turned to face the inquiring looks of Sheia and her father.

"It's coke all right," he declared, nodding. When he attempted to reach into the case for a second look, Captain Levine quickly closed and locked the case.

Daniel Msomi spoke without any hint of emotion.

"That is my son's case. You may keep its contents, all I want is his attaché case."

"Well, you won't get it!" The captain's temper flared again. "This case and its contents are evidence. It may be returned to you after the coroner's jury next week. You will be notified of the exact date, time, and place."

"I see," said Daniel Msomi in a quiet voice. "We have engaged Mr. Fowler to look into this matter for us. Unfortunately, we do not trust the police authorities to make a fair investigation. If one had been made, my son Joseph would already be cleared of this despicable charge."

Captain Levine leaned forward, fixing his eyes on Fowler.

"You know how we work around here. This is a police matter, and we handle it our own way. I don't want to hear you are getting in the way of my men and their investigation." He paused and, without taking his eyes off Fowler cautioned, "Is that clear?"

Fowler nodded. He had been through similar scenes

before with Captain Levine and other police officials. Besides, he worked as an officer on a beat for several years before becoming a private investigator.

The captain placed the case on the floor beside his desk. He rose from his chair and indicated the meeting was over. His three visitors arose as one and filed out of the office.

A voice was heard above the babble of the squad room. It came from a black, neatly dressed, plainclothes officer.

"Hey, T.J. Fowler, what the hell are you doing here this time of the day?" He quickly approached Fowler and the Msomis.

"Business, Jules." Fowler paused briefly. "I'll tell you about it later. Have you seen O'Donovan?"

"Over there by the coffee machine in the corner."

"See you later," mumbled Fowler as he gave his attention to the Msomis. "I've got to see O'Donovan. He was in on the drug bust and shooting. I might as well start with him. We've been friends for a long time, and I'm sure he'll give me the straight scoop. I'm going to check some of my contacts, and if you are available, I would like to come by this evening and let you know what I've picked up."

"That would be fine. Should we make it at seven o'clock?" asked Msomi. "We would be through with dinner by that time."

"Fine," said Fowler. He waved at the Msomis and made his way toward O'Donovan, who was leaning on a vending machine, drinking a cup of coffee.

"What brings you here, Fowler?" asked O'Donovan. "I thought you were on one of those cheating wife cases. Boy, you guys sure have it easy, sitting in front of motels, imagining the grunts and groans going on behind closed doors, while we real police do the dirty work in this city."

"Someone has to take on those interesting jobs while you eight-to-five guys enjoy your wives in your warm bed. It's a job like any other job, and it pays well."

"Want a cup of coffee?" O'Donovan pointed to the machine. Getting a nod, he put a coin in the machine, filled a cup and handed it to Fowler. "Are you on a case we're involved in?"

Over the years Fowler traded notes on certain assignments with O'Donovan, and each did favors for the other.

"You can say were in the same arena, but not on the same team—the Msomi shooting. His father and sister think there's more to it than has surfaced so far. They're paying me to look into it. They absolutely refuse to believe their Joseph could ever become involved in drugs."

"You're taking their money under false pretenses this time, ol' buddy. I guess you know I was on that drug bust."

"Yeah. I know. Sorry to hear about your partner Linsky. That was a bad rap. I went over every known thing about the case with the Msomis and told them I would bring out whatever was there, even if my investigation agreed with the police. I laid it on the line, pulled no punches. You know me. So that's why I'm here."

"You're up against a brick wall this time. I've been over what happened a thousand times, and I can't even suggest a different version of the shooting."

"What the hell happened? Give me quick run-down. The news we get on the TV and in the papers always leave me up in the air."

"Well, the captain got a tip there was going to be a drug movement on L Street and 20th—you know, near Marcel's restaurant Linsky and I staked out the place until the suspect came out of the restaurant carrying an attaché case. When he got to the other side of the street a woman in a late model Mercedes pulled up, stopped and talked to him at the curb. Must have been the contact, telling him where to take the stuff. Linsky and I ran up to them and told them to halt, that we were police officers. The woman in the car took off."

"Did Msomi attempt to run, to leave the scene?"

"No. Linsky was a little bit in front of me, and to the side. The suspect set the case down and started to reach inside his coat. I guess Linsky thought he was reaching for a gun. Before I could say anything, Linsky nailed him. Then all hell broke loose. Shots came from all around us, I think mostly from an alley across the street near Marcel's. I hit the sidewalk and lost sight of Linsky. Anyway, one of the shots hit him in the chest. It wasn't easy telling his wife about it. She was really broken up. They hadn't been married very long, planning to celebrate an anniversary that weekend."

"Was there any gun on Msomi?"

"No. When I searched him, all he had was his I.D.— you know, passport and things like that. I guess that was what he was reaching for when we asked him to stop."

"Anything else you can remember?"

"That's about it. As you can imagine, the captain's real uptight about this whole thing. He's got me on the case until I can find who shot Linsky and find the woman in the Mercedes. So far, no leads on either. Have you got anything on it?"

"Just started today. I'm checking my contacts. I'll get back to you if I turn up something."

O'Donovan threw his cup into the wastebasket and turned to leave.

"I could stand any help you can give me on this one.

One of these days, we'll catch the sonofabitch who did Linsky in. I think the woman is the key. Find her and we'll be able to clear up this case pretty quickly."

Fowler paused on the front steps of the building and pondered his next move. He always found O'Donovan to be a straight shooter, one to look a situation in the face and decide it strictly on its merits. Chances were slim of finding anything that would please the Msomis. He wondered if it would be better to drop the case now before he put a lot of time and effort in a losing cause. But the Msomis were so sure of Joseph's innocence. A wry smile crossed Fowler's face. Most relatives were like that. They could believe what happened if it happened to someone else. He trudged down the steps and made his way to his car, his mind still not made up as to his next move.

7

Dead Ends and Surprises

Fowler let his car guide him to the Lincoln Memorial, where he parked. He got out of the car, found a bench in the shade, and casually observed the passing scene. Suddenly his heart gave a quick beat and a warm glow slowly crept over him. His eyes fixed upon a female figure jogging toward him. As the figure drew closer, he saw it was not her.

"Her" was Mary Lou Dawson. They met in similar circumstances the year before. He had just finished a case and stopped in the park to relax. While out jogging on her lunch break, she sat down for a breather on the edge of his bench, perspiration streaming down her face.

"A hot one," remarked Fowler. Many close relationships begin with nothing more than a casual comment about something as ordinary as the weather. He had no thought about a conquest, but he did look favorably upon her blues eyes, smooth complexion, and rounded form. Fowler asked if she would like something cool. She smiled and said yes with a twinkle in her eyes. Mary Lou had recently arrived in the city from a small town near Jackson, Mississippi, and quickly found employment at the Internal Revenue Service. Thus, their brief and torrid romance began from nothing more than a chance meeting in a park.

Still contemplating the past, he walked over to a

nearby refreshment stand. While standing in line, he called to a smallish man hurrying past.

"Hey, Rat, homeboy." The man waved and joined him.

"What about a sandwich and drink?" asked Fowler.

"Sounds good to me."

"Find a table. Get one in the shade if you can."

Sandwich and drinks on a tray, he soon joined Rat.

Something about Rat reminded Fowler of a long-tailed, furry animal skulking in and out of garbage cans. He was a small man, perhaps five feet five or six, and, at most, 125 pounds. His long pointy face, big ears, and brown complexion, together with small beady eyes and darty movements complemented his nickname. Fowler wondered what brought Rat out into the daylight, because he was a night person, seldom seen during the day. When Fowler was on the police force, he turned him loose after an attempted burglary. He became one of his best informants.

Fowler learned Rat came from a small town in Alabama called Hartselle. During his youth he played a saxophone in a combo led by a rotund Chinese-looking black man. Wong's Rhythm Rascals played in many of the communities in north-central Alabama. Playing in the band did not return much money, nor was there much of anything else to be had for a black man with little skills. Eventually Rat left the south and came north. He occasionally played saxophone in a little combo in the colored section of Washington, led by a piano player by the name of Reel Foot Henry. Fowler had been in the club many times, and the little combo played what he called "foot patting" sounds.

Rat finished his lunch and broke the silence.

"What's up, m'man?" He shifted his eyes momentarily toward Fowler. "I've got some business to attend to and got to be on my way."

Fowler leaned forward and eyed Rat closely.

"What have you got on that shooting up on L a couple of weeks ago?"

"You mean that African dude, caught with a suitcase full of dope?"

Fowler's heart skipped a beat.

"Right, that's the one. Know anything about it?" He tried to sound casual.

"I was there when it happened."

"Go ahead."

"I was headed across L on some business, right in front of Marcel's, when *boom*, I heard shots coming from across the street. I turned to look when all hell broke loose. Motherfuckers were shooting all around the place. My ass hit the concrete in a hurry."

"Did you see anything in particular?"

"Like I told you, my ass was lying on the ground out of the way," snapped Rat. "All I was thinking about was getting away from there as soon as I could."

"I really thought you had something," said Fowler. "Think! Think!"

Rat looked skyward and scratched his head. "A guy ran down the alley on my side of the street just after the shooting. But the police know all about that."

"Did you talk to the police afterwards?"

"You must be kidding. I got away from there as fast as I could. Me and the police don't get along too well, as you know."

"Well, what have you heard on the street? Someone must know something about that drug bust. Who was the guy dealing with? How was he going to dispose of the stuff? Did you get a look at the guy who ran down the alley?" Questions tumbled from Fowler's lips.

"Too dark to tell what the dude looked like. Besides, as I told you, I was flat on the ground. I wasn't about to look up to see what he looked like. As far as I know, no one on the street's got any answers to any of your questions." Rat looked sharply at Fowler. "How come you're so interested in that case?"

"A client."

Without another word, Rat abruptly got to his feet and scurried away.

A jumble of unanswered questions raced through Fowler's mind. Rat was a funny one, he thought. Slim told him Rat was in jail, which he might have been. Knowing Rat, it was not hard to imagine him doing something to get himself arrested if things got too difficult. Still, he had ways of knowing what was going on even if jailed.

Thoughts of Mary Lou began to push aside his preoccupation with the Msomi case. There were times she would find him sitting in his usual place as she jogged by on her lunch break. They began to go to various clubs, mostly in the colored section of the city, movies, jazz programs, and football games. She did not want him to come to her apartment. He found out where she lived by simply following her home. She lived in a large apartment building in Rosslyn. It was not an area where one was likely to see many blacks. Given their different background, he black, she white, he accepted and understood her reluctance. Later, he found out it was not just a matter of race.

The imposing Lincoln Memorial loomed before him. Often, when faced with a difficult problem, he would find clarity with the huge figure of the sixteenth president.

It was slow day for visitors. A few gray-haired men and women wandered around, pausing now and then to take pictures or to read the Gettysburg Address. "Four score and seven years ago . . . dedicated to the proposition that all men were created equal . . . this nation under God, shall have a new birth of freedom."

Fowler stood with unseeing eyes fixed upon the words on the wall. Thus far, he had turned up nothing but blanks. There was one more possibility. Slim had mentioned Fat Susie who hung out at the State Department. Abruptly, he turned and quickly made his way to the exit and to his car.

He hurried to the State Department, and parked in a no-parking zone. Probing his glove compartment, he pulled out a card with "Press" on it and placed it on the dashboard, then went in search of Fat Susie. He was in luck. She was sitting in back of the State Department, where employees could eat, relax, or enjoy a smoke. A rope was tied around her wrist, the other end tied to a shopping cart piled high with her belongings.

Fat Susie was all the name implied. She was a very fat, black woman of indeterminate age.

"Can't talk right now," she said, as Fowler drew near. "As you can see, if you're not blind, I'm finishing my lunch. Whatever you want can wait."

Fowler sat down opposite her and waited. Fat Susie had contacts at a number of restaurants, where she received handouts, mostly leftovers scraped off the plates of customers. Breakfast, lunch, and dinner could find her making her rounds. Seldom did she come away without something to eat. During her meanderings, she also picked up information about what was going on in the city, especially the illegal activities of the citizenry.

"Okay, motherfucker, what do you want and how much is it worth to you?"

Fowler chuckled loudly as she untied her wrist from the shopping cart and waddled over to a trash can to deposit the remains of her meal. Fat Susie was not one to mince words. He watched the fat ripple underneath her dress as she retraced her steps to the table.

"Well, what is it? There's some kind of big time political group coming in this afternoon, so they're going to chase us away pretty soon. I'm thinking of heading down to the park to see what I can pick up."

"You got anything on that shooting on L Street a couple of weeks ago?" asked Fowler eyeing her intently.

"You mean that uppity nigger from one of those little African countries who got caught with a case full of dope?"

"Yeah"

"What's it worth to you?"

"Depends on what you've got. If it's something good, you know I'll take care of you. I always have, haven't I?"

She looked off as if trying to recall anything she might have heard about the case. After a moment, she fixed her eyes upon Fowler.

"Better save your money, m'boy. All I've heard is no different from what you read in the papers or see on TV."

"You mean none of your contacts can come up with anything about this case—who he was dealing with, how he was going to dispose of the stuff, and so forth?"

She nodded slowly.

"Right. Nothing. At least no more than what I just told you."

There was a sinking feeling in the pit of his stomach. Once again a dead end.

"If you come up with anything, let me know. You know how to get in touch with me," said Fowler as he rose and left Fat Susie sitting at the table.

Fowler racked his brain as to what he should do next. Finally, he slowly drove away, letting the car decide where to take him. Shortly he found himself at L and 20th, the scene of the shooting. Turning into L Street, he glanced in an alley near Marcel's restaurant. A ragged black man sat on a box in front of a pile of discards propped up to form a dwelling of sorts.

He found a liquor store, selected the cheapest bottle of wine he could find, and had the clerk put it in a sack small enough for the neck to be seen. He then hurried back to the alley. The old man was sitting in the same place, looking out into L Street. Stopping in a place reserved for the handicapped, Fowler hung a handicapped sign on the rearview mirror. Sack in hand, he sauntered toward the man in the alley.

"Hey, old man," began Fowler, "what's happening?"

"Not much," grunted the other, never taking his eyes off the paper sack dangling in front of him.

"I'm after some information. If you can—"

"What are you, the cops?" asked the old man guardedly. I told the last guy who came around here all I know about that shooting."

"Nope. Not a cop. Private investigator. There's something in it for you if you can come up with anything I can use."

"Don't know anything," muttered the man, licking his lips.

"Too bad," sighed Fowler shaking his head and turning as if to leave. "If you can remember anything about that night, I'd make it worth your while."

Seeing the sack and its desirable contents about to leave was more than the old man could handle.

"Wait a minute," he whined. "I just remember something."

Fowler paused.

"Go on. Go on," he snapped.

"How about a little swig of that stuff you got in the sack?" drawled the other craftily.

"Let me hear what you've got to say."

"This is between you and me. I don't want to get mixed up in any of this drug action. I'll deny everything if the cops come back to me."

"Okay, okay," said Fowler, never relinquishing his hold on the bottle of wine. "What have you got?"

The old man pulled off his dirty, once a gray felt hat, and scratched his bald head.

"If my memory serves me right, it had been raining that day but kind of slackened off along toward night. I heard someone running down the alley towards L, so I peeped out of my place to see what was going on. Just then, I heard what I first thought was a backfire from some automobile. When I heard more sounds, I knew what it was. It was gunshots."

"Then what did you do?" Fowler fumbled impatiently with the sack.

"What do you think I did? I pulled my head back inside as fast as I could."

"Did you get a look at the guy in the alley?"

"No. It was dark, as I told you, and the light from the street isn't all that bright. Besides, the guy's back was toward me."

Fowler, still not satisfied with the information he was getting, eyed the old man closely.

"Could you tell whether he was black, white, or Mexican?"

"Not too well. I think he was a white dude, but I'm not sure."

"Was he tall, short, fat? Was there anything about him you can remember?"

"He was kind of short, average build. That's all I can

remember about him."

"You say you first heard him running down the alley. Where was he coming from?"

"From the direction of M Street."

"Anything else?"

"Well, I heard someone running back down the alley toward M."

"Did you get a chance to see who that was?"

"No way! I kept my ass inside. I wasn't about to get in the way of bullets flying all around the place."

There was a brief silence.

"Do you remember anything else?" Fowler asked.

"Nope, nothing else."

Fowler gave the sack to the old man, patted him on the shoulder, and slowly walked away. He felt let down. The wine had elicited not much more than he already knew.

Since Marcel's was nearby, he turned in that direction, only to find the door to the restaurant locked. His persistent banging on the door brought forth a Latin-looking youth with a mop in his hand. "We are not open, senor," he said.

"I'd like to speak to the manager."

"I'm sorry. We are closed. There is no one here but me. Come back at five."

Fowler trudged back to his car, making a mental note to return later. Heeding the grumbling from his stomach, he headed for a small soul food restaurant on Florida near his office.

The owner and chef had owned a restaurant in the French Quarter of New Orleans, where he was reputed to serve the best red beans and rice in all New Orleans. Determined to improve his lot, he sold his restaurant and moved to Washington. He was shortly back in business under the name of Homer's Creole Cookery. The food was authentic New Orleans, the gumbo the best.

Fowler found a seat at the bar and reached for a chunk of sourdough bread, smothering it with butter. His order was strictly soul, a cup of seafood gumbo, red beans and rice, baked chicken, collard greens, and a cup of coffee. A slice of sweet potato pie finished his meal. On the way out of the restaurant be looked thoughtfully at a table in a corner, the table where he and Mary Lou usually sat. Creole cooking was one of her favorites. She was well acquainted with the sights, smells, and foods of New Orleans.

Threading his way through the milling crowd, Fowler stepped out into the gathering dusk, only to be slapped on the shoulder by Jules and guided away from those entering or leaving the restaurant.

"What brings you here, m'man?" began Jules.

"The same reason that brings you here. To get some of Homer's good food. What's happening?"

"Not much. I'm on the rapist case. Levine took O'Donovan off it and put him on the drug bust where Linsky got shot down. Have you heard anything from any of your sources about the rape killings?"

"Nope. You got anything on the drug bust?"

"No more than what you read in the papers and what's on TV. By the way I heard a good one the other day. Have you heard the one about the black guy on the scales in the railroad station?"

Fowler was sure he had heard it, but that was not going to keep Jules from telling it again. He was full of jokes, most of them old, and most of them told over and over again. Usually he would crack up before reaching the punch line, so those listening would have to wait patiently until he was sufficiently composed to continue.

"Hold it, Jules. Alzheimer's must have got you, and at your young age. You told me that same joke a couple of weeks ago."

"Well, have you heard—"

"Wish I could stay to hear it, but I'm late for a client. Next time." Fowler brushed by Jules and made his way to his car.

He drove slowly to the Old Post Office, where he parked, placed a press card on the dash board, and sauntered into the building. Fowler wandered around aimlessly, glancing into the shops and food stalls, his thoughts on Mary Lou. She never tired of popping in and out of the different shops. She was intrigued by the many tastes sampled from the ethnic food stalls along the way.

He learned that in her small town in Mississippi, she was viewed as colored, and her life revolved around that perception in many ways. With the breakdown of many rigid segregation barriers, she was able to obtain a sales job in one of the downtown stores. She told Fowler she found life in the slowly changing, but stifling racial attitudes more difficult to accept as she grew older. One of her brothers had crossed the invisible line that divided what was black from what was white in America. He was blond and blue-eyed, so had no trouble becoming what strangers took him to be, white. He accepted the fact he had to make a clean break with his past, including family, friends, and familiar places, and left home and settled in one of the northern cities. The family was not sure which one. Breaking all ties with her family was not easy for Mary Lou. Once a year, she went home for a holiday, sometimes Thanksgiving, sometimes Christmas.

Fowler's musings were interrupted by the sight of a pair of uniformed officers escorting a youth out of the building.

Wonder what the kid did this time, he asked himself as he followed the officers and their captive out of the building.

It was only a short distance to the Msomi apartment, and when Fowler arrived, it was a few minutes before seven. He hurried up the steps past the doorman and into the building.

"T.J. Fowler to see Daniel Msomi," he said to a young man in a uniform sitting behind a desk in the lobby.

"Just a moment." The man scanned a ledger. Looking up, he pointed toward a door leading to the elevators and murmured, "You may go in now."

Moments later Fowler knocked on the door of apartment 1212.

"Good evening, Mr. Fowler. Come in." Sheia's soft, accented voice flowed from a wide smile that revealed pearly white and perfectly shaped teeth.

Fowler followed her into the living room, admiring the graceful curve of her body and the cat-like rhythm of her walk. She was wrapped in a colorful, casual robe that split in the front enough to expose a well-shaped set of legs. He entered the room to find her father looking at the television.

"Come in, come in," said Daniel Msomi in his precise English voice. "Here, sit in this chair." He directed Fowler to a chair that faced the television. "The news will be coming on in a few minutes, and I wish to see it before we talk."

"Can I get you something to drink?" asked Sheia, looking at Fowler, as her father gave his attention to finding the news channel on the television.

"Sounds like a good idea," replied Fowler.

"Make mine the usual," called out her father as he settled into his chair.

"I'll take the same," said Fowler. He had no idea what the usual meant but was willing to try anything once. Sheia glided out of the room to fetch the drinks. Her father, remote control in hand, sat silently listening to the newscaster.

"This is a very violent country," remarked Msomi, directing his comment to no one in particular.

"I guess all newscasters start off the same way," said Fowler. "The first thing they give you are all the latest murders, rapes, and assorted crimes before they give you the rest of the news. Not much you can do about it since all the newscasters go about it the same way."

Sheia re-entered the room, bringing drinks, placed her father's on a table near him and handed a drink to Fowler.

She sat, curled her legs under her and sipped a drink, quietly shifting her eyes from Fowler to her father.

". . . and what we see now is the spread of protests in opposition to any form of weapons of mass destruction," droned the announcer. "These protests are now being seen in nations where such activities were not permitted only a few years ago." With these words, the screen filled with close-ups of men, women, and children marching around an installation of some kind, under the watchful eyes of uniform policemen.

"Look!" exclaimed Daniel as the camera panned the protesters. He rose from his chair and went to the television and pointed to a figure near the front of the mass of people. "Is that not Joseph?" he asked his daughter.

"I am not sure, Father." Sheia looked as the picture changed. "Perhaps—"

"Look! Look!" interrupted Msomi, once again pointing to a black man in the forefront of a protest group in another country. "That is my son. That is Joseph!"

"You are right, Father," agreed Sheia giving her full attention to the news broadcast. "That is, without a doubt, Joseph."

Fowler watched the two of them intently eyeing the screen. Father and daughter had completely forgotten about him in their common interest. In every occasion, Joseph Msomi was clearly seen among the protesters.

Msomi turned off the television and returned to his chair.

"What does it mean?" he asked, more to himself than to the others. "Why is Joseph in all of those protests?"

Fowler did not know what to make of any part of it. Nor could he conceive of any connection between antiwar protests and a drug bust.

Daniel Msomi sat, chin cupped in his hand, brooding over what he had just observed. Sheia, too, was quietly lost in her thoughts about the matter—both oblivious of their visitor's presence. After a considerable pause, Msomi turned, and his eyes lit up as if he had only that moment discovered Fowler.

"And what have you to report about this dreadful matter? What about the murder of my son?" he demanded irritably. "Have you found the ones behind this tragic situation?"

Fowler did not answer immediately.

"Speak up!" snapped Msomi impatiently.

"I'm sorry to tell you I have nothing new to report. Not one of my contacts gave me anything I could use."

Msomi thought long before responding.

"I see. What you mean to be telling me is that you believe, like the rest of them, that my son is guilty—that he is a drug pusher."

Fowler was aware Msomi and his daughter were observing him carefully.

"No. That is not what I mean," he said, shaking his head slowly. "I must admit this is one of the strangest cases I have ever dealt with. But, that is the problem."

"What do you mean?" asked Sheia.

"No one knows anything," replied Fowler. "That's the thing that bothers me. A drug bust and nobody knows anything. Who is the contact? Where was your son taking the stuff? Who were the big names in the deal? How did it get into his attaché case in the first place, and so forth. Nothing like this ever goes down without some of my sources knowing something about it."

"I, too, am not sure I understand what you are getting at Mr. Fowler," commented Daniel Msomi. "Continue."

"It's too pat. Keeping something like that quiet in this town is simply not done. I am convinced there is more to it than meets the eye."

"Then that means—" began Msomi.

"It means I intend to get to the bottom of it," interrupted Fowler. "Are you sure the attaché case he was carrying, that had the dope in it, was the case you gave him?"

"I am positive. It is the case I gave him. Iyanga, my good friend, made it for me many years ago. That was my son's signature: you noticed it on the inside of the case. Yes, it is the same case. There is none other like it in the world."

"One of the first things we have to clear up is how the stuff got into his case without him knowing about it. I'm going to start working on that first thing in the morning. I've got a couple of other contacts to look up, but I don't hold out much hope of anything coming out of them. I've seen my best ones, and if they haven't got anything ..."

"I'll get back in touch with you when I have something more to report," said Fowler, rising to leave. Msomi

111

was standing, looking out the window. The only indication of being aware of what was said was a wave of his arm.

Sheia followed Fowler to the door, her slippers barely heard as she glided across the thick carpet.

"You must excuse Father," she said as she opened the door to the corridor. "It is not often he finds himself confronted with a problem he cannot solve. Please let us hear from you as soon as possible. This matter is very difficult for my father and for me."

"I will. You can depend on it." He turned and walked swiftly the elevator. The question of the case full of cocaine occupied his thoughts as be drove to his apartment. After parking in front of the building, he sat for several minutes trying to sort things out. Finally, he shrugged his shoulders, left the car, and plodded into the building and to his apartment.

8

The Blonde and Mrs. James

O'Donovan watched the captain slowly weave his way toward his office, pausing now and then to talk to someone on the way. Pondering his next move, which took on more of a random aspect, he decided there was nothing to be gained by sitting in the office. He abruptly stood, reached for his raincoat and prepared to leave. At that moment, his phone rang.

"O'Donovan here," he answered.

A female voice responded.

"I think I have some information about that shooting on L Street a few weeks ago; you know, where an ambassador and a policeman were killed."

O'Donovan's heart skipped a beat or two. Could this be the lucky break they were waiting for?

"Go on," he said eagerly.

"I don't want to talk over the phone. Could you meet me somewhere?"

"Okay. Where? What time?"

"Arlington, at the Visitors' Center, at 1:30."

"How will I know you? What will you be wearing?"

"I'll have on a dark gray hat and a light blue raincoat. What about you?"

"Don't worry, I'll be wearing a tan raincoat and be seated near the front entrance to the building. When you enter, turn to the right and you will see me reading a paper."

O'Donovan felt his mood slowly turn to one of doubt. Why was she going to such an extent to make the meeting mysterious? Perhaps it was only a wild-goose chase; she might not show. Still, he had no choice. He had to follow every lead, and the mystery woman was the only one he had.

He let the car determine his next move, leaving him to focus upon the unknowns of the Msomi case. Finding himself at the Museum of Natural History, he parked and quickly ran up the steps into the building. A quick scan of the foyer failed to produce any of his contacts. Contacts seldom showed during bad weather. A hasty check of Jerry's refreshment stand across the street proved no more productive. "It's one of those days," he mumbled. If a contact had information, the phone was more likely today.

The race track was the best place to run into Duke, one of his best sources of information. There was plenty of time before racing began. The only action at that hour was the "Early Bird Betting" the track provided to let the public bet on their favorites.

O'Donovan spotted a tout who hung out at the track, giving tips, and tapped him on the shoulder. A small man, the size of a jockey, turned to face him.

"I haven't done a thing, captain. You got nothing on me."

A wry smile appeared on O'Donovan's face as he watched the man glaring up at him. According to Duke, Jake was at the track every business day to pick up a few dollars giving tips on the races. His method was to approach a patron of the races spinning a tale about his connection with someone in the stable area—a jockey, exercise boy, groom, or trainer. He claimed a particular horse was a sure thing to win a certain race. In order to eliminate the chance factor, he repeated this tale for every horse in the race for different patrons. If confronted by those who lost, he had a ready story for them: the horse stumbled at the gate, was forced wide at the turn, or was the victim of some other piece of chicanery.

Horse players generally took his explanations in good grace, shrugging it off and going about the business of trying to pick a winner in the next race. The race over, Jake reminded those who had the winning horse that a few dollars were in order.

"I'm thinking about running you in for operating an illegal scam on the public," growled O'Donovan sternly. "However, I've got better things to do. I'm looking for Duke. Have you seen him today?"

Jake was more than delighted to help as long as he wasn't the center of attraction.

"I saw him headed for the stables about an hour ago. There he is now," he said, pointing to a figure emerging from a tunnel.

Mud had began to build up on the track surface as the rain continued. Looks like a good day for those who bet on mudders, thought O'Donovan as he hurried away to intercept Duke. It was a busy time for Duke. He had been rambling around the stables, picking up tips: what horses were ready, which ones were out for the exercise, which ones were being prepared for a future race, etcetera. All those bits of information were used to make up his "Gold Star" selection tip sheet. Duke did not bet on horses, or anything else, as far as O'Donovan could ascertain.

"Duke, hold it. Wait a minute," he shouted. At the sound of O'Donovan's voice, Duke turned and waited.

"Make it quick, Inspector. I have to get my tip sheet ready for the day. If it's about that Msomi case, I haven't heard any more than what I told you the last time we met."

"Nothing at all?" questioned O'Donovan, fixing his eyes on Duke's face, watching every change of expression.

"Nothing," repeated Duke with finality. "It must be a new act in town. None of my contacts have any ideas, or are unwilling to talk about it." As he turned to continue on his way, he tossed a remark toward O'Donovan. "Bet Sassy Sue in the fourth to win. She should pay a good price." With that, he quickly disappeared.

On the way to the exit, O'Donovan stopped to place a bet on Sassy Sue. The odds were ten to one, a long shot. Just like the Msomi case, he thought.

In his hurry to look up Duke, he failed to carefully note where he parked his car. Irritation slowly built up inside him. Nothing had gone right this day. Nothing from Duke. He was committed to spend time with an unknown informant, probably a crackpot, and the rain was coming down in full force, soaking his shoes as he searched for his car.

Inside his car, listening to the patter of rain on the roof, O'Donovan wondered whether it was worthwhile to make the trip to Arlington.

On his way to Arlington, the rain began to slacken as the clouds moved off to the northeast. He parked in front of the Visitors' Center and sat, giving close attention to any female who resembled the description given by the caller. Failing when no one fit, he gave a sigh and stepped into the rain-soaked outside.

Once inside the Center, he meandered around the building covertly checking out all females. None fit the description. He found a seat near the front door pulled out a paper and began to read. The rain was enough to hold in check many who might have visited Arlington that day. It began to look like a wild-goose chase. The clock in the Center showed it was well past time for the meeting. Five more minutes he decided.

"Pardon me, are you Sergeant O'Donovan?" A soft female voice interrupted his musing.

O'Donovan looked up to see a pretty blond woman who appeared to be wearing a pink rain hat and a black raincoat. He had noticed her while walking around the room, but since she was not wearing a light blue raincoat, he dismissed her.

"The same," he answered motioning to her to sit down beside him as he showed her his I.D. card. "And what is your name?"

"My name is not important. I think I have some information that may be related to the shooting on L Street." She paused, arranged her hair, and evaded O'Donovan's probing eyes.

"Go on, go on," he whispered. He began to suspect there was more to this meeting than he thought. Perhaps she was the mystery woman who pulled away from the curb as he and Linsky approached Msomi that night.

"I happened to be in Washington that night. I . . . I . . . live in Winchester. You know where that is?"

O'Donovan nodded.

"Over in Virginia, not too far from the West Virginia border. I think."

"Right, about fifty miles from here. My husband has a publishing business there. We have a lovely home and two fine children. He is active in the affairs of the city."

"Did you see the drug bust involving an African ambassador, where he and a police officer were killed?"

"Yes. I didn't see the drug bust, but I did see the ambassador."

"Go on," prompted O'Donovan. "What were you doing

in the city that night?"

"It's a long story. Would you mind getting me a cup of coffee?"

O'Donovan hurried away to a drink machine in the hall. A few minutes later, he returned with a cup of coffee in each hand.

"I forgot to ask if you wanted cream and sugar," he said as he handed her a cup.

"Thanks. This is fine."

O'Donovan sat and waited for her to continue. She was attractive, nice legs, clear complexion, sky blue eyes, and well formed breasts, probably helped out by some kind of expensive bra. There was a hint of perfume, just enough, not too much, probably expensive too.

"Why were you in the city that night?"

"A private matter. I guess I'll have to tell you the whole story, then you'll understand why it has not been easy for me to come forward, even now." She finished her cup of coffee and handed the empty cup to O'Donovan. He placed the two cups on the floor beside him.

In a halting voice, she continued

"It was one of those things. I was active in politics in my city and you know . . . "

"What?"

"There was a political rally several years ago. A man from Congress was there to support the candidate I was working for. To make it short, we began to see each other whenever we could. My husband travels quite frequently. This man—I can't tell you his name—and I often met in Washington at some quiet place. The affair lasted for several years before we both decided it could not go on. He is married with a family. Any scandal would wreck his chances to get a very important position." Quietness descended over the two of them.

"Well," she continued, without looking at O'Donovan, "It was a night when my husband was away on a business trip. This man and I made arrangements to meet for the last time. We were going to exchange some very personal letters we wrote over the years."

Looking intently at O'Donovan, she added, "We parted in a friendly way. Both of us realized what we had was very special, but there was no future to it. Neither of us were willing to give up our present lives. You asked what I was doing there when that dreadful shooting took place. Well, it was just one of those things that happen. You know, when you find yourself in the wrong place at the wrong time."

"Go on, go on," murmured O'Donovan, impatient to hear what she knew about the shooting.

"There really wasn't much to it. We planned to meet at a small bar in an unfamiliar section of the city. I stopped a black man, carrying an attaché case and asked him for directions.

"I found out the next day he was some kind of ambassador. Anyway, he was not able to help me, so I drove off. I stopped a man further down the street who directed me to the place I was trying to reach. That is all there is to it, sergeant, I swear. When I saw the picture of the black man in the newspaper, I recognized him as the man I stopped that night."

"Why didn't you come in and tell us about it earlier? We've been trying to find a mystery woman for several weeks."

"I wanted to come in before now, but there wasn't much chance. My husband does not know about my coming here today. He went to Atlanta for a couple of days. You are the only one to know about my connection to that incident.

"You can believe me, sergeant, that is all there is it to it. You can understand why I do not want to tell you my name, or identify the other party to the police. Once the police get my identity, the news media will become involved. Believe me, I thought long and hard before deciding to see you."

O'Donovan's thoughts whirled around in his head. If what she said was true, and his instincts led him to believe her, the theory of a mystery woman was shot to hell.

"What kind of car were you driving that night?" he asked quietly.

"That's another problem with this whole incident," she said with a wan smile. "It was my husband's car. I use it whenever I have to travel some distance from home. It is a Mercedes, black, late model. If he found out it was in Washington that night . . . ."

O'Donovan noticed a Mercedes fitting the description in the parking lot. Although he tended to believe her story, he made a mental note to jot down her license later and run a check on it at the Department of Motor Vehicles. On the other hand, anyone bent on breaking the law, would know it is easy to trace a person by a license number. His thoughts were interrupted by her soft voice that appeared far away.

"Is that all, Sergeant O'Donovan?"

"Well, uh, I guess that's it. I will try to keep you out of this matter. However, I need your phone and address. Can you remember anything else about that night, anything?"

"No. I've told you everything as far as I was concerned. I have no interest in the reward money. I only hope what I've told you will help, although I don't know how it can. An ambassador involved in drug pushing. It is hard to believe, but so many things are happening these days." She rose, looked at her watch, and said, "I must go. I sincerely hope you will keep me out of the picture." O'Donovan followed to her car and made a note of the license number. The mystery woman was no longer a mystery. If she was telling the truth.

Sitting in his car O'Donovan decided to keep quiet about his interview, at least for the present. There must be some clue to what went on the night when Msomi and Linsky were killed. Not surprisingly, his car took him to the exact corner. He parked and looked up and down the street. He shed his raincoat and tossed it onto the back seat. Then he spotted Fowler leaning against the corner of a building, talking to a decrepit-looking black man sitting on a box near the entrance of the alley behind Marcel's. He watched them for a few minutes, then started his car and parked in the alley near the two men.

"Anything up?" asked O'Donovan, glancing at the old man whom he had talked to a few days after the shooting, but, but got nothing worthwhile.

"Nothing special," replied Fowler. "This old man was here the night of the shooting, but when the action got started he ducked into his place over there. He didn't come out until things settled down. He told me heard someone running, but didn't know who or where they were going."

"Yeah, that's about what he told me when I talked to him a couple of weeks ago."

Just then a marked police car pulled into the alley and parked behind O'Donovan's car. Jules, from the 77th Precinct, leaned out of the car window and eyed O'Donovan and Fowler.

"What are you two guys doing to that poor old man?" he jested with a smile.

"We're about to arrest him as a material witness in the Msomi case," declared O'Donovan with a serious expression, as he turned and looked meaningfully at the man sitting before him.

Fowler's attention was directed to the old man whose face reflected his misgiving about being involved.

"It may be his memory will improve if we promise we will keep his name and picture out of the papers if he cooperates," he added. "By the way," Fowler looked at the old man, but directed his question to Jules, "what brings you into this neighborhood?"

"The captain has me following a lead on the serial rapist case. It was the same night as the drug bust and about the same time." Looking at O'Donovan, he said, "How'd you like to come along while I interview a woman who called about some information that might be helpful in this case?"

"Well," after a pause, "okay. Not much happening around here. I'll follow. Is the place nearby?"

"Yep, right around the corner, 29th and M." The two men drove away leaving Fowler talking to the old man.

The apartment Jules pointed out was one of the oldest structures in the area. Some of the units had a small balcony and a trellis, half-hidden by a clinging vine that ran along the side of the balcony.

On their way into the building, Jules told O'Donovan about the call from Mrs. James who lived near the scene of the rape murder. Although the police questioned her earlier, she explained she was asleep and didn't hear anything out of the ordinary. Now, she had second thoughts and wanted to talk about it.

Jules went to the tenant listing board and rang her apartment.

"Detective Jules Williams, 77th Precinct," he said, when she answered.

Mrs. James lived on the third floor. When Jules knocked on the door, she opened it with chain connected and peered out at the two officers, and asked for identification. Satisfied, she admitted the two men.

"Please come in, come in, officers," said the gray-haired woman, who appeared to be in her late fifties, plumpish, and wearing a flowery robe.

"Come in," repeated the woman, as she led the officers into the living room. "Have a seat." O'Donovan walked over to the glass door leading to the balcony and stood looking out. Jules sat on a sofa, facing her. "I'm Mrs. James," she said. "And you?"

"Detective Williams." He added with a twist of his thumb, "Sergeant O'Donovan, my partner."

O'Donovan left the door, and he, too, sat facing Mrs. James. Both officers waited patiently for her to tell them what she remembered about the incident in the apartment near her.

"I'm not sure my information will help in your investigation," she began. "Still, it seems I should leave it up to you." she paused and eyed Jules.

"Yes, ma'am," replied Jules. "We understand and appreciate your cooperation in this matter. Did you know the lady who was killed?"

"No," answered Mrs. James softly. "I never met her personally. She lived in an apartment on the first floor below, such a lovely young lady—a model, I think. When I sat out on my balcony, I saw her going in and out of her apartment, or just sunning herself on her balcony. How could anyone do such a terrible thing to such a nice person?"

"That's what we ask ourselves all the time." O'Donovan shook his head. "We've got some crazy people in this society."

"Perhaps if we go out on the balcony, you might be able to understand what I am going to tell you a little better," said Mrs. James.

On the balcony, she pointed to an apartment on the floor below. It was the apartment where the rape and murder took place. Jules was there during the investigation.

"I'm not sure just where to begin." She looked apprehensively at the apartment. "Funny, it seems so long ago, almost as if it never happened." After a brief pause, she began to talk about the night in a halting manner.

"I had finished my dinner, and the TV show I follow had just ended. It was a nice, warm night, so I decided to sit out on the balcony for a while. I happened to look down and saw this man . . . "

"Yes," murmured Jules coaxing her to continue.

"Well, he was hanging onto the vines that run up the side of the building. I didn't think much of it at the time. We always have workmen cleaning up or doing something around the outside." She looked down at the apartment and shook her head before continuing. "The next day I heard about the lady being killed in that apartment. This sad incident stayed on my mind for days. I couldn't sleep thinking about it. Something kept bothering me that I couldn't put my finger on. And then it came to me."

"What?" asked Jules anxious for her to get on with rest of her recollections.

"The man I saw hanging in the vines. There was something about him. For one thing, workmen do not work that late at night. Secondly, he was in the vines near the poor girl's apartment."

"Could you describe him in any way? Was he short, fat, black, white?" broke in O'Donovan.

"The lights in the courtyard were low, so it was hard to tell. For a moment, the lights shone on his face. I don't think he was black. Anyway, I think he must have seen me watching him. He took off in a big hurry. The last thing I saw, he was going across the courtyard in that direction."

"Toward L?" asked Jules, his eyes following her out-stretched arm."

"Yes. It was dark, and I couldn't get more than a glimpse of his back," replied Mrs. James in a subdued voice followed by silence.

"Is there anything else you can recall about that night?" O'Donovan hoped to move the conversation along. "Anything else out of the ordinary?"

Mrs. James thought for a moment.

"No. It was so sad. She was so young and lovely." Turning to Jules, she asked in a low voice, "What kind of person would do a thing like this?"

Jules shrugged his shoulders and mumbled.

"We don't have too many answers either. We try to bring about justice. I wish I could say something positive, but that's the way it is."

O'Donovan located the manager and obtained a key to the apartment. He entered and went directly to the balcony. Looking down he saw Jules searching the ground and the clinging vines that ran beside the apartment. "See anything down there?"

"Not yet."

After several minutes of poking around, Jules called out, "Nothing down here. I guess we might as well call it a day."

"Hold it a minute. There's a bright reflection on

something in those vines, just above your head. Can you see it?"

"Not from here. I'll stand here, and you come down."

"Okay, stay put." O'Donovan hurried out of the apartment and joined Jules. "It was right about there," he said, pointing to a spot just outside their reach.

"Let me give you a lift," said Jules, cupping his hands to raise O'Donovan toward the object. "See if you can reach it."

"There's something in there all right. If you can hold me, I'll see if I can reach it."

"I've got you. Can you see what it is?"

"Not sure, but it looks like a knife. Hold on while I get a handkerchief out of my pocket. Okay. Let me down."

O'Donovan came down with a bloodied knife wrapped in a handkerchief in his hand. Both stared at each other.

"So that's what he was looking for," said Jules. "Maybe this is what we need to break this case. Let's hope there are good prints on it. The guy's been pretty slick up to this point, he's the serial killer we've been after the past year. I'll get back to the lab and have them run a check on it right away. Coming?"

O'Donovan thought for a moment.

"I guess not. I think I'll poke around and see what I can stir up on the Msomi case." He turned and walked briskly toward L Street and his automobile.

When O'Donovan looked around, he failed to see Fowler or the old man. It had not been a fruitful day as far as making headway in solving the Msomi case. His gut feeling told him the mystery woman was simply going to be another case of someone in the wrong place at the wrong time.

9

Some Curious Goings-on

It was one of those perfect September mornings. The rain slowly worked its way across the city, cleared the air, and left a sky devoid of clouds. Fowler paid little heed to anything that surrounded him. The Msomi case was getting on his nerves. He found himself waking up during the night puzzling over the unusual lack of information from his sources. None of his facts made any sense if Joseph Msomi was innocent of drug dealing.

Fowler, arriving at his office, mumbled a vague "good morning" to Henrietta as he walked past her to his small cubicle. She followed him into the room and stood as he sat staring into space.

"The Msomi case?" began Henrietta. "Without saying I told you so, that case was bad news from the start. They caught him dead to right with the goods on him. And what about the policeman who was killed? Besides, you're passing up some easy money from the Jackson case. He called this morning and complained about your friend Bill Jones."

Fowler turned to face Henrietta as if suddenly aware of her presence.

"What was that?"

"I said, Mr. Jackson wants you to handle his case. He doesn't have much confidence in Bill Jones. I don't blame him. I don't think much of him either."

"Well, call him back and tell him I'm tied up right now, but I'll get back to him as soon as I can."

"You mean you've got something going on the Msomi case?"

"Nope, not a thing," replied Fowler with a sly smile. "This case has me hooked. I've never been on a case where none of my contacts knows anything. Someone has to know something. It's up to me to find that person, or persons."

"By the way, I forgot to tell you, Mr. Msomi called this morning and wants you to call him as soon as you can."

"Okay, okay, get him on the phone. I'll talk to him now."

"Ah, Mr. Msomi," began Fowler in a breezy manner. "How are you? I've been intending to—what's that—yes, things are going fine. I'm on a good lead that ought to help us prove your son's innocence. I stopped by the office for a minute to check it out. How's that? . . . sure I can make it tonight. After dinner is fine—around seven is all right with me. Yes, sir. See you then." He hung up the phone and glanced at his secretary with a smirk.

"What are you going to tell him tonight?" asked Henrietta, a smile spreading across her face.

"No idea. Right now, I have to let tonight take care of itself. Who knows what might come up during the day?" He stood and wandered over to the window and looked out.

A short time later, Fowler strolled past Henrietta's desk. "If anything comes up, give me a call. Sometime today, I'll be at Marcel's restaurant. Other than that . . . who knows."

He left his office with only a vague idea of his next move. It was too early to go to Marcel's. The only ones likely to be there were the cleanup crews, and he had not gotten anything out of them.

Fowler revisited the haunts of those who had supplied him with information in the past. There was no new information about the Msomi case. All were in agreement, he was spinning his wheels. None of his contacts had a lead that cast any doubt on the story provided by the police department.

Intuition kept telling him Marcel's restaurant held the key to the problem. Yet, he had talked to all the employees, except the waiter of Msomi's table the night of the shooting.

He drove to Potomac Park and sat in his car, watching the passing throng. A familiar figure, with quick mincing steps, came into view in his rear view mirror. Moments later, Rat leaned into an open window.

"Got anything for me?" began Fowler, eyeing the other closely.

"On what?"

"The Msomi case—you know—the shooting up on L Street."

"You mean the African dude passing some dope? The one who was wasted by the police?"

"Yeah," answered Fowler quietly. He knew there were not going to be any tips coming from Rat. Whenever he had something to sell, he began by haggling over the price.

"You're wasting your time, m'man. It's like the cops put it out—the dude was caught red-handed. Anyway, his back-up man rubbed out one of the cops, too." A little small talk, and Rat was on his way.

Fowler's thoughts settled upon Mary Lou. It was still too early for government workers to take off for lunch, and if he waited around, there was little chance he would see her. She must have changed her usual practice of jogging around the Reflecting Pool. Lately, he had reached the uncomfortable conclusion that it was time for him to get on with his life and put her behind him. The deep hurt that persisted was more a matter of his injured pride rather than anything else. He turned the key in the ignition and slowly left the park.

Fowler headed toward Marcel's. Once again, he stopped at a liquor store and bought a bottle of wine. In the alley next to the restaurant was the old man he had questioned stretched out in a rickety chair. He was talking to a seedy character sitting on a box. Fowler approached them holding the neck of the bottle.

"What you got in that sack, boy?" asked the old man.

"Nothing much," was the sly response. "Only some cough medicine. Too bad you two don't have a cold or, at least, know something about that shooting."

"I told you all I know," whined the occupant of the ramshackle dwelling. "Are you sure that's nothing but cough medicine in that sack?"

"Could be. Of course it could change if you two come up with anything I can use." He watched as the two looked at each other intently

The stranger, looking away thoughtfully, spoke quietly.

"I was on my way here to see my man, Jake, when a little sonofabitch hauling ass ran into me in the alley down by M Street. He knocked a bottle of wine out of my hand and it broke."

"Could you recognize the man?" asked Fowler.

"Naw, at least, I don't think so. I was on the ground and it was dark in the alley. Besides, the guy took off like a bat out of hell. I hollered at him and told him to come back and I would kick his motherfuckin' ass, the motherfucker."

Fowler chuckled to himself as he looked down at the skinny, dirty old man, his legs stretched out, black toes peeping out from what, at one time, passed for shoes.

"He's right," broke in Jake. "Cephas here, came and got me out of my pad. By that time, people were all over the street. Police were running back and forth like chickens with their heads cut off. We laid low and kept out of the way. Besides, we were not about to check it out; could've been a lion or tiger loose on the street."

All three of them had a good laugh.

Fowler directed his attention at Cephas, while turning to leave. "Can you remember anything at all about the man? Was he tall, short, heavy, black, white—anything?"

Glancing at the sack, Cephas replied, "He was kind of short and stocky, a white dude, I'm sure. As I told you, he moved fast, and it was dark. If I could remember anything else, I would tell you." After a pause he continued. "I don't want to get mixed up in this thing. If the police come after me, I don't know nothing about nothing."

Fowler nodded to the two men, handed the sack to Jake, and left. At Marcel's, waiters and bus boys were bustling around in the final preparation for the lunch period. He wandered over to the bar and sat on a stool, eyeing the bartender as he prepared the bar for the day.

"I'm looking into the Msomi shooting a few weeks ago," ventured Fowler. "Private investigator."

"Nice man," muttered the bartender, never pausing in his preparations. "Quiet, polite—a real gentleman." Shaking his head. "Too bad."

"Do you know who waited on him that night?"

"I think it was Jim Bush. Mr. Msomi usually sat at the same table, it was Jim's table, so I guess he was the one who waited on him."

"Know anything about Jim Bush?"

"Good buddy of mine. He went to Florida to visit his folks and do some fishing, and maybe take one of those cruise ships and do a couple of islands in the Caribbean. He should be back now."

"What can you tell me about Mr. Msomi, anyone you saw him with, just anything?"

"He was pretty regular whenever he came to town. As I said, he usually sat in the corner near the kitchen door. Come to think about it, several weeks ago, he came in with a couple of men, one white, the other Oriental. They had dinner and a few drinks and talked a lot. The reason I remember, it was different from his usual practice. I cannot recall him being with anyone except those two. It's a damn shame."

At that moment the bartender noticed the manager hurrying by.

"Tony," he called, "what's with that plumber who was supposed to come and take care of the leak under the bar?"

"My brother-in-law. He'll probably come in tonight when things slow down a bit."

Fowler felt there was nothing else to be gained by spending more time at Marcel's and got up to leave. He casually asked, "Did you notice anything unusual happening the night of the shooting?"

The bartender thought for a few moments before answering. "No. I can't think of a thing."

Fowler turned to go, but stopped in his tracks when the other said, "Wait a minute. There was something that happened that day—no, come to think about it, it was the next morning."

Fowler watched silently as the bartender mulled over the events of the night of the shooting.

"Yeah, it was the next morning just after we opened

for the day and were getting the place ready for the noon meal. Some immigration guys came in and picked up the cloakroom attendant. I haven't seen him since."

"Doesn't surprise me," chuckled the bartender as he gave a finishing touch to a glass and hung it on a hook above the bar.

"Why not?"

"Tony, the manager, isn't likely to broadcast the fact he hires illegal aliens. That's not the first time. Every now and then a bus boy, or cloakroom attendant comes up missing. Sooner or later it gets around the Feds got him. Anyway, I can't figure out what that might have to do with the shooting."

"You never know. Got any idea where this cloakroom attendant lives?"

"No. I think it's over near-the railroad station. Hold on a minute. He was pretty buddy-buddy with Carlos over there. He might be able to help you." At his call, a slight built youth came over to the bar. "Carlos," said the bartender. "This man would like to get Pablo's address. He's okay. He's looking into the shooting of Mr. Msomi, you know, that nice African man who sits in your section."

Fowler thanked the bartender and followed Carlos to the cloakroom. Carlos looked round.

"I live at 977 K Street NW. He lived next door to the right." Giving Fowler a quizzical look, he added, "You won't find him there."

"I know." Fowler jotted down the address. "Do you remember anything out of the ordinary that went on in the restaurant the night Mr. Msomi was shot?"

"The only thing I remember was someone telling me Mr. Msomi and a policeman were shot outside the restaurant."

"Thanks for your help. If you think of anything,

here's my card. Give me a ring."

On his way out of the restaurant, Fowler met O'Donovan as he was entering.

"Any luck with your investigation?" asked O'Donovan.

"I haven't come up with anything solid yet. It's a funny case. None of my reliable sources have been able to pick up a thing. That's what puzzles me. Somebody should know something."

"It's got me, too. I keep coming back here hoping to find something I've overlooked. So far, nothing."

"Did you know immigration picked up the cloakroom attendant the morning after the shooting?"

"No. No big deal. Every once in a while, they come around and make a sweep of these places. They all use illegals for their low-paying jobs. It's a never-ending action. The day after they make a sweep, the managers or owners have more illegals on the job. Where you headed?"

"I think I'll see what I can find out about the other cloakroom guy. Immigration picked him up the day after the shooting. Want to come along?"

"Not this time. I think I'll mosey around here and see what I can pick up."

"What about the rapist case?"

"Not much. The prints on a knife we found don't match any we have on file, or any they can come up with at the FBI."

Still at loose ends, Fowler drove to Potomac Park and parked near the Lincoln Memorial. Suddenly he froze. His heart pounded violently. There she was, sitting across the Reflecting Pool from him. The slender blond youth in a jogging outfit, sitting so close to her, confirmed his worst fears. He watched as they embraced each other. Nor was he too surprised to find the one who captured her heart was white. Early in their affair, she explained why she left Mississippi and her life as a black person. With a sigh, he ended his focus on Mary Lou and searched for a familiar face. Finding none, he started the engine and drove slowly out of the park.

Fowler could not think of any reason to connect Pablo's situation with the Immigration Service to the events of the drug bust. Missing a clear course of action, he drove toward the State Department. He pulled over to the curb when he saw Fat Susie sitting at a table in the rear of the building. Honking the horn, he beckoned to her. She rose with difficulty and shuffled over to the car, dragging her cart behind her.

"As you can see motherfucker, you're interfering with my lunch," mumbled Fat Susie angrily. "If it's about that drug bust, you can forget it. Like I told you the last time, there's nothing on the street that says the African dude wasn't caught dead to right."

"Anything on the back-up man?"

"Nothing on that either. Must have been somebody from out of town. By the way, my big toe tells me it's going to rain pretty soon and I'll need some change to get me out of it."

"You must be bull-shitting! The weatherman said we're in for some sunny, warm days for the rest of the week," protested Fowler while reaching into his pocket for a couple of dollars. Besides, he was in no mood to argue the merits of a big toe versus the high tech prognostications of the local weatherman. Fat Susie swooped the money out of his hands without so much as a thank you and retraced her steps to her table.

Since he could not think of any other leads to follow, he headed for 977 K Street NW. It was a neighborhood of old two- or three-story flats that had seen better days and were mainly occupied by Hispanics. Weaving his way among children at play, Fowler wondered which house was to the right of 977. Trusting to luck he selected one of them, climbed to the top of a flight of steps and knocked loudly on the door.

A middle-aged Latin woman poked her head out the door.

"*Que quiere usted, senor,*" snapped the woman.

After a few minutes of limited communication, frustration and irritation were building up inside him.

"Does anyone here speak English?" Fowler asked loudly.

He feared the worst since the old woman gave no indication she understood what he was asking. Just as he was about to give up and leave, a young man came to the door and said a few words in Spanish to the woman, who then turned and padded toward the back of the house.

"What do you want?" asked the youth, making no move to open the door any wider.

"Does Pablo Rodriquez live here?" asked Fowler, placing his foot inside the door to keep it from being closed.

"Who are you? Are you the police?"

"No. Private investigator." Fowler pulled out his identification card. "I'm on a case, and there's a chance Pablo can help me clear it up."

There was a brief pause as the young man eyed Fowler suspiciously.

"Pablo doesn't live here anymore," he said, reluctantly.

"Can you tell me where I can find him?"

"No. How can I tell if you are not from the police?"

"Read my ID. I'm just what it says, a private investigator. Why are you so worried about the police?"

"Well, the day after he was picked up by the immigration officers, a man came by who said he was a policeman. He turned everything upside down, pulled everything out of the dresser drawers, went through Pablo's closet and threw his stuff in the middle of the room. He even turned the bed upside down."

Fowler's senses became fully alert.

"Can you tell me what he looked like?"

"I wasn't home. My grandmother let him in."

"Do you think she can tell me what he looked like?"

"I don't know. I'll call her and see." When she came in response to his call, the two of them talked several minutes in Spanish. "She said he was kind of short, but she didn't have a chance to look at him closely because he told her to go to the back of the house and he would call her if he needed her. She said he spoke a little Spanish. He asked where Pablo's room was and went in and closed the door. When she came back up front, he had left and the room was like I told you it was."

"What about the immigration people?"

"They brought him by the day before. I was home that day. One of them brought him in and waited for him to pick up some of his things. Then they took him away. We have not seen him since then. I think they sent him back to Mexico."

"Can I see his room?"

A moment later, the youth the door opened. Fowler entered and followed the youth to a room just off the kitchen. It was a small room, plainly furnished. It had been put back in order and showed no signs of things having been tossed around. There were a few items of clothing hanging in the closet but little else.

"We've got someone else staying in the room," said the youth, looking intently at Fowler.

Fowler nodded, looked around the room a moment more, then made his way to the front door. He mumbled a "thanks a lot" to the young man as he brushed by him and down the steps to his car.

10

Tom Nkombo

Sitting in his car, Fowler's thoughts wandered over all he had found out about the Msomi affair. *Who came by Pablo's house? What was he looking for?* He considered Joseph Msomi, the object of his investigation, essentially unknown to him. He knew Joseph was an ambassador from some small African country called Niberia, but that was about all. He reached for the phone, called his office, and asked Henrietta to find the address of Niberia's embassy. Minutes later, she called with the address—F near 22nd—a few blocks away.

"May I help you?" greeted a receptionist as he entered the embassy.

"Mr. Khumale, please."

"Your name."

"T.J. Fowler."

A few minutes later, Mr. Khumale appeared in a doorway.

"Ah, Mr. Fowler, come into my office," he requested with a sweep of his arm. His visitor followed him into an office just off the main hall that ran the length of the building.

"Please be seated," said Mr. Khumale, pointing to a leather-covered chair at one side of his desk. He waited for Fowler to sit before he took a seat behind his desk. Both were silent for a few moments, as if waiting for the other to initiate the conversation. Finally, leaning forward on his desk, Mr. Khumale broke the silence with his precise tone of voice. "Now, what can I do for you, Mr. Fowler? How are things going with that dreadful Msomi situation?" He leaned back with his hands folded across his chest, eyeing Fowler.

"Not as well as I would like. I need more information about Joseph Msomi. What were his main duties as an ambassador? Was he on any important project you know about? In short, I can use anything you can tell me about his affairs, or anything he was doing."

Mr. Khumale shifted his weight and looked away as he hesitantly replied.

"I am afraid there is little I can tell you about the activities of Joseph Msomi."

"You must realize an ambassador is a political appointment. You must also realize Mr. Daniel Msomi is a man of wealth and power in my country. When he decided his son was to be an ambassador . . . need I say more. It has caused some hard feelings in those who felt they were better qualified, but that is life, my friend. As for your question about what he was doing, quite frankly, I do not know. On occasion, he put in an appearance at some diplomatic function or some similar affair. Generally speaking, we seldom saw him, and were not at all privy to what he did when he was not here. In addition, we—"

"You mean to tell me that he was an ambassador from your country and you don't know what he was involved in!" Fowler began to feel one more possible source of information was about to come to nothing.

"Well, we heard rumors about his involvement in certain peace movements around the world. That is the extent of it. I would be glad to help you if I could. What I have told you is all I know."

Mr. Khumale and Fowler engaged in small talk for a short time. Nothing of substance coming out of it as far as Fowler was concerned. He took his leave of the embassy once again with a feeling of frustration. It seemed, every way he turned he faced a solid wall he could not penetrate. His gut feeling told him it was too pat. Somewhere out there was a simple key to the puzzle. Meanwhile, what was he going to tell Mr. Msomi? He had suggested some new information, but what?

There was little purpose to Fowler's drive across the city streets. Passing the Old Post Office, he swerved and parked in a no-parking zone. He placed a card that read, "Post Office, Official Business" on the dashboard. It was early afternoon, and since the lunch period was over, there were only a few stragglers roaming in and out of the shops and restaurants. He wandered aimlessly from floor to floor, hoping to see a familiar face. Another wasted effort. He left the building and ambled out to his car. A motorcycle policewoman pulled alongside of him and stopped as he reached his car. Leaning against it, he looked down at the officer in her three-wheeled vehicle with a traffic control insignia on the side of it.

"What's happening?" asked Fowler. "How're the clowns who call themselves drivers and make this city a dangerous place to live?"

"About the same as they are every day," responded the officer, a light-skinned colored woman.

"I understand there's a big flack in the public about you traffic folks having to write a certain number of tickets a day—a quota, if you know what I mean," mentioned Fowler wanting to get away, but not wishing to appear to be in a hurry.

"Between you and me, that's about it. They'll slow it down for a while, but as soon as things quiet down, they'll be on our asses for more tickets." She winked at Fowler as she said, "Traffic Control has got to provide the, you know what, to run this city. By the way," she asked, glancing at him with a serious expression, "what office do you work out of?"

He was feeling uncomfortable with the situation, but did not hesitate before answering.

"Downtown."

"Did you know you've got one of the old cards in your window?"

"Well, I'll be damned," said Fowler. "That goes to show you how efficient the post office is. Here I am in the main office, and I still don't have my new card. I'm going to get on somebody's ass as soon as I get back to the office." With that last comment, he got into his car, waved at the officer, and pulled out into traffic. He made a mental note to contact a friend who worked in the post office to obtain one of the new cards.

Once again his driving was without purpose, down one street, up another. The Mall had the usual assortment of late summer vacationers who wandered in and out of the museums. Young lovers meandered about arm in arm, along with an occasional jogger and the ever-present beggars. He drove slowly, scanning faces and figures along the way. Life in the city, he reflected.

Noticing two police vehicles parked near a small lunch stand, he found an empty space in a no-parking zone, placed a press card on the dashboard, and walked over to the stand. Just as he surmised, he found O'Donovan and Jules leaning on the counter, a drink in front of them.

"My man, Fowler," greeted Jules. "What's happening? What brings you here? You must be following us."

Fowler nodded to the two officers.

"I saw your cars parked down the street and thought I'd see how the police force is spending us citizens' hard-earned tax money. I can see by the sweat on your face you're hard at work trying to catch those scoundrels who make life difficult for us law-abiding citizens." That being said, he looked at the two with as serious an expression as he was able to muster.

"Since when did you start paying taxes?" asked O'Donovan with a smirk. "One of my sources tells me the IRS is asking questions about your financial affairs."

"Okay, okay," said Fowler with a smile. "Have you guys come up with anything new?"

"We're working on the fingerprints of the rapist," said Jules. "The FBI is running a check on his prints, but we don't have their report yet. Any of your people got anything for me?"

"Haven't heard a thing. No one seems to know anything. What about you, Pat, any leads?"

"A funny case. Whoever orchestrated this thing sure did a good job putting a cap on any info getting out."

"Things sure has gotten quiet," remarked Fowler. "Even the news has quit saying anything about it."

"Not that quiet," broke in Jules. "The commissioner has been on the captain's ass for results. He passes it down to us."

"Same thing here," agreed O'Donovan. "He's been raising hell with me about finding the guy who killed Linsky. Just like I'm some kind of magician."

Fowler checked his office and found there was nothing that needed his immediate attention. He turned the nose of his car toward Homer's Creole Cookery, deciding to eat and relax before his meeting with Daniel Msomi.

Leaving Homer's place, his thoughts roamed over the case—still no solid answers. He promised Msomi some

143

new evidence about his son's killing. Should he mention Pablo, the cloakroom attendant? On second thought, he would be hard put to connect Pablo with the shooting. It seemed he was no closer to solving the shooting than the last time they met. He was also sure Daniel Msomi was someone who did not take too kindly to reversals or failure. Maybe the best thing he could do was play it by ear.

Darkness began to fall over the city when Fowler parked in front of Msomi's apartment building. He walked slowly up the steps.

"Good evening, sir," said the attendant as he opened the door for Fowler.

"Good evening. Thank you."

"T.J. Fowler, to see Daniel Msomi," he told security, seated at a desk in the lobby.

"Go in," said the uniformed employee, pointing toward the elevators. "He's expecting you."

Sheia opened the door of their apartment and, with a wave of her arm, invited him in. She was dressed in a colorful, loose fitting robe with a slit in front, probably some kind of African dress, he thought. His eyes took in the grace and curve of her back as he followed her into the living room. He saw Daniel Msomi standing, looking out the window. Also present was a very black man, neatly dressed, including coat and tie and shiny black shoes. Fowler knew, without being told, he was an African.

"Have a seat, Mr. Fowler," came the precise intonation of Daniel Msomi. Without turning from the window, he said, "Please meet Mr. Tom Nkombo. I will explain his role in this dreadful affair in a moment."

Fowler extended his hand to Mr. Nkombo.

"T.J. Fowler, pleased to meet you." Tom Nkombo stood and offered his hand to acknowledge the greeting, then sat and reached for a drink on a small table.

144

"Please sit, Mr. Fowler," said Sheia. "May I fix you a drink?"

"Sounds good," replied Fowler. "Gin and tonic will do." Sheia glided silently out of the room.

Daniel Msomi abruptly turned away from the window and made his way to his chair and drink. A moment later, Sheia returned and handed a drink to Fowler. She then walked across the room and sat on a cushion near her father, legs crossed under her. All waited quietly for Daniel Msomi to open the discussion. He did not keep them waiting very long.

"When we talked this morning, you mentioned you were looking into some new facts that would shed light on my son's murder," began Msomi with a sigh. "I trust you have found the key to this distressing matter, the key that will clear my son's good name and bring justice to those who masterminded this appalling affair." His eyes bored into Fowler's face as he waited for a response.

Fowler knew, without looking around, Daniel Msomi's eyes were not the only ones fixed upon him. There was no way he could put a positive face upon his efforts to date. He would have to level with them; his efforts had not produced a single thing that could be viewed as a solid lead to help him solve the matter in a way satisfying to his client. Racking his brain, he searched for the exact grouping of words to fit the occasion.

"I am sorry to say—" began Fowler.

"It is just as I have said, the problem—" interrupted Nkombo.

"Just a minute. Let Mr. Fowler finish," admonished Msomi, raising his hand to quiet Nkombo, who was sitting with hands clasped across his ample belly, a derisive smile lighting his black face. Msomi lowered his arm and turned to Fowler, nodding for him to continue.

"I found out there had been an unusual happening at the restaurant the day after the shooting," began Fowler, in as clear and convincing a voice as he was able to bring forth. "The man who took care of the cloakroom was picked up by the immigration service, and no one knows what became of him. I went out to the place where he lived and talked to the people there. The funny thing about it was that someone came by a day or so after he was picked up by immigration claiming to be a policeman, and tore up his room, looking for something."

Fowler knew he was grasping for straws, since there was nothing unusual about the immigration service making a call at Marcel's and taking out an illegal alien. "Besides, I've got two reliable witnesses to the shooting," he continued, thinking about the homeless winos in the alley.

"You say you have two eye witnesses to the shooting of my son?" asked Msomi, eyeing Fowler closely.

"Yes, two very reliable witnesses."

Tom Nkombo leaned forward and spoke softly to Msomi.

"I still maintain the key to this dreadful affair is to be found in our country. I have the word of six highly respected citizens who were present when Mr. Lumbabwa threatened to kill your son if he came back and ran for the presidency. As you know, Mr. Lumbabwa has been priming his son for that position, and he is a dangerous man to cross. There are many who believe he is the one behind the deaths of those other candidates. If you will recall, both were assassinated during a political speech, assassins unknown." When Msomi did not respond, he continued. "As you are aware, Mr. Msomi, Mr. Lumbabwa is a man with a violent temper. He is also quite wealthy

146

and, as some are quick to point out, unscrupulous when it come to getting what he wants."

"But, this is happening in the United States," protested Msomi.

"Money has a long arm," retorted Nkombo.

"What do you think of that, Mr. Fowler? Perhaps we have been following the wrong trail. Could it be that my good friend Nkombo is right? What do you make of that?"

Fowler raised his glass and slowly finished the contents. His thoughts pondered this latest turn of events. Finally, he turned and faced Msomi.

"I cannot give you anything definite, but somehow I find myself in disagreement with Mr. Nkombo." He paused and shifted his eyes in Sheia's direction. It was impossible to know the thoughts behind those smokey brown eyes of hers as she sat impassively watching him. Turning to Nkombo he added, "There's something about this case that bothers me, that makes me sure there's more to it than a conflict over a political office in your country."

"And what is that?" asked Msomi.

"I've been on many a case, but I have never been on a case where there is less information on the street about it."

"The very point I have been making," countered Nkombo. "The answers to this puzzle lie in our country, not here in the United States. It is a waste of Mr. Msomi's money for him to continue on this fruitless line of investigation. I am convinced I will be able to provide him with an answer to the affair within a few weeks."

"It is time to refresh your drinks," said Sheia, interrupting the conversation.

Fowler welcomed a breather before responding to Nkombo. Msomi wandered over to a window and looked down on the passing scene. Nkombo leaned back in his chair, his head cradled in his clasped hands. Without a word, Sheia returned and placed each drink on its respective table. Fowler's eyes met hers briefly as she placed his drink beside him. He imagined a hint of support for the point he was trying to make, but he couldn't be sure. She returned to her cushion, Msomi back to his chair. All eyes were upon Fowler, waiting for him to respond. He began hesitantly.

"I guess I don't have more than gut feelings that there are big operators behind the shooting of your son. Whoever they are, they covered their tracks better than anyone in any case I've ever been on." He glanced at Msomi before continuing.

"Then you are convinced my son is innocent of this outrageous charge," interrupted Msomi.

"I must admit I had some doubts when I first took on the case. The more I looked into it, the more I began to suspect it was too pat. Nobody knows anything. In every drug case I've been on, it has never been this difficult to find someone who knows something about it." Shaking his head he added, "Nope. Nope. Your son was set up. We are faced with the usual problems: how was it done, why was it done, and who did it."

"What about the possibility of police involvement?" questioned Msomi.

"I gave that some thought, but I know the officer who was in charge that night. O'Donovan is a good cop. I cannot imagine him in on some kind of setup. Then there is the matter of the policeman being killed. We've seen your son on TV at a number of protest demonstrations, but there were a lot of people involved. Why your son? Other than protest movements, can you think of anything else he might have been involved in . . . that might have led to

148

his being murdered?"

After a long pause, a subdued no came from the lips of Msomi.

Fowler looked at Sheia, hoping she might provide a clue to her brother's death.

"I can think of nothing that might be of help to you," said Sheia in a soft voice.

Fowler remembered he wanted to go by Marcel's before closing and talk to the waiter who waited on Joseph Msomi that eventful night.

When Sheia led him to the door, leaving her father and Nkombo talking about events in their native country, she placed her hand on his arm. He felt it was an attempt to assure him she was aware of his efforts to resolve the matter. In a moment, the door closed and he was on his way to Marcel's. He had no other leads and could not get rid of the thought that a clue to solving the shooting was somewhere in the restaurant.

Hurrying down the steps of the building, Fowler felt the humid night air closing in on him. Looks like another day of rain, he thought as he entered his car and drove away.

When he got to Marcel's, he parked and sat for a few minutes, going over known and unknown aspects of the Msomi case. Finally, with a shrug, he slowly got out of the car and entered the restaurant.

11

The Key

A few tables were occupied with diners lingering over coffee and dessert when Fowler entered Marcel's restaurant. He glanced toward the bar where raucous laughter was intermixed with clouds of smoke that drifted toward the ceiling of the cocktail lounge. Only one person sat at the bar when Fowler walked over to it: a youngish, sandy-haired man of medium build wearing glasses. On taking a seat at the opposite end of the bar he noticed the bartender was the same one he talked to earlier.

"Jim Bush back?" asked Fowler, ordering a drink.

"Yeah. He came in this morning. Here he comes now," said the bartender pointing toward a slender man in a dark uniform, with white shirt and black bowtie. "Jim. Jim," he called. "Wait a minute." Pointing to Fowler, he said quietly, "This man has been here several times to see you."

Jim Bush stopped and came over to the bar.

"Fowler, private investigator," said Fowler, rising to shake hands with the waiter. "I'm on the Msomi shooting that happened shortly after he left this restaurant."

"I heard about it when I got in last night," said Jim Bush shaking his head. "A really nice man. Quiet like, a real gentleman. What can I do for you?"

"I understand you were on duty that night and waited on Mr. Msomi. Can you remember anything unusual that might help me with this case?"

Bush thought for a few minutes before replying.

"Mr. Msomi always tried to get a table in my section of the dining room. As far as I remember, he came in about his usual time, sat down, and ordered a drink—scotch and water I believe. I usually let him finish his drink before giving him the menu. He looked it over and ordered, I don't remember what, probably some kind of lamb dish. He was partial to lamb."

"Did he act upset in any way? Was there anything out of the ordinary that night?"

"Not a thing. Mr. Msomi generally brought papers with him to read, and he could get so involved with them, I would have to remind him about the menu."

"Was there anyone with him?"

"No. He usually ate alone. I only remember one time when there was someone with him. A couple of weeks ago, he came in with two men, one an oriental, the other, white. They had dinner and talked almost to closing time."

Fowler wanted to bring the conversation to a close, especially since man on the other end of the bar was inching the closer and listening intently to what was being said. After a few more questions, Fowler thanked Bush and watched him stride away.

"Can I buy you a drink?" asked the sandy-haired man who was now sitting nearby. "My name is Jim Marshall. I overheard you and the waiter talking about the Msomi shooting."

Fowler eyed the other carefully before accepting the invitation to have a drink.

"T.J. Fowler," he muttered. "Sounds like a good idea."

"What'll you have?"

"Gin and tonic is my drink." Marshall ordered the drink.

"I guess you're wondering why I'm interested in the Msomi case?" He received a gruff nod from Fowler.

"I'm a reporter for Don Nestor of World Broadcasting Company. He had me looking into the Msomi shooting. I don't think be was too satisfied with the police version of the drug bust."

"I'm looking into the matter for a client of mine. What have you got on the case?"

For several minutes, the two discussed what each of them knew, at least, what each was willing to share. Fowler concluded Marshall did not know as much as he did about the shooting.

"I'm off the case now. Nestor thinks it's a dead issue, and the public has lost interest. I'm on the bank fraud case that's in the news."

"I know what you're saying. I'm about to give up on this case myself. I keep coming back here thinking there must be something I've missed. But I'll be damned if I can find it." The two drank in silence as they watched a tradesman approach the bar, place his tool box on the counter, and lean over to talk to the bartender.

"I'm the plumber you called about some leak in the bar," stated the man quietly.

"At the other end." The bartender pointed to the far end of the bar. "Somewhere under the counter."

The plumber picked up his tools and moved as he was directed. Fowler and Marshall returned to their drinks and small talk.

"Did you know Msomi was scheduled to speak at the UN the day he was killed?" asked Marshall, looking closely at Fowler.

"No. What was he going to talk about?"

"I'm not sure. The scoop from the UN had something to do with arms and the problems of the Third-World countries. There was a rumor he was going to lower the boom on some high placed people in our government. Msomi was supposed to tell, in detail, about them being behind a worldwide organization that promoted disorder in many countries in order to profit from the sales of arms. But I could never pin that rumor down, so I don't know how much it was worth. Anyway, it was too fuzzy for Nestor to use. I looked—"

"What the hell is this?" came the voice of the plumber from the other end of the bar.

Marshall and Fowler turned to see what occupied the plumber's attention. He had placed some kind of briefcase upon the counter.

Fowler's heart gave a quick beat as he got up from his stool and hurried to the other end of the bar, Marshall at his heels. Fowler recognized the case, or one like it. It was a replica of Joseph Msomi's attaché case, or a perfect likeness of the one he saw in Captain Levine's office, the case Daniel Msomi positively identified as the one he gave his son.

"That's just like the case I saw in Captain Levine's office the day he gave a press conference about the drug bust and shooting," said Marshall. Fowler did not respond, his eyes transfixed upon the object sitting on the counter.

"What's this about?" asked the bartender.

"This case is one of the missing pieces of the puzzle surrounding the shooting of Joseph Msomi," said Fowler.

Jim Bush passed by on his way back to the dining room.

"Jim, Jim," called Fowler. "Come over here for a minute." Bush stopped and walked briskly over to the small gathering at bar. Pointing at the case sitting on the bar, Fowler asked quietly, his eyes fixed upon Jim Bush's face.

"Do you know whose case this is?"

Bush looked at the case for only a few moments before replying firmly.

"Sure, it belongs to Mr. Msomi. I've seen it many times. I've never seen another one like it."

"Does he bring it to the table with him?" asked Fowler,

"Very seldom."

"What was his usual procedure whenever he came to Marcel's, I mean where this case was concerned," continued Fowler.

"He usually left it at the cloakroom when he came in and picked it up when he left."

"Do you remember whether he had it with him at his table that night?"

"I'm not sure, but I don't think he did. He had some papers he was looking over, but I don't remember seeing his case."

"What about those papers? What happened to them? Any idea what they were about?"

"I have no idea. He sometimes gave me papers to throw away when he was through with them, but I couldn't tell you what they were about."

Fowler thanked Bush for his help and pondered this new development. Marshall, the bartender, and the plumber watched for him in silence waiting for him to explain what was going on.

He shook himself out of his preoccupation with unanswered questions.

"Is there a phone around here?" he asked.

"On the wall, at the other end of the counter," volunteered the bartender.

Fowler hurried to the phone. He collected his thoughts when he heard Sheia's voice on the other end.

"Something important has come up," he told her. "I can't tell you about it over the phone, but I would like you to be there when we meet this evening."

The three men looked expectantly at Fowler when he returned, waiting for an explanation. "I wish I could satisfy your curiosity, but I can't. I can tell you this case is very important to me and my attempt to get at the bottom of the Msomi shooting. To show you how tight this whole thing is, this is the first break I've had since I've been on this case. Whoever is behind it made sure there were no loose ends."

"I wonder whether I should tell the manager about this case?" questioned the bartender.

"Let me tell him about it," said Fowler sharply. "The one thing I should make clear to all of you is the danger we face just because we found this case. Two people have been killed. I am convinced the guys pulling the strings would think no more about wasting us than they would about stepping on an ant. Besides, I'll have a better chance to put a squeeze play on them if they don't know I have this briefcase. No matter. I'm a cooked goose if the word gets out I have a case that's a duplicate of the one at the police station."

"What about Don Nestor? We've put a lot of hours on this case," mumbled Marshall peevishly. "Besides, if this is an exclusive, I want to be the one who springs it first."

"You've got my word. I'll turn the whole thing over to you as soon as I can put my finger on the ones in back of the shooting. You'll get your exclusive. Don't worry about it."

Fowler knew the briefcase was hot property, and the thought of walking around with it, all of a sudden made him uneasy. What should he do with it? It was too dangerous to leave with the Msomis. His thoughts were interrupted by Marshall.

"Anything wrong?" asked Marshal eyeing Fowler.

"Naw. Just trying to make up my mind what to do with this thing. Nothing that can't be worked out."

Fowler fingered the lock on the case as if, for some reason, it would change from locked to unlocked. Noticing the plumber had finished his job and was preparing to leave, Fowler directed his comments to the three men. "I've got an appointment with my client with this case. Although I don't expect all of you to keep your mouths shut about this matter, I want to say one more time, this is dangerous stuff, and it would be best for you to keep out of it. Don't mention it to anybody—wives, girlfriends, buddies, *nobody*."

Fowler picked up the briefcase and made his way rapidly to the door of the restaurant. Stepping out into the cool, damp, night air, he paused for a moment to look around him. A slight shiver ran up and down his back as his eyes settled upon his car. With deliberate speed, he made his way to his car and to the Msomis.

Many thoughts flooded Fowler's mind as he drove across the city. He pulled up and parked in a no-parking zone in front of the Msomi apartment building. The doorman indicated he could leave his car where it was. Fowler had formed a good relationship with all the doormen during his visits to the Msomis. Then, too, apparently Sheia and her father were held in high repute by the doormen.

His senses were on full alert as he stepped slowly out of the car and carefully scanned his surroundings. Satisfied, he strode stiffly up the steps and into the building. Security must have been put on alert—as soon as he mentioned Msomi, he was waved through to the elevator.

The door of the Msomi apartment swung open to his knock, and the musical voice of Sheia was heard.

"Come in, Mr. Fowler, We are anxious to hear this news you are bringing us."

Fowler followed Sheia into the living room, where her father was seated, clad in an expensive-looking robe. At a glance, Msomi's eyes fixed upon Fowler and the case he was carrying. Sheia curled herself, catlike in a chair and waited to hear the reason for the late night visit.

"I see you have brought my son's attaché case," began Msomi impatiently. "How did you get it away from that most disagreeable fellow at the police station?"

Fowler handed the locked case to Msomi.

"Is this your son's case?" he asked. Msomi gave the case no more than a cursory glance before turning to face Fowler

"Of course it is," snapped Msomi. "Do you think I do not know my son's case, the case I gave to him so many years ago!"

Fowler remained silent, his eyes upon Msomi, who was tenderly fingering the exotic-looking object, a far-away look in his eyes. Sheia was quiet, her eyes riveted upon the case her father was holding.

"The case is locked," murmured Msomi, looking at Fowler in a questioning manner.

Fowler nodded.

"Would you have any of your son's keys?" he asked. "Perhaps there might be a key that would fit the lock."

Msomi gave a sharp look at Sheia. Without a word, she rose and glided from the room. In a few minutes she returned with a key ring containing a number of keys.

"My brother left this set of keys with us some time ago," said Sheia, handing the keys to her father.

Fowler watched Msomi try key after key in an

157

attempt to open the case. Finally, one worked. Msomi opened the case, flipped the lid and stared at papers, magazines, and newspaper clippings.

Puzzled, Msomi looked quizzically at Fowler.

"What does this mean? The last time we saw this case it was full of cocaine. These papers were not in it." Without waiting for Fowler to answer, he growled angrily, "Speak up. Speak up! What is this about? I can see from your face there is more to this than meets the eye."

Fowler answered in a slow and deliberate manner.

"You are right. There is more to it than meets the eye. Are you sure this is your son's case? What makes you so sure? Are there any identifying marks that you can point to?"

"What are you talking about?" demanded Msomi, his voice rising. "Of course this is my son's case! There is his name printed in gold letters across the back of the case, Joseph Ngemi Msomi. It is a one of a kind case. In all the world there is no other like it."

Sheia, who was sitting quietly and observing the two men, leaned forward.

"Are you suggesting, Mr. Fowler, that this is not my brother's case," she asked.

Fowler directed his comments to Msomi.

"If you will remember, you positively identified the briefcase you saw in Captain Levine's office, with the dope in it, as your son's case, a case you bought for him years ago."

Turning to Sheia, he added, "No, I am not suggesting that this case is not your brother's case. As a matter of fact, this *is* your brother's case. The case we saw in the captain's office was not your brother's case. It was an exceptionally good fake." Fowler paused to let this new development sink in.

"Continue," muttered Msomi sharply.

"Part of it is beginning to make sense. That is how it was done. Just as I thought, the key was in the restaurant all along. Your son's case, this case, was switched with the case containing the dope in the restaurant. The law of unintended consequences finally caught up to them, whoever is behind this tragic affair."

"And what does that mean?" asked Msomi.

"I happened to be in the restaurant when this case was found. It was hidden under the counter in the bar. The brains behind this slick caper never intended for it to be found. Something got fouled up. I've got a good idea who did the switching. I'll check it out in the morning-"

"Well, who was it?" said Msomi angrily. "I will get the authorities on it right away so that we can quickly clear my son's name of this miserable charge."

"I'm sure the switch was done by the cloakroom attendant."

"If you are so sure, why is it we cannot have him arrested and make him tell what this is all about?"

"Not so fast," protested Fowler. "In the first place, we cannot locate that cloakroom attendant. He was picked up by immigration the day after the shooting. Right now, he is somewhere in Mexico—but where, nobody knows. Besides, I'm pretty sure he played a small part in this deal. We've got to find the big wheels behind this affair. So you see, there are still many questions to be answered."

"Well, at least I have my son's case in my possession." Msomi gazed at the case with a perplexed look on his face.

Fowler was quick to respond.

"We need to talk about that too."

"Why should we discuss my son's case?" asked Msomi firmly.

"This is one of the few things of his that I have left. There is nothing to discuss." His tone made it clear the issue was closed, as far as he was concerned.

"I need to point out that two men were killed and that that case is pretty important to someone," insisted Fowler. "I went to the house where the cloakroom attendant lived, checking up on him. Someone beat me to it and ransacked his room. My guess is they were looking for this case."

"Let us listen to Mr. Fowler, Father," interrupted Sheia. "Perhaps he—"

"Sheia is right. Until I get at the bottom of this thing, anyone with that case is going to be in a dangerous spot. Although I warned those who saw the case not to talk to anyone about it, my experience has taught me it is difficult to keep people from talking about something that should be kept secret.

"All the way over here, I racked my brain, trying to come up with a safe place to put this case. If you keep it here, both you and your daughter will be in real danger. You are paying me to take over the danger aspect of this situation. I know how you feel about your son's things, but believe me, I know best in these matters. Trust it to me. I'll take good care of it."

Msomi wandered to the window and looked out as he mulled over Fowler's comments. After several minutes of silence, without turning around he spoke.

"What do you think, daughter?"

Sheia shifted her position in her chair, glanced at her father's back and replied.

"I think we should follow Mr. Fowler's advice. We need to get at the bottom of this horrid affair. If he thinks this attaché case might help him solve the shooting, then he should have it."

160

"All right, all right," agreed Msomi, returning to his chair. "What about my son's papers? Is there any need for you to keep them?"

"I don't know. It might be best to leave them just the way they are. I'll need the key, too."

Msomi took the key off the key ring and handed it to Fowler.

"What is your next move?" he asked.

"To be truthful, I don't know. But, I do feel better about what we're up against for the first time since I started. We now know your son had nothing to do with dope. He was set up. That's for sure."

"What about the police?" remarked Msomi. "I do not trust that police captain. Could it be he is behind it?"

"I doubt it. I gave that some thought after I went out to see the cloakroom attendant. I was told the person who turned his room upside down said he was a policeman. He pulled out some kind of identification, but the people in the house didn't get a good look at it. There's no way to tell who, or what he was. Besides, there's one thing that shot holes in that notion. The policeman killed during the shooting was a favorite of Captain Levine." Fowler paused to let his words sink in.

Sheia placed her hand lightly on Fowler's arms as she let him out the door of the apartment.

"I have faith you will soon get at the bottom of this mess," she said softly. "It has caused my father a great deal of suffering. His sleep is frequently interrupted by unpleasant dreams. I am sure they are about my brother." She reached into a pocket of her robe and pulled out her business card and handed it to Fowler. "If you have need to get in touch with me at any time, please feel free to call me."

161

The touch of her hand lingered in his mind as the elevator glided to the ground floor. Those thoughts were surpassed as he brooded over this new predicament. What was he going to do with Joseph's case? When he walked out onto the steps of the building, he took a deep breath, carefully checked his s surroundings, and then hurried to his car and to his apartment.

Safely behind locked doors in his apartment, he placed the case on a table and stared at it for a few minutes. Sooner or later, and most likely sooner, the word would hit the street he had evidence bearing on the Msomi shooting. He was aware he was on a precarious time table. Either he got to the ones who were searching for Joseph's briefcase before they got to him, or . . . His mind refused to contemplate the likely choices available to that mystery person or persons. He was convinced of one thing, the case could not remain in his apartment. But where could he put it?

Fowler's thoughts were put on hold when he noticed the light flickering on his answering machine. The message from Tom Nkombo indicated important news about the Msomi incident. After several minutes of indecision, he returned the call. Nkombo flatly refused to discuss his information over the phone. Reluctantly, Fowler agreed to a visit from Nkombo that night.

He picked up the case, hurried to his bedroom, and slid it under the bed, then to the kitchen to fix a drink. Drink in hand he settled into his favorite chair and waited for his guest. This had better be good, he mused.

Shortly afterwards, he pushed the buzzer to let Nkombo into the building and stood by the door to wave him into the living room of his apartment.

"Have a seat. Can I get you something to drink?

You've got a choice between gin and tonic and bourbon. That's it."

"Gin and tonic sounds very good. A sliver of lime would be fine, too."

"No can do. What about a slice of lemon?"

"A good substitute. That will be fine."

Fowler returned shortly with a drink in hand.

"Now, Nikombo." He liked the way many African names rolled across his tongue. "Just what is this new development that's got you excited enough to call me at this hour?"

"My contact in Niberia has come into information that reinforces my theory that the answer to the shooting of Joseph Msomi lies in my country."

"And what's that evidence?" Fowler wondered whether Nikombo was aware of the second attaché case. His uneasiness evaporated quickly. He would have mentioned it right away. "All right, Nikombo—"

"Nkombo! Nkombo! You fail to pronounce my name as it should be."

"Okay, okay, Nkombo. Now, get on with it. It's late and I have a big day tomorrow."

Nkombo paused to sip his drink before continuing.

"Are you aware Mr. Lumbabwa was in this city during the time Joseph Msomi was killed?"

No," replied Fowler, rapidly trying to remember who the hell was Lumbabwa.

"Mr. Lumbabwa, if you will remember, was priming his son for the top administrative position in my country."

"I can't see what his coming to Washington has to do with the shooting. Lots of people come to this city at all times of the year and for all kinds of reasons."

"True. But he was overheard to say he had to remove the last barrier that stood in the way of his son occupying the seat of power in my country."

"So?"

"It is so clear. The only one left to stand in the way of his son's advancement is, or was, Joseph Msomi. Mr. Lumbabwa, as I told you, was known to have removed other contenders for the position."

"You—"

"Let me finish. Through my investigations, I found out Mr. Lumbabwa flew back to my country the day after the shooting. He went to some trouble to hide the fact he was in Washington, or even left my country. He was here under an assumed name and traveled back to Africa under an even different name. Would you not consider that strange, very strange, indeed?"

"Perhaps, but let me finish what I started to say. Have you forgotten that Joseph Msomi was shot by a police officer while he was holding an attaché case full of cocaine? In addition, an officer was killed during that shooting."

"It is, as I have said before, all doors are open to money. You would hardly argue that policemen are not immune to the enticement of large sums of money?"

Fowler half-listened as Nkombo rambled on, occasionally nodding his head as if in agreement. A possible solution began to form in his mind about what to do with the briefcase. Finally, taking charge of the conversation, he ended it. He ushered Nkombo out the door with vague promises to get back to him as soon as anything turned up.

Once rid of Nkombo, Fowler retrieved the attaché case and methodically assembled wrapping paper, twine, scissors, and an old suitcase. The briefcase was put in the suitcase and wads of newspapers placed round it to prevent it from moving. He then wrapped the suitcase with brown wrapping paper and firmly tied it with twine. When he sidled off to bed, his moves for the next day were, for the most part, fixed in his mind.

12

Thin Ice

The sun streaming into Fowler's bedroom window indicated it was going to be a pleasant day. His thoughts bounced back and forth on the Msomi affair as he took a shower. Finished, he headed for the kitchen and prepared a cup of coffee. Although he understood how Joseph Msomi had been set up, there were many details that needed to be resolved. Who was the supposed back-up man who shot Linsky? Clearly, the official version was wrong. He recalled Nkombo's comment about the police not being above the charm of money. It didn't make sense for the police to shoot one of their own. Joseph Msomi must have stepped on some powerful shoes. Fowler's eyes settled upon the package carefully concealing the attaché case. The first priority was to put that package in a safe hiding place. He finished his coffee and was on his way to his office.

Henrietta glanced up from the papers on her desk as he entered the office, and immediately shifted her attention to the package he was carrying.

"Morning, boss," mumbled Fowler as he hurried past on the way to his cubicle.

Henrietta gave little more than a muffled greeting before he passed out of sight into his room. Her curiosity was quickly obvious when she appeared in the doorway.

"What in the world have you got wrapped in that

166

package?" she asked with hands on hips.

"This package contains an important piece of evidence that will solve the Msomi case," answered Fowler with a straight face. "Anything new?"

"All's quiet on this front. Are you kidding about that package?"

"I'm on to a good lead. I'll let you know about it in a few days, if it pans out the way I hope it will. Right now I need to get in touch with a couple of people, O'Donovan and the immigration office."

"By the way, some of those bills on your desk need to be taken care of. We're behind in a couple of them." Henrietta returned to her office and soon called out, "O'Donovan on the line."

"Hey, O'Donovan, let's kick around some ideas about the Msomi case." After a pause, he said, "the Old Post Office at ten o'clock is fine."

The call to immigration was not fruitful. They deported Pablo the day after he was picked up at Marcel's restaurant. Where he was in Mexico was anybody's guess.

"If anything comes up, give me a call," said Fowler as he passed Henrietta's desk on his way out of the office, package in hand.

"By the way," reminded Henrietta. "When are we going to get some money from the Msomis?"

"I'll mention it to his daughter. She probably takes care of money matters." Fowler waved and left.

He had plenty of time before he was to meet O'Donovan. As he rounded the corner of Rhode Island and 10th Street, he became aware of someone honking a horn. Looking into his rearview mirror, he saw Jules gesturing for him to stop. Fowler was in no mood to waste time, but he pulled over to the curb. In a moment, Jules stuck his head into the window of the car.

"What's the rush, ol' buddy?" asked Jules. "What's happening?"

"Not much. What's up with you? Anything new on the rapist case?" Fowler's mind raced to find some way to end this unplanned interaction.

"Things are pretty quiet."

"Are you still on the case?"

"Yep, the captain's been giving me hell about not coming up with something on that killer. I told him the other day I had a solid tip that might be the one thing we've been looking for."

"What have you got?" Fowler gave Jules a searching look.

"Nothing, a little bullshit. I had to give him something. I can always go back and tell him it didn't work out. Incidentally, a couple of days ago, I saw that blond gal you were running around with. She was snuggled up with a white dude over near the pool. Whatever happened with the two of you?"

"We decided to call it off. Just one of those things."

"I heard a good one the other day." Jules was barely able to smother a laugh as he relished the joke.

"Some other time," winked Fowler, putting his car into gear. "I'm on to a lead. Don't know how good it is, but I'm running a little late. Save it for me until the next time."

"Right, you'll get a charge out of this one. I hope I can remember it until I see you again. See you later."

Fowler entered the mix of passing vehicles, his mind flooded with memories of his brief affair with Mary Lou. His absorption with the Msomi case gave him some relief from recollections of the many good times the two of them spent together. A glance at the package brought him back to the present. He had not made up his mind whether or not to mention the case to O'Donovan. In addition, Nkombo's comments about the power of money could not be disregarded. He pulled to a stop at the Old Post Office, placed a press card on the dashboard and stepped out. He locked the package in the trunk, turned and hurried into the building.

Some of the shops and restaurants in the converted post office were just completing preparations for the day. Fowler was just finishing the last morsels of ham and eggs at a short order café, when he saw O'Donovan enter the building. It was exactly ten o'clock. That was the thing about O'Donovan; he could always be expected to be right on time or call if unable to do so. Fowler finished his meal, paid the bill and left to intercept his friend, who was making his way around the other side of the building. When he came upon him, he tapped him on the shoulder.

"On time as usual, Pat," observed Fowler. "Had your breakfast yet?"

"Yeah. I ate earlier with the family. I could stand another cup of coffee though."

"Get a table over there in the corner," said Fowler, pointing to a spot in the large open room on the first floor.

He left to get a couple of cups of coffee. Minutes later, he joined O'Donovan at a table somewhat hidden in a corner.

"What's up?" questioned O'Donovan, as Fowler placed a small tray with two cups of coffee on the table and sat down. "It's not often you call me for a meeting away from the station. You've come up with something. What is it?"

Fowler nodded. He thought for a few moments before responding. Even now, he wasn't sure whether it was the smart thing to take O'Donovan into his confidence. Still, he had been on a number of assignments with him when

169

he was on the force and . . . trusted him.

"You're right. It's about the Msomi drug bust," said Fowler. "He was set up. It was only a matter of luck that I found out how it was done." He paused and finished his coffee.

"Go on. Go on."

"There was an identical briefcase involved. A switch was made in Marcel's restaurant." Fowler related the events of the previous evening. When he finished, O'Donovan leaned back in his seat, his eyes fixed upon an empty cup of coffee on the table.

"I'll be damned," said O'Donovan. "That sure puts an entirely different fix on the whole thing."

"You remember telling me that after Msomi was shot, you took some keys out of his pocket and tried to open the case, but couldn't get it open? You had to force it with a screw driver. Well, the captain opened that case without any trouble at all."

"Hold it! Are you trying to tell me the captain is mixed up in that shooting?"

"I don't know. It bothers me. I can't imagine Captain Levine having anything to do with something like this, the shooting of an ambassador."

"You're right. And if you remember, Linsky got killed in that shooting."

"Yeah, I know."

"Linsky was one of the captain's boys. He was grooming him for a promotion. What about the supposed back-up man, or hit man?"

"Haven't a clue about that one. None of my contacts have come up with anything. It's too quiet. Whoever is behind this caper is sure keeping a lid on it. An African friend of Msomi thinks politics in his country is behind it. But I don't buy that notion. There will be some bigger fish shaking the line before we find the answer to this mystery."

"What about the cloakroom attendant?"

"Deported, somewhere in Mexico. No one at immigration has any idea where he went."

"You mentioned going out to the guy's house and being told an officer had been there and trashed the attendant's room. Couldn't they identify the person?"

"I doubt it. The only person who spoke English told me an old lady at the house said the person looked kind of odd. My bet is the guy was disguised. For all we know, he probably wasn't an officer. He flashed an I.D. at the old lady, who, even if she could see it, probably couldn't read it. She doesn't speak a word of English."

A long silence.

"Where is the briefcase now?" O'Donovan asked.

"In the trunk of my car."

"You called me—"

"I know, you want to know how you fit into this puzzle. Well, the first thing I want from you is a promise you won't say anything about what I've told you to anybody, not even your wife. There's already been two people killed. I doubt—"

"I think you're forgetting something else, if we're going to get to the bottom of this case."

"What?"

"It wasn't some unknown who shot Msomi. It was my partner Linsky."

"I know, I know. Until I get more facts, there are only a few people I can trust, and you're one of them. I haven't told my secretary about this briefcase. As it stands, there are too many knowing about it now, and you know how people talk. I've got to find a safe place to hide this case, and that's where you come in."

"Me," mumbled O'Donovan, giving Fowler a long, searching look. "Just what do you want me to do with it?"

"The more I think about it, the more it seems the best place to hide it is in the police station. You've got a good buddy in personal effects. Maybe we could get him to put it away in some far corner, out of sight. I've got Msomi's attaché case in an old suitcase that is wrapped and tied up. Outside of you and me, no one else would have any idea what it's about."

"I don't know," countered O'Donovan. "I don't know. It'll be my ass if the captain finds out about it. He's already giving me hell about the back-up man who shot Linsky." Looking sharply at Fowler, he added, "If I go along with it, you'd better level with me. What else have you got?"

"I wish I could tell you I've got more, but this is the first good lead to come my way. Not a single contact has come up with anything. You and I know that is most unusual in this city. It's just too quiet." The two men spent a few more minutes talking before leaving the building.

Standing on the steps of the Old Post Office, O'Donovan suggested they go to the station in his squad car. After getting the package from his car, Fowler joined O'Donovan. He quickly removed the wrapping paper and twine, opened the suitcase and showed O'Donovan the attaché case.

"Identical?" questioned O'Donovan after inspecting the case.

"Yep," said Fowler as he rewrapped the package. "Mr. Msomi told me the attaché case he gave his son was one of a kind. He was wrong. This one is exactly like the one he gave his son, in every detail. I'll be glad to get this thing in a safe place as soon as we can." Moments later, they were on their way to the 77th Precinct.

The two men hurried to the personal effects office at the station. O'Donovan greeted the personal effects clerk.

"Hi, Bert, it looks like you've been swamped this morning, from the looks of all that stuff on the counter."

Bert looked up from his paperwork and smiled.

"One of those days—be with you in a minute." Several others entered the room. Bert looked inquiringly at O'Donovan, who indicated they'd wait until he was finished with the new arrivals.

When only O'Donovan and Fowler remained, Bert asked, "What's up."

O'Donovan picked up the package and placed it on the counter. He replied in a quiet voice.

"I'm on to something pretty big, and I need your help. I'd like you to put *this package* in some far corner and forget it. Forget I gave it to you. Got it?"

"Don't worry. I'll take care of it."

"Guess I'd better check my desk for messages," said O'Donovan as he and Fowler left the personal effects office. "Get yourself something to drink, and I'll take you back to your car in a few minutes."

Fowler wandered over to a drink machine, placed a coin in it and listened as a Coke went kerplunk into the holder. Just as he finished the Coke and turned away from the machine, Captain Levine came out of the squad room.

"Fowler! Fowler! Hold on a minute." He hastened over to him.

"How are things?" asked the captain.

"So, so," responded Fowler noncommittally. He felt a certain wariness welling up inside him. He had only a gut feeling, but ... until he was sure one way or another whether the captain was mixed up in the Msomi affair, he was going to be careful whenever he was around him.

"Got a minute? I have a couple of things I'd like to discuss with you. Let's go into my office."

"Okay, after you." Fowler followed the captain across the squad room. He touched O'Donovan on the back as he came abreast of him sitting at his desk.

Captain Levine closed the door of his office after the two men and motioned to a seat in front of his desk. He walked around it and sat down. Fowler watched him deliberately select a pipe from a rack, fill it with tobacco, light it, and take a few puffs. Moments later, the captain broke the silence.

"I hear you are still on that Msomi incident." Fowler made no comment. "I can't imagine what you're finding out there when even the FBI gave up on the case. Unless of course you've come up with some facts we don't know about. That African sonofabitch was caught red-handed with the goods. Other than the Linsky matter, the case is closed. Why are you still fucking around with it?"

"Playing out my hunches, Captain. There's something about the shooting that smells, and I mean to find out what it is."

"Have you got anything more than a hunch?" asked the captain in a low voice.

"Nope."

"I need not tell you that messing around with police business is not good for your health," snapped Captain Levine, his voice rising. "Now, I'm asking you again! What have you got on the Msomi case? I know damn well you wouldn't still be asking questions all around town if you did not have something, and I want to know just what it is."

"But, Captain," responded Fowler in a mocking tone. "You just got through saying as far as the department was

174

concerned, the case was closed."

"I know what I said!" The captain pounded on his desk with his fist. "If I think a case needs to be opened, it will be opened. Is that clear? It doesn't matter what you or anyone else thinks about it."

Fowler sat quietly, waiting to see if the captain had anything else to say. He sensed the less said the better.

"Anything else, Captain?" he finally asked.

"No." The captain replied in a crisp tone as his attention wandered to some papers on his desk. Without looking up he growled, "Remember, if you come up with anything important, I want to know about it. I'm sure you are aware I can get your PI license revoked if I want to. If I were you, I would cooperate with this department."

Fowler left the captain's office and walked across the squad room. He motioned to O'Donovan, indicating he was to follow. On finding a convenient wall, he leaned against it and waited. Shortly after, O'Donovan passed by him on his way out of the building. Fowler followed him to his car.

"What was that all about . . . in the captain's office?" asked O'Donovan as the two sped on their way.

"Nothing much. I think the captain was trying to find out if I had come up with anything new on the Msomi drug bust."

"What did you tell him?"

"You mean about the duplicate briefcase? Nothing. He tried to convince me the incident was closed and the department satisfied with the FBI decision about it. Didn't you say you were still trying to find the guy who shot Linsky?"

"Yep. The captain has me on another assignment, told me to keep trying to find the one who shot him. I'm supposed to keep quiet about it, so keep it under your hat.

"What the hell's going on over there?" O'Donovan snapped, pointing to a crowd of angry shouting youths gathered on a corner.

"There's Jules," noted Fowler. "Must be some kind of traffic violation." O'Donovan got out of the car and hurried to the scene. After a brief chat with Jules, he ordered the throng to disperse. Another squad car arrived, and two officers helped to clear the area. A handcuffed prisoner was placed in the back seat of the squad car and the officers quickly sped away.

"What's going on?" Fowler directed his question to Jules, who came over to the car with O'Donovan.

"Not much. One of those unpaid traffic ticket cases with a warrant for the guy's arrest. Things got a little out of hand. I responded to the call for back-up. That's it. What are you and O'Donovan up to? I'm beginning to see so much of you that you might as well be back on the force."

"Out for a joy ride on the people's money," drawled Fowler with a smirk and a wink.

"Yeah, yeah, I know. None of my business, eh."

"We've got to go." O'Donovan entered the car and started the motor.

"Funny thing," mused Jules. "There was something familiar about the guy we just picked up. Oh, well, maybe it will come back to me later. Did I mention we found a gun in the glove compartment of the car?"

"Doesn't surprise me these days," muttered O'Donovan. "A lot of these kids have a gun somewhere in their cars. See you later." The drive to the Old Post Office where Fowler's car was parked took only five minutes. "Let's keep in touch," he said as he let Fowler out of his car. "Call me if anything else comes up, okay?"

"Will do."

Fowler called his office and received two messages. The client in a divorce matter was dissatisfied with the assigned investigator. The second was from Daniel Msomi requesting a return call as soon as possible. There was no answer when he called Msomi. The divorce problem could wait.

Fowler drove around aimlessly, finally stopping at the Lincoln Memorial. He ordered a soft drink at a snack bar and chatted with the clerk, mostly to pass the time of day. He was about to call it a day, when his eyes picked up the form and action of one of his contacts, Ace High Jackson. This enterprising man of the streets was plying his usual trade. He was dressed in clean but tattered clothing, leaning on a cane as he looked out at the world from behind dark glasses. The placard hanging on a string tied around his neck stated, "Help a Blind War Veteran." He was neither blind nor a veteran. Occasionally, well-wishers would drop a coin into his container.

"Hey, Ace High, m'man. What's the good word?" said Fowler when he came alongside him.

Ace High, who played the role of a blind man quite well looked around as if to locate the direction of the voice.

"I think I hear the voice of my good friend Jasper." He knew full well who he was talking to.

"Nope, this is your good buddy, Fowler. I can fill that bucket of yours with bills if you can give me some solid information on that Msomi shooting. Anything coming down the street as far as you know?"

"If you'll help me to that bench, I might have something for you." Ace High turned to thank a kindly old lady who dropped a coin or two in his cup.

Fowler took Ace High by the arm and directed him to

a nearby bench, where he sat, folded his hands on top of his cane and tilted his head slightly upwards as if to better hear what Fowler had to say.

"Okay. What have you got?"

Ace High spoke in a quiet voice.

"There's no back-up man."

"How's that?"

"I said, there's no back-up man."

"Where did you pick that up? Besides, you know a policeman was killed that night." Fowler was skeptical, but not ready to discount Ace High's comments entirely. He had been a reliable source of information.

"A crazy dude by the name of Coky Jim laid it on me. I don't know where he got his information. The old guy has been pretty straight . . . and, when he comes up with anything, you can be sure there's something to it."

"Where can I get ahold of this guy?"

"Right now, you can find him at the central police station. He was caught trying to hustle some stolen watches to a plainclothes officer at the Mall. I suspect he'll be out of circulation for a while."

Ace High stood and indicated he was to be taken back to his office. Fowler waited until a steady stream of pedestrians was passing before taking a dollar bill and putting it into Ace's cup with a flourish. Since he had not heard any coins dropping into his cup, Ace High continued to look upward, his head cocked to the side and facing away from Fowler.

Sitting in his car, Fowler tried to make sense out of the information he got from Ace High. If there was no back-up man, then who shot Linsky, and why? What was the connection? The winos in the alley near Marcel's said they heard someone running away just after the shooting. One said someone ran into him in the alley just before the incident. He pondered the matter then decided he would go to Joseph Msomi's apartment. Perhaps a lead could to be found there.

13

The Idealist

Fowler phoned Daniel Msomi before getting out of his car at Joseph Msomi's apartment building. Still no answer. Placing a press card on the dashboard, he got out, sauntered over to the doorman, and waited until they were alone.

"Howdy," said Fowler.

"How are you, sir? Can I help you?"

"That depends." Fowler pulled out his ID and handed it to him. "I'm investigating a shooting of one of your former tenants, a Mr. Joseph Msomi. Do you remember him?"

Handing Fowler's ID back to him, the doorman answered cautiously.

"Msomi, Msomi. Yes, I remember him. The police were here asking a lot of questions about him. I told them all I knew, which wasn't very much. Are you connected with the police?"

"No. I'm on my own. I don't—"

"Hold it a minute." The doorman hurried down the steps to assist a middle-aged woman out of a luxury automobile. Several cars later, he returned. "You were saying?"

"I have nothing to do with the police department. Joseph Msomi's father hired me to look into the matter. I'm sure you are aware the police claim he was carrying an attaché case with cocaine in it when the shooting took place."

"I know, I know. I can't believe a nice man like Mr. Msomi would be involved in drugs. But I don't know how I can help you."

"Who knows? Were you on duty the day Joseph Msomi was killed?"

"I've got no problem remembering that day. I talked it over with a buddy of mine several times. I told him I had seen Mr. Msomi that morning, the morning of the shooting."

"Can you—"

"As a matter of fact, I got him a cab that morning."

"Do you remember anything about the cab. What company it was or anything?"

"It was a Yellow Cab, but I don't remember anything special about it. There was something, though."

"What?" asked Fowler sharply, sensing a possible lead.

"He dropped a card as he was walking to the cab. I picked it up and handed it to him as I was opening the door of the cab. I happened to glance at the card. It was the same name and address he gave the cab driver."

"Can you remember the name of the place?"

"No problem. I couldn't forget that. A lot of my tenants shop at that store. It's one of the most prestigious jewelry stores in Washington. Aldrich is the name. You might have seen it during your way around town."

The name was familiar to Fowler. He thought of the nights when he and Mary Lou were out for a drive. They stopped at that store and browsed, admiring the jewels of every description. The prices were far beyond their reach. The salesman quickly left them to talk to other customers.

"Anything else? Did you see Joseph Msomi after that?"

"No. That was the last time I saw him. Too bad. Such a gentleman, too."

The doorman had no more to add, and Fowler had no more questions to ask. He thanked him and left.

Fowler sat in his car and mulled over the information he just obtained. He wondered what Joseph Msomi would be doing in a jewelry store, especially on the last day of his life. Having no answers, he decided to head for Aldrich's in the exclusive section of Georgetown.

Fowler found a parking space across the street from the store and sat for a few minutes observing the automobiles and pedestrians passing by. Finally, he climbed out and weaved his way through traffic to the other side of the street.

He entered the store and walked briskly to a salesman standing behind a counter.

"May I help you?" greeted the salesman.

"I'm looking for Mr. Aldrich." Fowler spoke in a blunt and businesslike manner.

"Over there." The salesman pointed to a well-dressed man bending over a counter, arranging jewels in a tray. He looked up as Fowler approached.

"Mr. Aldrich?" The man nodded, his piercing blue eyes fixed upon Fowler's face. "T.J. Fowler, private investigator." He produced his I.D., which Aldrich read and handed back to him.

"What can I do for you?" asked Aldrich in a guarded tone with no hint of a smile.

"I'm investigating the shooting of a Mr. Joseph Msomi. Would you by chance know the man?"

"Joseph Msomi," mused Aldrich. "The name does not strike me as one I am familiar with. Joseph Msomi." He stroked his chin as he looked off, as if trying to connect the name with some familiar memory. "Can you tell me more about him? What does he do?"

"He does—he was ambassador from Niberia. He was shot and killed several weeks ago. The police claim it happened during a drug bust. A police officer was also killed at the same time."

"Ah, I remember something about that shooting. It was all over the news for a while. Dreadful affair. An ambassador, too. Back to your question. The name does not ring a bell with me. Perhaps you might ask my salesmen—They may be able to help you." Aldrich turned abruptly and strode quickly to the back of the store.

Fowler waited patiently for the salesmen to finish with their clients before approaching them. None could provide any light on the Msomi affair. For some reason, he felt all was not what it seemed to be. Perhaps it was the way the salesmen answered his question, disclaiming all knowledge of Msomi without making an effort to check the records of purchases made by their clients.

Deciding to push a little further, Fowler approached a salesman who appeared nervous when questioned.

"It would help me if you would check your records of recent purchases and see if the name Msomi shows up. It's an unusual name, so it would not be difficult to find if it is there." He eyed the salesman closely. It was obvious the request made him very uncomfortable.

"Well, I don't know—" began the salesman.

"What is it, George?" asked Aldrich, re-entering the showroom.

George seemed relieved and more than glad to shift the conversation to the owner.

"Mr. Fowler wanted me to check our books to see if I can find the name of Msomi among our recent sales."

With a wave of his long tapered hand, Aldrich dismissed George.

"I will take care of Mr. Fowler. You may return to the counter. There are things to be rearranged before our next shipment." Turning to Fowler, he asked softly, "You wish me to check our books to see if I can find the name of Msomi among those who recently made a purchase?"

"Yes." Aldrich was some cool cat, Fowler thought. It was not going to be easy getting information from him.

"Just how far back do you want me to go?"

"The past month will do." Aldrich walked to the back of the store and shortly returned with a thick ledger.

"The past month you say. Let us go over to that desk in the corner. We can check the list together."

Fowler was fairly certain, giving the agreeable turn of events, the name Msomi was not going to show up in the record file Aldrich had in his hand.

Both men sat close enough to be able to follow the entries together. When their search failed, Fowler cupped the back of his head in his hands and spoke quietly.

"A place as fancy as this would have all this information on a computer." He looked for a change of expression. There was none. Aldrich quickly responded.

"You must realize, showing these books to you is not good business practice since you have such an honest face, I am doing something I would not ordinarily do. However, as a law-abiding citizen, I feel it necessary to help in any way I can to solve the unfortunate shooting of Mr. Msomi."

Fowler was sure he was hearing a lot of bullshit. He was becoming more fixed on the notion that the owner and his employees knew more about Msomi than was being said. A furtive smile floated across his face as he waited for Aldrich to continue.

"You are right. We do keep some records of this kind on a computer. Come with me. Perhaps we can find out if

184

we have a record of Msomi being a customer of our store."

Among the fixtures of the small office in the back of the store was a computer. "We have our records of purchases filed by year and by alphabet," said Aldrich.

Fowler watched as Aldrich punched a key to retrieve the information. Names, purchases, and other data about each transaction began to flash on the screen. There was no Msomi among the names. In order to make sure, he asked to run the list over again. No change. The records did not show a Joseph Msomi had purchased anything from the store within the past year.

Aldrich eyed Fowler closely.

"Is there anything else I can do for you?" he asked.

"No. I guess you've done all you can. It looks like the person who told me about Msomi visiting your store must have been mistaken. Thank you for your time and help." Without another word, he walked swiftly to the front door and left the store.

Fowler threaded his way between traffic to his car, deep in thought. Something did not fit. The doorman was positive about overhearing Msomi giving the address of the store as well as picking up Aldrich's card when it fell out of Msomi's pocket. Yet, Aldrich and his salesmen professed not to know anything about Msomi, and their records seemed to back them up.

On getting into his car, he sat slouched over, deciding his next move. Finally, he drove off and turned into the alley that led to the back of the jewelry store. As he passed it, he noticed a black Mercedes parked alongside several smaller cars. The alley made a right angle and came out on Wisconsin. He parked where he could see the jewelry store, as well as any cars coming out of the side streets. Sunk down in the seat, he waited. For what? Perhaps it was just a hunch, but he had time to spare.

Shortly after, he sat alertly upright. A black Mercedes was coming out of a side street. The driver was William Aldrich the Third. He turned north on Wisconsin and sped away. Fowler followed close enough to keep him in sight, but not so close he could be spotted.

Aldrich set a swift pace as he left the commercial section of Georgetown and was soon passing a section of homes that clearly belonged to the well-to-do. They were huge, gated homes that sat well back off the street, surrounded by a large expanse of grass, trees, and shrubbery. Aldrich turned into a driveway, and a massive iron gate swung shut as he drove by.

Fowler made a U-turn several hundred yards down the street and parked. He felt uncomfortable sitting in such a wealthy neighborhood. It would be difficult to come up with a reasonable excuse for being there if a security officer were to come by. He knew he had to do something or leave. Yet, intuition told him one of the pieces of the puzzle was here with Aldrich. Just as he was about to give up, Aldrich drove out of the driveway and hurried away.

Playing it by ear, Fowler reached into his glove compartment and searched until he found a badge that identified him as a reporter for a not-so-well-known newspaper. He walked to the gate, now closed, and rattled the bars to find out if the noise attracted any guard dogs, When none came, he looked around and easily climbed the fence. Moments later, he walked boldly to the door of the mansion. He rang the doorbell and listened to the chimes coming from within the house.

A young, burly man appeared at the door.

"Who are you and what do you want?" he demanded in a gruff voice.

Fowler responded quickly, sensing trouble ahead.

"Dabney Washington of the *Rockville Post Herald*. I'm doing a story on that Msomi shooting a while back—you know, the ambassador from that little African country. We understand there is a mention of a Mr. Aldrich among his notes—"

"How in the hell did you get in here?"

"That's all right, Bob. Let him in," directed a female voice

Fowler barely set foot inside the house before he was grabbed by a man standing behind the door. The next thing he felt was a hard blow to the side of his face and another to the pit of his stomach. He vaguely heard someone say, "Take him to the basement," before passing out.

Fowler came to and found himself sitting in a chair, hands tied behind his back. Facing him were the two men he saw when he first entered the house. Standing to one side was a youngish, willowy, blond woman who was eyeing him closely.

"Once again," snapped the man called Bob. "How did you get in here?"

Fowler groaned aloud while thinking of an answer "There was a man leaving your place as I drove up. I managed to get in the gate before it closed."

"We find you came here under false pretenses," said the woman, parting her lips in a smile that seemed to be plastered on her face. "You are also a private investigator, under another name."

"Okay, okay," responded Fowler. "How about untying these ropes. They're cutting into my hands. I'll be glad to tell you anything you want to know."

"Not so soon," Bob said. "You've got to come up with a lot of answers as to why you broke in here asking questions about someone named Msomi."

"That man you passed was my husband, William

Aldrich," murmured the woman. "We will decide what to do with you when he returns."

Fowler was sure his gut feeling was right. There was some kind of connection between Msomi and the Aldriches. Bob stood staring with menacing eyes at the subdued figure in the chair.

"Keep an eye on him. He's pretty slippery," said Mrs. Aldrich with a smile as she left and went upstairs. Finally, Fowler heard shuffling of feet overhead, followed by someone coming down the steps. It was William Aldrich and his wife.

"So, it's you again!" barked Aldrich angrily, as soon as he saw Fowler. His wife looked at him sharply, but said nothing. Aldrich growled, "He came to the store earlier today, asking all kinds of questions about someone named Msomi. I even showed him the books for the past year to prove to him no one by that name had ever purchased anything from the store. Now he's bothering us at our home. By the way, how did he get in here?"

"Claims he came in when you left, came through the gate before it closed," replied Bob, looking at Fowler in a threatening manner.

Aldrich pulled up a chair and sat facing Fowler, with his arms dangling over the back of the chair, a cold, angry look on his face.

"You can save us a lot of trouble, and yourself a great deal of pain by telling us exactly who you are and what you are up to." He waited a minute or two for an answer. When Fowler was hesitant, Aldrich nodded toward Bob.

"Perhaps you and Jerry can persuade our dear friend we mean business." Jerry stood on one side of Fowler and Bob on the other. Mrs. Aldrich, with a scowl, went upstairs.

Fowler had no stomach for further punishment. His

thoughts had been racing ever since he entered the house. The Aldriches did not seem to be the type to be involved in a setup leading to the shooting of an ambassador. But he had little choice. He had to level with them, at least to some extent.

"I was hired by Daniel Msomi, Joseph Msomi's father, to look into this matter. When I first took this case, I thought it was mostly a father refusing to accept the police and FBI findings that his son was caught red-handed with an attaché case full of dope. But it was too pat. That's what kept me going." Fowler noticed Aldrich was listening with a great deal of interest. In addition, Bob and Jerry backed off a little from his sides.

"Go on. Go on," demanded Aldrich.

"Well, as I was saying, the whole thing was too pat. None of my street contacts came up with anything on the incident. That was most unusual. There had to be a loose end somewhere. I finally found it a few days ago." He paused to let his ramblings set in.

"And . . . " whispered Aldrich.

"Joseph Msomi was set up."

"How?" asked Aldrich calmly.

"I'd rather keep it to myself for the time being. There are some powerful and dangerous people in back of this caper, and the fewer who know about it the better."

"You said you were hired by Daniel Msomi to look into this affair, right?" remarked Aldrich. Fowler nodded. Aldrich abruptly rose from his chair and hurried up the stairs.

Fowler sensed the mood in the room had changed. Bob and Jerry sat, casually keeping their eyes on him. Moments later, Aldrich slipped back into the room.

"Untie him," directed Aldrich. Bob quickly untied Fowler.

189

As soon as he was free, he stood, stretched his legs and wrung his hands to get the circulation going. Aldrich sat and motioned for Fowler to do the same. Mrs. Aldrich re-entered the room just as he sat down.

"And now, Mr. Fowler," said Aldrich quietly. "Tell us what you know about this unfortunate matter."

Fowler, in measured tones, related his efforts and results, leaving out the part about the attaché case. He felt much of what he had to say was already known to Aldrich.

Aldrich studied him.

"Do you think the police had more to do with this killing than we are led to believe?"

Fowler was quick to answer.

"I can't figure out how or why. There was also an officer killed. I know the officer in charge that night. He's a good cop. As of now, I've got nothing to tie the police with this case, other than that Msomi was shot by a policeman and a policeman was killed at the same time."

"You mentioned you thought Joseph was set up. What made you think that?"

"No definite facts. A gut feeling, I guess. I'm sure you must feel, as I do, that someone with Joseph Msomi's reputation would never be involved in drugs." Aldrich nodded in agreement. Fowler leaned back in his chair and asked, "What kind of man was Joseph Msomi? What was he doing that made him so dangerous to somebody that they wanted him killed?"

Aldrich thought for a while before answering. Then with a faraway look in his eyes, he began to talk about the Joseph Msomi he knew.

"I guess the time for maintaining a high degree of secrecy is past," he said, in a quavering voice. "Joseph Msomi was a most unusual man—quiet, thoughtful, trusting. I could say many more things about him and still not entirely describe the man." He leaned back in his chair and pointedly asked Fowler, "How much of this do you want to hear? It could be a long tale."

"Up to you, especially anything that might help me solve his shooting. I was told some political problems back in his native country might have had something to do with the case. What do you think of that idea?"

"Although it cannot be ruled out completely, I do not attach much importance to that suggestion. No, my friend, this killing, murder, if it pleases you, was done by someone a great deal more powerful than someone you will find in Niberia. I know Joseph was preparing to expose some very important people on the international scene."

"Where and when did you first meet Joseph Msomi?"

"We were students at one of those prestigious universities in England. His father wanted him to get the best education money could buy, like mine and most of the students' at the school. For most of us, getting an education was not as relevant to the world of work as it was to most college and university students. If we went to work at all, it would be in a family business or some big corporation, no matter how much education we had.

"Some of us were very idealistic about our role in our particular society, and the world beyond. Without a doubt, Joseph was the most idealistic of the lot. There was a kind of messiah air about him. He really believed he was put on this earth to save mankind. We used to joke about it until we found out he was in earnest. He finally convinced some of us to join him in a struggle against those who would destroy the hopes of a good life for men, women, and children, no matter where they lived. Well, to make a long story short, twenty of us made a pledge that

191

we would get together following graduation and do what we could to improve the lot of citizens of the world. Although there were twenty of us who made such a vow while in school, only twelve of us carried through on that pledge after graduation."

"Who were those who joined Joseph Msomi in his plan to save the world?"

"I can say the group was fairly representative of the peoples of the world—Asia, Africa, Europe, South America, India, and the United States. It was a good group of idealistic young men and women.

"It took us several years before we were able to put together an international organization of like-minded people willing to confront those who would destroy society for profit. Our little band has been behind many of the protest movements you may have seen on television. Our efforts have been mostly against the development and spread of weapons of mass destruction."

"I heard Joseph was scheduled to give a talk before the United Nations a day or so after he was killed. Do you know what that was all about?"

"I know a little, but not much. I had not seen Joseph for several months until he called and wanted to come out and have a chat with me. If I am not mistaken, it was the same day he was killed."

"Did he give any names or any details about his talk at the UN?"

"Not too much. He did not seem to be in a mood to go into details about his talk, so I did not push him."

"Do you think he wrote down what his speech would be about . . . and the names of those involved?" Fowler persisted.

"I doubt it. Joseph was rather strange that way. I remember him telling us many times that it was risky to

192

put certain of our activities down on paper. He felt there was always a chance something important would fall into the hands of those who were opposing our efforts.

"His approach was to review every detail of a situation until he was certain it was clear to him. Once that was accomplished, he felt there was no need to write anything down on paper. It was all in his head, to be brought forth at the proper time. If you were to find any of his papers, you can be sure he did not consider what he wrote to be of any significant importance to our cause. He did mention a worldwide organization that promoted assassinations, false rumors, media control, and anything else they could use to create disorder between states and within states, all in the interest of selling arms and making profits. I cannot say whether or not that was the subject of his talk.

"It was one of those busy days, and I could not spend a great deal of time with him. He left promising to get together with me a few days later." His wife came over and placed her hand on his shoulder. He placed his hand on hers, looked up and gave her a smile before turning to Fowler. "That was the last time I saw him," he said softly.

14

A .38-Caliber Pistol

Fowler left Georgetown and drove leisurely toward the Mall, stopping at a small stand near the Museum of Natural History for a drink and sandwich. In a few minutes, O'Donovan walked up to him.

"I didn't think I would see you any more today," said O'Donovan. "What are you up to?"

"Not much. One of those days. What about you?"

"I've been following a hunch about that guy Jules stopped this morning. Let's mosey over to my car. I'm waiting for a call from the station—running a fingerprint check. Pick up a new lead today?" asked O'Donovan as he opened the car door for Fowler.

"A possible. But, I'm not sure how important it is. I found out the ambassador was part of an international group of people promoting protest movements against the arms industry all over the world.

"I had an idea along that line from some shots I saw on a TV program. Those people are facing some serious power. Msomi was to speak at the UN the day after he was shot, dealing with some crooked activities by high-level figures in the arms field, even giving names and specific actions."

"That sounds hopeful. All you need to do is go through his papers and follow up on those he mentions."

"Not that easy. Joseph Msomi was a funny guy. He

had a thing against writing down anything important. He kept the real important matters locked in his mind. There was nothing in his attaché case about the arms industry. It looks like—" His remarks were interrupted as a call came over the radio.

"Pat," said the voice over the call box. "You hit the jackpot. The guy's fingerprints match the ones on the knife found at the scene of the rape."

"Hey, it looks like you've got your man," commented Fowler. "How did you catch him?"

"It was the little sonofabitch Jules stopped. I don't know what made me ask the lab to compare his prints with the prints on the knife found at the scene. Luck, I guess."

"You can say that again. There was some strange things happening during the Msomi shooting."

"Like what?"

"Well, you said Linsky tried to tell you something the captain said, just before he passed out. Then there was the matter of the attaché case. You had to force it open because the keys found on Msomi did not fit the lock. Yet the captain opened it easily the next day. I don't know," said Fowler shaking his head, "but for some reason, I'm getting bad vibes about the whole deal."

"If you're still hinting the captain might be involved, you're barking up the wrong tree. I've known Captain Levine a long time. He's a good cop. A little heavy on the military side, but good just the same. I'll stake my reputation on it."

"You might be right. And another thing. That rape took place on the same night as the Msomi shooting and only a block away."

"So."

"I talked with those old guys who were sitting in the

alley across the street from the scene that night. They remembered someone running from the direction of the apartment about the same time the shooting started."

"I talked to those same winos too. They told me they ducked down into their makeshift pile of cardboard as soon as they heard the shooting. I've got my doubts about what they saw or heard."

"You mentioned a hunch," said Fowler. "I've got one, too."

"What?"

"Jules said they found a gun in the glove compartment of the suspect's car. I'd like ballistics to check it and see if it might be the gun that killed Linsky."

"Sounds like you're reaching. But I'll go along with you if only to prove you're wrong about the captain. Leave your car here. We'll go to the station in my car."

Just as O'Donovan pulled into his parking space at the station, he saw the captain leaving the building. "Let's hope be doesn't see us. From what went on in his office this morning, I don't think he's too excited about you being involved in the Msomi shooting. You know how he is, straight from the book.

"He doesn't think PI's have any business in police affairs. As far as he is concerned, you guys should stick to peeking into bedroom windows to get evidence in divorce cases. You worked here long enough to know how he feels about that subject."

Fowler smiled and nodded. He had listened to Captain Levine rant and rave about private investigators interfering in police affairs many times.

"Watch out, here he comes," cautioned O'Donovan. "Keep low." Fowler slid low in his seat. Moments later, he saw O'Donovan wave his hand, followed by "It's okay, he's on his way."

Fowler sat upright in time to see the captain's car pull into traffic.

"There used to be a black guy by the name of Ted who worked in the lab. Is he still there?" he asked.

"Still there."

"He was a good buddy of mine when I was on the force. Let's go in and ask him to run a check on the gun and the bullet taken from Linsky's body."

They walked quickly to the rear door of the building, down the steps to the basement, and a large room with the usual paraphernalia of a police laboratory. There was a joint sigh of relief as they found only one person in the room, a black man in a long white coat.

"Hey, O'Donovan," greeted the man. "Who is that you've got with you?"

"Ted, you know Fowler. He claims you two were good buddies when he was on the force."

Ted walked deliberately over to Fowler, took out a handkerchief, and began to clean his glasses, all the while eyeing him solemnly.

"I'll be damned," he said. "if it's not my man, Fowler. I hardly knew you. You've got uglier since I last saw you."

"Time does some strange things, Ted. I can't figure it out, but you were so ugly back then that there was no way for you to go but up," retorted Fowler with a smile as he reached out to shake a hand. "How is the family—Lucy and the children?"

"All fine. The oldest boy is in college. I'm finding out how much it costs to get a higher education nowadays. How is the private investigator business?"

"So, so. I'm making a living out of it, so I guess I shouldn't complain. Glad to hear about your son in college—Ted Junior, isn't it?"

"Right. The other two are still in high school. I've got

my fingers crossed. So far, they haven't become involved in the drug scene. That's the torment of most parents these days."

They continued to engage in small talk before Ted turned to O'Donovan who was standing to one side during the interchange. "What can I do for you, Pat?"

"Let Fowler tell you what this is all about." O'Donovan pointed a thumb at his companion.

"You remember that shooting a few weeks ago where an ambassador was killed? Officer Linsky was also killed during that shootout."

"A drug bust, wasn't it?"

"That's what the record states. Anyway, would you still have the bullet they dug out of Linsky?"

Ted frowned and stroked his chin.

"It's around here somewhere. I'll have to look it up in my files. What do you want with it?"

"I want to check it with a gun found on a rape suspect. You know, to see if that gun was the one used to shoot Linsky."

"I wouldn't have the gun down here, probably in the guy's effects. O'Donovan would have to get it for you. In the meantime, I'll look up the bullet in my files."

Fowler looked sharply at O'Donovan who mumbled, "I'll see what I can do."

He quickly left the room. It seemed to Fowler that it took O'Donovan a long time to find the gun. Perhaps it was no longer at the station.

"Ah, here it is," said Ted, as he reached into a box and brought forth a tightly wrapped plastic bag. He took it to a table, unwrapped it, and displayed a used bullet. "This is the one."

Ted and Fowler were looking silently at the article that had taken a human life, when O'Donovan reentered the room, carrying a small box.

O'Donovan's eyes assured them of his success in finding the gun.

"They've already checked the registration. It belongs to the suspect." He walked over to the table, took the gun out of the box, and placed it on the table beside the spent bullet. He also brought forth a sack containing the bullets found in the gun during the arrest.

Fowler looked from the gun to Ted.

"This is it. Do your thing, and tell us if this is the gun used to kill Linsky."

Ted picked up the gun and sack of bullets and headed for the back of the office. Fowler and O'Donovan waited for the results. A short time later, they heard a muffled sound from the rear.

Ted re-entered the room with a small object in his hand—the bullet he had just fired. He took a marking pen and made an identifying mark on it. O'Donovan and Fowler came closer as he placed the recently fired bullet and the bullet from Linsky under the microscope. After several adjustment, he spoke to O'Donovan.

"Take a look."

O'Donovan looked a long time before motioning to Fowler. Fowler looked quickly and turned to Ted with a smile.

"One more piece of the puzzle. It looks like we've got the sonofabitch that did Linsky in." As an afterthought, he commented, "We'd like you to keep quiet about this, at least for the time being." Ted looked sharply at O'Donovan who nodded agreement.

"Come on," snapped O'Donovan, "Let's get the hell out of here." Without another word, he turned and headed for the door. Fowler, with a last "thanks" to Ted, quickly followed O'Donovan up the steps and out the back door of the station. Seated in the car, O'Donovan said to Fowler, "Let's get going. I think it's best we not trust our luck too far." When he put some distance away from the station, he slackened his pace and drove in the slow lane to the Mall and Fowler's car.

At the Mall, they sat in the car without speaking. Finally, O'Donovan spoke.

"I've been thinking it over. I've got to level with Captain Levine. He has to know that we have the back-up man who shot Linsky. I can't withhold that kind of information from him."

"Yeah, but are you sure we have the back-up man?"

"About as sure as we can get. We've got the gun. It's the one that fired the fatal shot, and it's registered to the suspect. How much more do we need?"

"You've also got the rape suspect. Now, what is he? The rapist or the back-up man?"

O'Donovan thought about Fowler's questions for a few moments.

"Maybe we should have a talk with the suspect. Captain Levine seldom stays past six at the station. Can you come down, say about seven, and we'll have a talk with our man?"

"I don't think so, unless I can get out of my appointment with the Msomis. Hold on a minute and let me go to my car and see what I can do." He used his car phone to call his office. Henrietta told him Sheia had tried to reach him several times and wanted him to call her as soon as he could. Sheia's soft voice answered his first ring. She explained that her father had left that morning on an unexpected trip to Niberia and would be gone for a few days. Their meeting would have to be postponed. Promising to get in touch, Fowler sauntered back to O'Donovan. "Looks like I'm free tonight."

"Seven, okay?"

"No problem."

Fowler drove to the Old Post Office, deciding to get something to eat and watch the action unfold around him. He placed a press card on the dashboard, ambled into the building, and in and out of the numerous eating booths, trying to make up his mind what he wanted to eat. Deciding to try something different, he stopped at an Indonesian booth and ordered a meal and beer. Whatever he ordered was spicy hot, his tongue barely cooled by a cold beer. A black, slender young woman caught his eyes as she walked gracefully past his table. She reminded him of Sheia.

Fowler let his mind freely roam over images of Sheia—her walk, her smooth satiny skin, her soft voice with accent of her native country. He felt a warm glow come over him as he recalled the touch of her hand on his arm during his last visit. Perhaps there might be more than an employer-employee relationship there.

The hour passed without his seeing a familiar face. It was time to get started for the 77th Precinct and O'Donovan. He pushed open the door leading to the street and came face to face with Jules.

"Hey, m'man," greeted Jules. "What's the rush? Come on back and have a drink with me. I've got some interesting news you might like to hear."

"Sorry, not this time," responded Fowler. "I'm on my way to a pretty important meeting. Some other time." He turned to go, indicating the brief encounter was over.

"At least you could hold on a minute while I lay some late-breaking news on you," persisted Jules, following Fowler out the door. "The news media will have it tonight. We caught the rapist."

"No kidding! Great. One more lunatic off the streets.

How did you catch him?"

"Luck. You remember the guy we picked up this morning on that traffic violation?"

"Yeah."

"When we got back to the station, we ran a check and found his prints matched the ones on the knife found at the rape scene. Anything new on your Msomi shooting?"

"Nothing new like your case. Catch you another time. Keep me posted on your rapist."

He listened to the engine's silken purr for a few moments before merging with traffic. It was only a short distance to the 77th Precinct, and he was early. Shortly after seven o'clock, O'Donovan came out the front door and looked up and down the street. Fowler got out of his car and hurried over to the building.

"Things are all set up," said O'Donovan as he pushed the door open and entered, Fowler close behind him. "I had a couple of officers bring the suspect to the interrogation room. We might as well go on up and get it over with."

The interrogation room was a small room on the second floor with a minimum of furnishing—several hard-backed chairs and a long table with a few ashtrays on it. A window ran the length of one of the walls.

A smallish, defiant-looking, sandy-haired man who appeared to be in his early thirties sat at the table smoking. Standing nearby, arms folded, were two uniformed officers. "Thanks, guys," muttered O'Donovan, dismissing the officers. "We'll take it from here. I'll see that the prisoner gets back to lockup."

O'Donovan slid a chair over to the table and sat facing the suspect. Fowler stood, leaned on the back of a chair and eyed the man intently. The room remained as quiet as the cigarette smoke that curled its way toward the ceiling. The prisoner's eyes shifted from one or the other of the two men as he extinguished one cigarette and lit another. Fowler sat and watched O'Donovan in action. He had seen him in similar situations before. In his quiet but forceful manner, he would state his case clearly and move the suspect in the direction he wanted him to go. His method was to keep at it until he had obtained all the information he could get from a suspect.

O'Donovan sat, eyes glued on the face of the suspect without saying a word. The man took a few puffs on the cigarette then mashed it out in an ashtray, only to light another and repeat the process. Fowler sat impatiently wanting O'Donovan to get on with it.

Finally, O'Donovan began softly.

"Mr. Jankowski, you are in some serious trouble. You—"

"I don't know what you're talking about," interrupted Jankowski. "I don't know nothing about no rape. You've got the wrong man."

"I'm not talking about any rape," continued O'Donovan, his voice still at the same low level. "You shot and killed a policeman. That's another matter entirely."

"A policeman? I never shot no policeman. You've got nothing on me."

"Our investigation has you as the back-up man for a Mr. Msomi, accused of dealing in drugs. During a drug bust a few weeks ago, you shot and killed Officer Linsky while he was in the act of carrying out an assignment."

"Missomi, Missomi, I don't know no Missomi," whined Jankowski as he mashed another cigarette in an ashtray.

"Let me tell you what we know about you," snapped the officer. "You knew you had plenty of time to commit that rape since you knew Msomi would spend about an hour in the restaurant. The rape didn't go smoothly so you ended up killing the girl."

The suspect attempted to interrupt, but O'Donovan raised his hand. "Let me finish, then we will give you all the time you need." Once again he was back to his soft-speaking, emotionless approach to the suspect. "The gun we found in your car, registered to you, is the same gun that killed Linsky. We've had the lab check it out. There is no doubt about it." O'Donovan paused to let his words sink in. Fowler, who had remained quiet, now saw a chance to become involved in the proceedings.

"Jankowski, my boy," drawled Fowler with a derisive smile. "Let's cut out the bullshitting. We've got two witnesses who place you at the scene of the shooting. You ran into one of them and knocked him down. Now, we know you were not in this thing by yourself. How about telling us who the big man is that is behind this caper? How much were you paid to protect Msomi?"

"You guys are wasting your time. I don't know nobody by the name of Missomi, and I never shot no cop. If I'm not mistaken I was out of town when those things happened."

"What things?" broke in O'Donovan with a wry smile.

"You know, that rape and shooting you guys are talking about. I was surprised when that gun showed up in my glove compartment. I was planning to come to the police department and report it stolen, but I haven't had a chance to get around to it. You can see, somebody's trying to set me up."

Neither O'Donovan nor Fowler were swayed by the suspect's explanations for his whereabout at the time of the shooting, or the gun found in his car. O'Donovan waited for Jankowski to light another cigarette and take a few puffs before continuing.

"We have a witness who can identify you when you came back to get the knife you dropped after you killed the model, the knife with the victim's blood on it and your fingerprints on the handle. What do you say to that?"

"I got nothing to say," Jankowski replied in a subdued voice. "I'm not saying anything else without my lawyer."

More attempts to get the suspect to talk failed. He sat mute while aspects of the case were pointed out to him.

Fowler left O'Donovan putting handcuffs on the suspect. He walked slowly to the stairs leading to the lower floors. Once outside, he leaned against the building and waited. Shortly afterwards, O'Donovan came through the doors and started down the steps. Fowler hurried after him.

"Let's sit in my car and kick around a few things," said O'Donovan without slackening his pace. Seated in the car, he remarked, "It doesn't look like we got much from our suspect."

"Looks like it. I guess it was too much to expect the guy to confess and make things easy for us, even with all that evidence laid out before him."

"Yeah, I know. Right now all we've got is some circumstantial evidence and nothing to say for sure the captain had a hand in what went on that night."

"I know, but my gut feeling still tells me he's into it in some way."

"Gut feeling or no gut feeling, I've got to have more to it than that, especially to accuse an officer of being an accomplice to a shooting where a fellow police officer was also a victim. Nope. Nope, we still have more work to do before we can wrap up this case."

"What's our next move?"

"I don't know. I'm having problems keeping what we've discovered from the captain. Without having anything more solid, I have to level with him."

Fowler thought and then spoke.

"It doesn't matter what you tell him about the suspect we just saw. He'll find out about him anyway. What do you think of this idea? Tell him one of your contacts told you about me going to Mexico to try to bring back the cloakroom attendant for questioning. That will give me more time to follow through on my hunches."

O'Donovan mulled over the request a few moments.

"Okay. But I think you're barking up the wrong tree." The two men parted to go their separate ways. It had been a long day.

15

Is He or Is He Not?

O'Donovan's preoccupation with the Msomi and rapist cases was an unseen barrier to a comfortable evening with his family. When he finally went to bed, he lay awake for hours absorbed in thought as he listened to water pouring over a broken gutter pipe and cascading to the walk below.

The rain continued its torrent the next morning, as he sat reading the morning paper and gulping cup after cup of hot coffee. He barely noticed the good-bye kisses of his children when they left to go to school.

Questions kept flooding O'Donovan's mind as he drove along on his way to the 77th Precinct. He pulled into the parking lot just ahead of Captain Levine. The two walked briskly to the door of the building.

"I'd like to see you for a few minutes," said O'Donovan to the captain as they entered the building. "I have some information on the Msomi and the rapist cases I think I should go over with you."

"Fine. Give me a half hour to go over my reports, and I'll be with you."

At his desk, O'Donovan shuffled a few papers, occasionally glancing at the captain's closed door. At last the door opened and Captain Levine came out and beckoned to him. He hurried over to the office and stood as the captain closed the door behind him.

Captain Levine sat down at his desk and motioned for O'Donovan to sit facing him. He selected a pipe from a rack, filled it with tobacco and lit it. After several puffs, he leaned back in his chair.

"Go ahead. What do you want to tell me about those two cases?" he asked.

Face to face with the captain, O'Donovan was not sure where to start. Clearing his throat, he began softly.

"It was one of those lucky things. Jules made a routine traffic arrest yesterday, and when we followed it up with a fingerprint check, the prints matched those on the murder knife found at the scene of the rapist killing. And, there was something else."

"What?" The captain brought his chair to an upright position.

"When Jules checked out the suspect's car, he found a .38-caliber pistol in the glove compartment."

"So?"

"I happened to run into Fowler and we got to talking about the Msomi case. He had a hunch the gun was the one used by the so-called back-up man when Linsky was shot. He felt Linsky's shooting was one of those unfortunate things, where someone was in the wrong place at the wrong time."

"I'm not sure I know what you mean."

"Fowler thought it was a coincidence that put the rapist in the alley at the time the drug bust was taking place. His idea was that the rapist thought someone was shooting at him and fired back, killing Linsky. I kind of laughed it off, but Fowler kept after me to check the gun against the bullet we took out of Linsky."

"And did you?"

"Yes. I had Lab run a check on the pistol. Fowler was right. It was the gun used in the shooting."

"What else did you learn from Fowler?" Captain Levine fixed his eyes upon O'Donovan's face.

"He said something. I can't quite put my finger on it, but I think he's come up with an attaché case identical to the one Msomi was carrying when we made the drug bust."

Captain Levine slowly tapped the used ashes into an ashtray, refilled his pipe, lit the tobacco, then leaned back and took a few puffs.

"Got any idea where he might have found such a case or where he might have it now?"

"He was pretty close-mouthed about it. I pushed him to tell me more. Nothing doing. Said he was following up another lead and would fill me in on everything as soon as he gets back."

"Gets back, from where?"

"He's got a lead on the cloakroom attendant who worked at Marcel's and plans to go down to Mexico the first of the week and bring the guy back. I don't have any idea what he expects to get out of him."

At that moment, a phone rang in a drawer in the captain's desk.

"I'll talk to you later," he said, dismissing O'Donovan with a wave of his hand. "Close the door behind you?"

On passing the captain's closed door, he wondered whether the call was from the commissioner of police, pushing for closure on the two cases. When O'Donovan got back to his desk, he found a message from Fowler, asking him to call him on his car phone. After a brief conversation, they arranged a meeting around noon at a small sandwich stand at the Mall. Jules walked by just as O'Donovan hung up the phone.

"Hey, old buddy," began Jules in his usual breezy manner. "Looks like we hit the jackpot on that rapist

209

case. Another one of those difficult cases the police department solved by thorough painstaking efforts," he said with a smile and a wink. "With that bloody knife and his fingerprints, it looks like we've just about wrapped this case up. Don't you think?"

"Not so sure," replied O'Donovan, momentarily undecided as to how much to tell him about the gun. Still, he had told the captain and Jules was assigned to the case. "When you arrested that suspect, you found a gun in the glove compartment—right?"

"Right."

"I ran a check in the lab and guess what."

"You got me. He shot the president."

"Nope. That gun was used to kill Linsky."

"Whoee!" exclaimed Jules. "You mean we've got the rapist, who also turned out to be the back-up man, too?"

"Not so fast. All I've said is we have the gun used in the shooting. The guy denies knowing anybody named Msomi. Claims he was out of town during the time."

"Yeah, but I ran a check on the gun. It was registered to him. Let's see him get his ass out of that."

"He admits the gun is his but maintains it was stolen. Says he has no idea how it got back into his car."

"Hah! I don't think he'll get too far with that defense."

"We'll see."

Jules mumbled a "see you later" and was on his way.

It was too early for O'Donovan's meeting with Fowler, but he needed to be anywhere but in the station.

He drove methodically across the rain-streaked streets to Union Station. The large entrance hall was bustling with employees at work and the general public rushing to and fro when he entered the building.

"Hey, Sarge, what brings you here this time of the

morning?" O'Donovan turned to face a black, uniformed member of the station's security police.

"Morning, Randy." O'Donovan reached out to shake the outstretched hand. "It's been a long time since I've been here. Where's the nearest rest room?"

"Straight ahead and left at the next corridor."

"I'm surprised to see so many people, especially with this miserable weather."

"Trouble on the line from New York. A freight jumped the track. A lot of these folks are waiting for arrivals. Then there's the usual crowd leaving town for the weekend, too."

"I didn't realize what a soft job you guys had. Maybe I should put in my application for the next opening."

"You got to be kidding." Randy smiled. "The little dudes don't usually gather until later in the day and into the night. Believe me, we've got our hands full. I think one night messing with these clowns would be enough for you."

A message came over Randy's walkie-talkie. "Gotta go," he said, heading for another section of the station. Me, too, thought O'Donovan hurrying to the rest room.

He blended with the crowd and strolled down the stairs to the lower floor with the many fast food shops He left the station and went across the street to the post office to get stamps for his wife. On leaving there, he hurried to his car and sat listening to the patter of the rain on the roof. Although he could not accept the captain as a major player in the case, he was well aware that Fowler had placed himself in a precarious position if his hunch was correct.

Shortly after he got to the Mall and parked he saw Fowler running under the trees toward a fast-food stand. O'Donovan jumped out of his car and hurried after him.

They joined under an overhang.

"The weatherman would have to be right today," said Fowler pulling his raincoat collar around his neck. "I'm for going somewhere else out of this cold dampness. What about you?"

"Suits me fine. Where to?"

"What about the Natural History museum? It's close, and we could get something hot to drink."

In the foyer, a scattering of visitors milled around a massive bull elephant that stood on a pedestal facing the front door. Fowler and O'Donovan removed their raincoats, tossed them an the back of a bench, and sat down.

"Well, how did it go?" said Fowler, his eyes following a well-shaped pair of legs that flounced across the floor.

O'Donovan thought a moment before answering.

"Hard to tell. If Captain Levine had anything to do with the Msomi incident, he sure didn't show any sign of it."

"Did you tell him about the identical case?"

"Yep."

"What about my trip to Mexico to get the cloakroom attendant? How did he act when you told him about that?"

"Nothing special. He just sat and smoked his pipe, the way he usually does whenever we make a report."

"Didn't he act surprised or angry?"

"Nope. The time he had that shouting spell with you was one of the few times I've ever heard him raise his voice with anyone. The captain is one cool customer. He just sits back and smokes that pipe of his. Leaves us trying to figure out what's going on in that brain of his hidden behind the smoke."

"You mean to say he didn't ask any questions?"

"Very few. He listened to what I had to say, and

that's about the extent of it."

Fowler's eyes wandered over the crowd circling the elephant in the center of the room.

"Funny, I thought he would have more interest in what I was doing. Nothing else?"

"No. A call came in for him on the phone he keeps in his desk. He had me leave at that point."

"Wonder who was on the phone. Got any idea?"

"None. It could have been the commissioner. But that's only a guess."

Other than an occasional comment, they sat quietly for ten or fifteen minutes. Finally O'Donovan decided it was time for him to leave. The few stragglers from the outside brought evidence the rain had not ceased.

Fowler trudged over to a telephone and called his office. He listened patiently to Henrietta castigating him for spending so much time on the Msomi case while letting some easy money go to another investigator. Other than her criticism, there was nothing that needed his immediate attention.

The exuberant voices of schoolchildren bounced off the walls, drowning the cries of their teachers trying to maintain a semblance of silence and order. He caught the eye of one of the teachers and flashed a smile as if to let her know he understood her plight.

Fowler found the exhibits full of pleasure and wonderment. He stopped beside an attractive teacher who was explaining an exhibit to her charges.

"Do you think they understand what you're talking about?" he asked with a smile.

"Some, but not likely all. We hope we can stir interest in places like this so that they will get their parents to bring them back. Perhaps we can kindle a spark that may be helpful to them."

"Here's my card. If you are in need of a private investigator to find a lost child, or simply to go out for a night on the town, call me." He noticed she looked at the card, opened her purse, and put the card in it. Fowler kept his eyes on her shapely back until she and her students disappeared around a corner. You never know what might turn up, he mused. He had made a number of interesting contacts using that same technique.

On leaving the museum, he drove slowly in the direction of Lafayette Square. As he drew near the square, he noticed a familiar figure. That scrawny frame hurrying along underneath a tattered umbrella belonged to Alabama Slim. Pulling alongside him, Fowler lowered the window in the passenger side and called loudly.

"Slim, Slim, over here." Slim looked around, recognized him, and came over to the car.

"Jimbo, what the fuck are you doing out on a day like this?" greeted Slim, leaning into the car. "I thought you affluent guys holed up with some broad, enjoying the good life while we disadvantaged have to hustle no matter what the day is like." With that, Slim, apparently overcome by the injustice of it, pulled out a dirty handkerchief to wipe some nonexistent tears from his eyes.

"I could ask the same thing of you, you old motherfucker. How come you're not holed up in your palatial mansion at the police station instead of out here trying to con someone? Get in out of the rain. If you've got anything worth while, I might take you where you want to go."

Slim quickly accepted Fowler's offer. He folded an umbrella that was letting in more rain than it kept out.

"Anything stirring, outside the rain?" asked Fowler.

"I'm not sure you want to know about it." Slim tried to stretch his legs. "Why in hell don't you buy a real man's car, one you can stretch your legs out, like a Cadillac or Buick?"

"Some other time. Now, about the piece of information you don't think I want to hear."

"This is an exclusive, worth more than the usual. I'm the only one on the street who has it."

"Has what?" asked Fowler impatiently.

"There's a contract out for a black PI."

Fowler weighed the words for a moment before replying.

"I'm not the only black PI in the city. Besides, where did you get your information?"

"I didn't say it was you. All I know is one of my contacts in Chicago got in touch with me a little while ago and laid it on me."

"How in hell did someone in Chicago get in touch with you in Washington?"

"There is such a thing as a telephone. My man called me at my office."

Fowler snickered derisively. He was aware that Slim's so-called office was a telephone booth at the corner of 9th and T.

"Okay, okay. What else was said about the contract? Don't worry, I'll take care of you, you know that."

"Some big-wigs hired one of the best hit men in Chicago to do this job. Whoever it is must have stepped on some pretty big toes. Probably not you, since you specialize in peeping into bedroom windows to get evidence in divorce cases."

Slim's information was disquieting to Fowler. It was one thing to mull over possible danger in the abstract. It was something else if a contract was attached to it.

"Did your man know anything more about it? Who the hit man was?"

215

"Nope. I've told you all he told me. If I was you, I would keep my eyes open, especially around strangers."

Little more could be learned sitting in the rain with Slim. Fowler pulled out a bill and handed it to him. Slim fingered the bill and gave Fowler a reproachful look.

"Where was it you wanted to go?" Fowler asked, before he had a chance to say anything.

"9th and T is okay with me."

When they got to 9th and T, Slim said, "This is fine. I'll get out here." He opened the door and ran to a coffee shop on the corner.

Fowler pointed his car in the direction of his office. A few minutes later he parked beside Henrietta's little car.

Henrietta looked up from her desk as he entered the office.

"Anything I need to take care of?" said Fowler on the way to his small cubicle.

"Some bills need to be paid. All of our retainers and the Msomis have come through. That's about all."

All of a sudden, he felt tired, lonely.

"Boss, get me Miss Msomi on the phone." While she was dialing he entered his room, excitement building up inside him for some reason. He remembered the soft touch of Sheia's hand on his arm that last night he was at her apartment.

Henrietta interrupted his thoughts.

"Miss Msomi on the line."

Several minutes of small talk finally led into his asking her out for dinner and a show. She agreed to both. He was to pick her up at seven o'clock.

"Boss," called out Fowler as soon as he hung up the phone. "See if you can get me a reservation for dinner and the show for two at that new jazz club upon Georgia."

Having settled his evening, Fowler was soon out of

the office with a cheery, "I'm off, have a good weekend. See you Monday."

He stopped at a florist and bought some flowers for Sheia, leaving it up to the shopkeeper to select the proper ones.

The rest of the afternoon seemed endless to Fowler. Eventually, the hands on the clock on the wall rolled around to the time he should be on his way. It was a relief to be on his way and out of his apartment.

Sitting in his car in front of her building, he saw a familiar figure, a very black man holding an umbrella high over his head as he hurried into the building. That very black man was none other than Nkombo. "I'll be damned." The words escaped Fowler's lips. The lively imagery of the evening had not included Tom Nkombo. He was sure that black African was headed for the same apartment he would be headed for in a few minutes. He reflected upon the truism of Murphy's Law—if anything could go wrong, it would.

When Fowler was admitted to the Msomi apartment, he found his apprehension about Nkombo was accurate. Sheia took his hat and coat and ushered him into the living room where Nkombo was seated.

"Ah, Mr. Fowler. And how are you this dreadful evening?" began Nkombo in his precise intonation. "This is indeed a coincidence. I have just these few minutes arrived. I am sure you are here to advise Sheia about any new developments in the case. I shall be pleased to learn of them myself."

"I hate to disappoint you. As a matter of fact, I am here to take Sheia out to dinner and a show. So you see, I haven't anything to advise her—and you—about."

"Where are you going for dinner?" asked Nkombo.

"The Kit Kat Club," said Fowler sharply. "We'll have

to leave shortly if we are to be there in time."

"I am sure Mr. Fowler would not mind it if you were to join us," remarked Sheia.

Nothing could have been more distant from the truth. Fowler spoke up before Nkombo could respond.

"No problem, but we have reservation just for two."

"What did you say was the name of the club?"

"Kit Kat."

"I do not think that will be a problem. The head-waiter is a countryman of mine. I will see to it that he arranges a plate for me at your table. I do hope this meets with your approval." He first looked at Sheia, who smiled, and then at Fowler who nodded weakly.

Sheia left to make a change of dress. She returned in a colorful outfit that accentuated her charms. Shortly, the door of the apartment closed behind the three of them.

Fowler drove quickly to the club. When he pulled up in front and gave his keys to the valet parking attendant, he saw Nkombo pull up in back of him and stop. When they were seated at their table, he noticed the head-waiter, followed by Nkombo, making their way toward them.

"Sir," began the headwaiter in an apologetic tone. "Mr. Nkombo tells me he is a good friend of yours and would like to join you. Is that all right with you?"

"Of course it is," said Sheia before Fowler had a chance to answer. The headwaiter motioned to a waiter who came over and fixed another setting for Nkombo.

"I have found the wine to be in good taste, contrary to some of the other restaurants in this area," remarked Nkombo. Looking at Sheia, he added, "Would you like to try one of my favorites?"

"Of course." Turning to Fowler, she asked, "Would that be all right with you?"

"Fine," answered Fowler, who had begun to feel left out of his own party.

The evening was a total waste of time as far as Fowler was concerned. Nkombo monopolized the conversation and was not at all reluctant about giving his advice on what they should eat and drink, as well as favor them with his opinion of the musical part of the evening.

Finally, seething inside and finding it difficult to maintain a civil attitude toward Nkombo, Fowler excused himself with a "I have to visit the room para hombres." He threaded his way among employees and patrons to the men's rest room, feeling it necessary to moderate his emotions.

After allowing himself a reasonable time to get under control, he left the rest room and headed back to his table. As he drew near, he noticed neither Sheia nor Nkombo were there. *What the hell*, he thought, *now what*. Then he noticed Sheia's purse was on the table.

"She went to the ladies' room," came the voice of a woman sitting at the next table. "She said to tell you she would be back in a few minutes."

"Thanks," said Fowler. He wondered what had become of Nkombo. He did not have long to wonder. He noticed Nkombo making his way to the table.

"Strange," murmured Nkombo as he sat down.

"What?"

"While you were away, there was a call over the loud speaker saying there was a telephone call for you. Since you were not available, I decided to answer it."

Just like him, mused Fowler, *meddling in somebody else's business.*

"Who was it? What was it about?"

'That is the point. When I answered the telephone, I said hello several times. No one said anything."

"Maybe there was a bad connection?"

"No. I do not think so. Whoever it was on the other end listened to me say hello several times and then hung up."

Fowler looked up to see Sheia approaching. He got up to assist her in being seated. A few fleeting thoughts about the telephone call floated across his mind before he forgot it and melted into the mood of the evening. He did not allow Nkombo to drag him into any more contentious discussions.

At the end of the jazz program, Fowler stood behind Sheia's chair, indicating it was time to go. Sheia joined him, leaving Nkombo sitting at the table.

"The table is all yours," said Fowler. "We'll see you later."

They joined the lines of patrons filing out of the club to get their cars. Shortly, he pulled out into traffic, his windshield wipers playing a rainy night tune for those who wished to listen.

"I really did enjoy the evening," said Sheia as she placed her hand lightly upon his arm. "I am sorry you found it difficult being with Mr. Nkombo, but he is my countryman and—"

"I understand," interrupted Fowler. "I did not make the situation any easier with my childish behavior. Maybe I was a little jealous of the attention you were giving him."

"There is nothing there. He is a business acquaintance of my father, and that is all," said Sheia giving his arm a pinch. A smile drifted across her face.

It did not take a whiff of exotic perfume to make Fowler's whole body become aware of her nearness. Abruptly, he drove over to the curb and stopped. He pulled her over to him and kissed her, first gently, then as he felt her respond, his ardor rose to a fever pitch along with the intensity of his kisses. Both groped fiercely for the other until drained of the passion of the moment. Sheia leaned back in her seat and stretched, not unlike a contented cat. Fowler searched her face closely and liked what he saw. Without a word he re-entered the traffic and drove with deliberate haste.

"Where are you taking me Mr.—? I do not know just what to call you."

"I know. Most people simply call me Fowler. Try it."

"It would be best that we remain on a more formal level when we are with my father."

"I understand that, too. My apartment is just around the corner." Moments after parking in the rear of his building, he was guiding her up the stairs to his apartment.

The door had barely closed before he began to peel her garments off her, to fling them wherever they may fall. He swept her into his arms and felt her melt against him until it seemed they were one. She curled her arms around his neck as he picked her up and headed for the bedroom. Kneeling on the bed, he let her roll off his arms onto the bed. Abandon was then tossed to the wind. Fowler ran his hands over her satin-smooth body, stretched out and waiting for him, black and lovely as an African night.

Sheia's passionate moanings, and wild gyrations found them rolling off the bed locked in exhilarating awareness, to reach the pinnacle of satisfaction on the floor. Back on the bed, Fowler held her in his arms as he strove to convince himself he could tame this wild beast that lay quietly beside him. When he rolled over, exhausted after a long period of lovemaking, he listened to her soft cooing of delight as she snuggled close to him.

They had given each other a night of intense pleasure that would not be forgotten. The sleep that followed could only have come from complete satisfaction.

16

Mistaken Identity

Fowler was in the depths of a dream, where he was barely holding his own in a battle with a pack of wild cats, when the telephone ended the struggle. He yawned, rubbed his eyes, and pulled the phone toward the bed.

"O'Donovan. I tried to reach you at your office. Forgot you guys close on Saturdays."

"What has you calling me at nine o'clock on a Saturday morning? I thought you were off this weekend."

"Jules came down with the flu, so I had to fill in for him. A report just came into the precinct that I think would interest you. You know that Douglas Hotel up on Vermont?"

"Yeah."

"Meet me there as soon as you can. I'll leave word downstairs to let you in."

"Hold on. Hold on. What's this all about?" barked Fowler, but O'Donovan had hung up the phone. O'Donovan's tone made him a little uneasy. Thoughts bounced back and forth as he tried to guess what might have happened. It had to be important.

His speculations were interrupted by a soft purring from Sheia lying beside him. She reminded him of a sleek feline, who, well fed and rested, stretched and curled its body in every direction. He fondled an uncovered breast before planting his lips upon hers. She wrapped her arms around his neck and pulled him down on top of her yielding body. Disengaging her arms from around his neck, he leaned back and looked at her.

"As much as I would like to spend the entire day here with you," he sighed, "I just got a call from O'Donovan. Something very important has come up. He wants me to meet him, immediately."

"Is it about my brother?"

"I don't know. He didn't give me any details. We'll see."

Fowler showered and dressed as rapidly as he could. He gave Sheia a number to call for a taxicab and, with a quick peck on the cheek, promised to get in touch with her later in the day.

The sun shone brightly out of a clear blue sky. He quickly drove the few blocks to the Douglas Hotel and parked across the street. Three or four officers were maintaining crowd control as a station wagon from the coroner's office pulled up. Fowler made a wry face. Whoever was involved no longer had a need for an ambulance. O'Donovan appeared at the front door of the hotel and scanned the street. Just as Fowler opened the car door, the car phone rang. It was the Boss.

"I've been trying to get a hold of you," said Henrietta. "I called your apartment. No answer, so I guessed you must be out galavanting around somewhere in your car."

"Give it to me quickly, Boss. I'm in a hurry and don't have time for details. What's up?" Fowler kept his eyes fixed on O'Donovan, who had stepped out of the hotel to say something to an officer holding the crowd back from the entrance.

"Did a Mrs. Jefferson from the office of the President of Howard University get in touch with you? She called late yesterday afternoon just as I was about to leave. She said there was a very sensitive matter facing the school and needed someone to handle it over the weekend. Your name had been given as a person who could be trusted with a matter of great importance and that had to be handled tactfully."

"The answer to your question is no."

"I told her that if she couldn't get a hold of you at home she could reach you at the Kit Kat Club."

"No matter. No one got in touch with me," snapped Fowler.

"I've got to go now, Boss. I'll get back to you later." He hung up the phone and walked swiftly toward the hotel, showing a press pass to an officer as he passed by. Fowler came abreast of O'Donovan, who nodded in recognition and kept walking. They hurried through a lobby slowly filling with media types and crime-hardened detectives, repeating a far-too-familiar scenario.

"I think you will find something upstairs of interest to you," said O'Donovan, as the two climbed the stairs leading to the second floor. Plainclothes detectives were milling around the floor near a room with an open door.

A team of police workers were methodically going about their tasks, when Fowler entered the room. Several officers were looking down at a figure lying on the bed, a figure almost hidden from Fowler's view. A photographer was busy taking pictures of the room, while a couple of officers checked for fingerprints.

O'Donovan stopped to talk to an officer. Fowler pushed his way through to the bed. As inured as he was to death and violent death, he was momentarily stunned when he saw the rigid figure lying on the bed. It was Nkombo, even blacker than in life, and naked as the day he was born.

"I thought you would find something of interest

here," said O'Donovan, stepping beside him.

"What have you got?" Fowler struggled to gain control of himself.

"Not much. As you can see, there's no sign of a struggle, and from the way he threw his clothes on the chair and the floor, he must have been looking forward to a good time. There's a bottle of wine and a couple of glasses on that table. One of the glasses has traces of wine. The other is as clean as a whistle. My bet is that the only fingerprints they'll find will be those of your boy, or some previous occupant of this room. Whoever did this is a pro."

"A woman hitman, why?"

"No reason a woman couldn't do this job. As for the why, you may be able to help us find the motive, since you've been working with him on the Msomi case."

Fowler looked down at Nkombo's open, but sightless eyes.

"Looks like a .38," he muttered, pointing at the small hole that entered one side of Nkombo's head and exited the other side, leaving a trail of dried blood on the pillow.

"Looks like it. Must have used a silencer, too. No one reports hearing anything like a shot."

"I was with Nkombo last night at the Kit Kat Club until the show ended. It must have been close to midnight. He was still there when I left. What about the night clerk who was on duty last night?"

"I sent a man to pick him up. He should be back by now. We might as well get out of the way and let these guys do their job." O'Donovan sauntered out of the room, Fowler close on his heels.

The lobby was buzzing with people when O'Donovan and Fowler re-entered. Two men from the coroner's department were lounging against a wall, their body bags and other paraphernalia in front of them, awaiting orders to take the body to the morgue. Fowler tried to sort out what happened as he watched O'Donovan make a round of the room, talking to one person after another. Who would want to kill Nkombo? Did it have anything to do with the Msomi situation? O'Donovan beckoned to him. Fowler joined him and a youngish, sleepy-looking man badly in need of a shave. He guessed this was the night clerk, which it turned out to be.

"Bob Williams, night clerk," said O'Donovan in a quiet voice.

"Hi," mumbled Fowler, eyeing the man closely.

"Is there a room where we can talk in private?" asked O'Donovan to a wary Bob Williams. Fowler surmised that O'Donovan wanted to get Williams away from some curious glances coming their way.

"Down the hall." He led them to a small room a few doors away from the front desk. As soon as they entered and closed the door, he turned to O'Donovan and asked, guardedly, "What's this all about?"

O'Donovan made no attempt to answer the question. "You on duty last night?"

"Yes. Why? What's all the fuss about? Did somebody commit suicide or something?"

"Not exactly," said O'Donovan. "There was a murder in room 210 last night, and we're trying to get a fix on it."

"A murder? In room 210?"

"Right, Do you remember anything about that room?"

"I checked them in. It was pretty slow last night. He was one of those funny-talking dudes, a West Indian, or an African. Did he kill the chick?"

"No. He was the one who got killed. We want you to tell us all you can remember about the woman who was with him. Describe her to us."

"Can't tell you much. She kept her back to me most of the time while he was checking in. I think he signed it James Jones and wife. No luggage."

"Can you give us any kind of description of her?"

"As I said, she stood with her back to me. When he got through checking in, they went to the elevator. Must have changed their minds about waiting for it, because they headed for the stairs to the second floor. She sure had a fine-looking pair of legs, and ass to match."

"I can understand your interest in the lower part of her anatomy," growled O'Donovan, "but what else can you tell us about her. How was she dressed? Was she tall or short? Skinny or fat? You know what I mean. Give us everything you can remember."

"I'd guess she was about five-ten or so, well built, but not fat. She had on one of those tight skirts, you know, the kind the young girls are wearing these days, way above their knees. Let me see . . . high heels. Those high heels do something to me. I think her skirt was black, and she had on some kind of white jacket."

"Was she a white or colored broad?" broke in Fowler.

"Couldn't tell too well. From the little glimpse I had of her, I'd say she was either white or a very fair-colored woman. Oh, yeah, she had long black hair that hung down to her shoulders. Boy, I can tell you, you should have seen her walk. Talk about an ass shaking . . ." Williams paused as if reflecting upon the vision of the previous night.

O'Donovan gave a sidelong glance at Fowler and winked while waiting for Williams to continue.

"Anything else?" he asked, after a long pause.

"Can't think of anything else. It's hard for me to believe that chick did the guy in. Maybe he was her main man and she wasted him in a fit of jealousy. You know, the thing you read about in the papers all the time. Have you two thought of that?"

Fowler gave a quick look at O'Donovan. As quickly as he considered the notion of Williams, he rejected it. Nkombo's murder was too professional, not the work of a jealous lover. He guessed O'Donovan would take a dim view of the idea, too.

"Anything more?" snapped O'Donovan impatiently.

"That's all I can remember." Williams shook his head. "I can't believe she did him in."

O'Donovan dismissed Williams with a "thank you" and a wave of his hand.

"Well, what do you make of it?" he asked Fowler

"Can't figure it out. Who would want Nkombo knocked off? I wonder if he was mixed up in some kind of African politics. Whatever. I have a hunch we're getting close to the end of the road."

They spent a few minutes talking about the Nkombo shooting before going their separate ways. On his way out of the hotel, Fowler noticed the men from the coroner's department bringing the body down the stairs. The curious and sensational seekers were still loitering outside the barriers set up by the police.

When Fowler got back to his car he remembered the call from Henrietta. He dialed Howard University and asked for Mrs. Jefferson in the president's office. There was no Mrs. Jefferson in the president's office, nor as far as the records showed, none among the faculty. He wondered whether Henrietta got the message right. Whoever it was would call back if it was important. There was enough on his mind trying to understand this latest development. Was it connected with Msomi?

Fowler's thoughts rambled over the twists and turns

of all that happened since he began his investigation of the Msomi shooting. He wondered how he was going to break the news to Sheia, and to Daniel Msomi. His gut feeling told him that, somehow, this latest incident was another part of the puzzle.

The crowd began to drift away, following the departure of the coroner's station wagon. He reached for his phone to call Sheia, changed his mind, and hung up the receiver before making the call. He was not ready to talk to her about what happened.

Fowler dawdled along in the slow lane trying to recall anything that might have a bearing on the death of Nkombo. He suddenly wheeled the car around in the middle of a block and raced back to the hotel. He was in luck. O'Donovan was coming out the front door with a couple of officers. Honking his horn, he caught O'Donovan's eye and motioned to him. After a few comments with the officers, O'Donovan came over to the car and leaned into the window.

"What's up Fowler? I thought I had seen the last of you, at least for a day or two."

"I'd like to try a couple of ideas on you."

"Okay, but I've got a meeting with the captain at the station as soon as I can get there."

"I ran into Alabama Slim, one of my contacts, yesterday. It was raining so I gave him a lift. He told me that someone is importing a hit man from Chicago to carry out a contract on a black PI here in Washington."

"Must be someone pretty important. Who do you know among black PI's who would be likely to get that kind of attention?"

"I have no idea. Slim didn't know any more than what I've just told you. But there's more to it."

O'Donovan opened the door and sat down.

"Go ahead."

"Last night, I took in the show at the Kit Kat Club. You know, that new club not far from my apartment. Well, I was having dinner with a young lady before the show and who should horn in, but Nkombo. He got the head waiter to make a seat for him at our table."

"So?"

"During the evening, I had to go to the rest room. While I was away there was a call for me. Nkombo went to answer it. He told me about it when I got back to the table. No one answered the phone." Fowler paused. "Nkombo was still at the club when we left. I didn't think any more about it until a little while ago as I was driving along."

"Nothing too exciting about a phone call where no one answers. I've had plenty of those and nothing ever came of them."

"Then, this morning Henrietta, you know, my secretary, told me a Mrs. Jefferson, supposedly from the president's office of Howard University, called late last night and wanted to get in touch with me about a very hush-hush matter at the school. Boss couldn't get a hold of me, but she told the person where I was likely to be. I called the school, and they didn't have a record of a Mrs. Jefferson in administration or on the faculty." He looked sharply at O'Donovan for a moment then said, "You know what I think?"

"I've got an idea."

"That call was made by someone who didn't know me and didn't have a lot of time to get a fix on me. When Nkombo answered the phone, they took him for me. That bullet in his head was meant for me."

"Makes sense. What are you planning to do?"

"You're on your way to meet with Captain Levine, right?"

O'Donovan nodded.

"I want you to keep what I just told you to yourself."

"I'll go along with you, but you know how I feel about that hunch of yours."

"I know, but just go along with me. If I'm wrong, I'll be quick and ready to tell you."

"Okay. I've gotta go." O'Donovan stepped out of the car, and walked swiftly away.

"I'll keep you posted on what I come up with." Fowler was sure another attempt would be made to correct a mistake and that would not be long in coming.

An inner voice told him there was no need to spend any time looking for Nkombo's killer. Whoever it was would find him. He was sure of that. Still, his eyes kept stock of his surroundings as he drove along. A small coffee shop around the corner from his apartment caught his eye, he swerved and parked in front of it. After a close scrutiny of the street, he got out of the car and quickly entered the restaurant. Fowler felt more at ease after his examination of the room revealed nothing but familiar faces.

"Hey, Fowler," hailed a black, wooly-haired man sitting at the counter. "What brings you out so early on a Saturday? Got to be something up to see you this time of the day."

"Everything's cool. Had one of those days when I just couldn't sleep, so I decided to come here and listen to some of your lies." He found an empty table where he could look out the window and keep an eye on his car. His order was sausage and eggs and whatever went with them. "Don't let me stop your discussion of the world's problems. I'd be pleased if you didn't ask my opinion while I'm eating. Most of you know that I get mighty upset when I'm interrupted while eating." This brought a round of snickers.

"Did you hear the news about some African dude that got done in by some gal up at the Douglas Hotel last night?" asked a little, stringy-haired, light-skinned woman sitting at a table in the back of the room.

"Tell me about it," mumbled Fowler between bites of food.

"You can't trust anyone nowadays," growled the wooly-haired man who was known as Girly. "You take a gal to a room for a little pleasure, and you take your life in your hands these days." His comments were treated with good-natured derision.

"When was the last time you took a gal to a room for what you call a little fun, Girly?" asked the stringy-haired woman, with more than a little sarcasm in her voice. "Maybe the woman had to protect herself from this guy. Who knows. People are too quick to blame the woman. They forget all about it when the true facts come out. I'll be willing to bet, you'll find there's more to it than we've been told by the news reporters."

Fowler finished his breakfast and leaned back completely absorbed in his own particular problem. He had no desire to enter the opinions that floated about him. Neither did he think that letting them in on his role in the shooting would produce anything more than a lot of questions that he was in no mood to answer. Finally, he paid his bill.

"Let me know if you find the answer to the shooting," he said to the group.

Fowler paused in front of the coffee shop and looked all around. Satisfied, he ambled over to his car. He thought about calling Sheia, but changed his mind. He still wasn't in the mood to go into details about the shooting. Besides, he felt more convinced than ever that whoever it was would contact him in some way and before the day was over.

He let the car lead him to his apartment as his thoughts ranged over the Msomi situation. Contrary to his usual habit of parking in back of the building, he parked in front, where his car could be seen. A quick glance around the street and he was into the building, taking the steps two at a time to the floor of his apartment.

Fowler locked the door and went directly to the window. Someone was watching, he could feel it. Nothing came from scanning the street, but the premonition persisted. The telephone rang interrupting his brooding.

"Fowler," he said sharply.

"I finally caught you," Henrietta began. "Did that Mrs. Jefferson ever get ahold of you?"

"No. As a matter of fact, I don't think there is a Mrs. Jefferson. I called the university. They didn't know anything about any problem or anyone on the staff by that name. Probably someone playing a game on us. You know these telephone freaks—they look in the book and find a name and then call with all kinds of foolishness. Let's just forget about it."

"Did you hear the news about the murder of that Mr. Nkombo? It's on all the TV stations. They claim some unknown woman is the prime suspect."

"I heard about it on the radio just a few minutes ago. I'll check on it as soon as I can get in touch with O'Donovan. Maybe between now and Monday I'll know more about it. See you Monday." He hung up the phone and hurried back to the window.

A late model car was parked a few doors down the street, he hadn't noticed it before. He squinted his eyes to see if there was anyone sitting in it.

He hurried to his bedroom and got his binoculars. The high-powered glasses did not reveal anyone in the car, unless they were lying down. Scanning the street failed to indicate anything out of the ordinary. He placed the glasses on a table and walked over to the television with the intent to turn it on just as the phone rang again.

"What's up, Fowler?" said O'Donovan.

"Has the captain said anything about the Nkombo killing?"

"He's been behind a closed door all morning. Nothing to report there. Do you still think it was a case of mistaken identity?"

"I'm positive of it. I've got a plan I'm going to try out. I'll fill you in on the details as soon as I get it worked out." He hung up the phone and returned to the window.

Fowler was startled to find the car he noticed earlier had moved from where it was parked and was now parked on the opposite side of the street, several doors away. Once again, he was not able to discern anyone in the car. Goose pimples raced up and down his back. Whoever it was out there was watching every move he was making. He was sure of that. He stood for several minutes hoping to see someone get into the car, then dragged himself to a chair where he flopped down with a sigh.

Fowler picked up the phone and dialed Sheia's number. He listened to it ring a number of times. Just as he was about to place the phone on its cradle, her sleepy voice answered.

"Msomi residence."

"Fowler. Where were you?"

"Asleep." Then with a gay tone, she added. "For some reason I find myself completely worn out this morning. Could you tell me why I find myself so exhausted?"

"You probably spent the night cleaning some offices in one of those new buildings downtown." He searched his mind briefly for some way to break the news to her about Nkombo. Realizing words could not fit at such a time, he blurted out, "I have some bad news to tell you." Then, before she could respond, he went on. "Nkombo was shot and killed last night." He paused and listened to her gasp as the shock of it hit her. Wishing to conclude the conversation as quickly as possible he added. "I haven't found out all of the details about the shooting, but as soon as I know more, I'll let you know."

"But, but—"

"I've got to go now. I'll get back to you as soon as I can find out anything. In the meantime, you'll hear a lot of guesses from the media. Don't get too upset over what you hear. Wait until I get back to you." With that last comment, Fowler hung up the phone.

He hurried across the room to the window and scanned the street from corner to corner. The car he had noticed earlier was nowhere to be seen. Perhaps he was getting paranoid, he thought. Yet, he knew he had good reason to feel that way.

Turning away from the window, Fowler wandered to the kitchen, obtained a cold bottle of beer, and sat at the table. He took several sips, sat the bottle on the table and stared at it. What to do? It was too early to go to the Kit Kat Club to see what clues he could stir up about the shooting. He pondered what the evening held in store for him.

Leaving the kitchen and the beer, he ambled into his bedroom and made his way to a little end table alongside his bed. Opening a drawer he took out a small-caliber revolver and tossed it on the bed. He held the pistol upside down until all the cartridges had been ejected. After checking them, he reloaded the gun and flipped on the safety catch.

Going to the closet, Fowler felt along the shelf until he found a holster that fit around his leg. Slipping off his trousers he placed the gun in the holster and fastened it on his leg. When he pulled up his trousers he decided there was a bulge that could be noticed by a discerning person. Finding a pair of trousers with fuller legs took care of that problem. The gun was well concealed.

He returned to the front room and sat looking out the window until it was time to leave for the club. At this point, he was preparing himself for action. There was no doubt in his mind that he was faced by an implacable, shadowy figure, and the only clue he had was that it was a woman, and very likely, an attractive woman, too. His eyes settled upon a flashy jacket hanging in the closet. It would be the coat he would wear to the club, providing a moving target for a pair of unknown eyes.

Fowler walked leisurely down the stairs and out the front door of the building. He stood and casually glanced up and down the street. The car was still nowhere to be seen. Yet, a rumbling feeling in the pit of his stomach told him that even then he was being watched.

He paused to speak briefly to a neighbor who was entering the building before sauntering over to his car, each step heavier than the previous one. The possibility his car might be set to explode when he opened the door filtered into his mind. He did not believe the person trailing him would resort to that method of eliminating him. Nevertheless, he breathed a sigh of relief when he opened the door and sat down.

There was only a fuzzy outline of a plan as Fowler drove along toward the Kit Kat Club to begin his investigation of Nkombo's murder. On occasion, he would glance into his rearview mirror to see if he was being followed.

Although he had the distinct feeling there was someone there, he could not be sure. Whoever it was knew how to keep out of sight.

Even as he brooded over his ghostly pursuer, the thought of his approach to the evening would not stand aside for any other thought. His mind flooded with first one approach then another. Initially, he thought of taking Sheia to the Kit Kat Club and wait for developments while they ate, drank, and watched the show. He was not comfortable with Sheia playing a role in his plan. She was present the past evening, sitting at the table with Nkombo. She would be recognized, and by a very dangerous killer. Sheia would not be the right one to place in such a spot. Even as he was wrestling with these thoughts, the framework of another idea was forming in his mind. But he needed the assistance of a woman friend.

Fowler racked his brain until he came up with someone who could be expected to go along with his plan. He finally settled upon Karen Sue Edwards, the wife of a good friend. She was sure to enthusiastically embrace anything that had the earmarks of intrigue. Bill Edwards had a cleaning shop on 9th Street near Howard University. Shortly, Fowler drove up, parked and hurried into the shop. Saturday was a busy day for the Edwardses and there were several customers waiting for service.

"Afternoon, Bill, Karen Sue," greeted Fowler when the shop finally cleared and he was alone with the two of them. "How about that blue suit of mine I brought in a week ago? Don't ask me for my ticket. You know me when it comes to tickets." He waited patiently while Bill checked his files for the number, started a line in motion, and shortly after, reached up and took down Fowler's suit. Bill looked quizzically at Fowler who made no move toward paying for the suit.

"That suit is not my main reason for coming here today," murmured Fowler softly. "I'm investigating a murder, and I would like to borrow your wife for a few hours this evening. I'm sure you would like to be on your own for a while."

This brought a chuckle from Bill, who was not certain if Fowler was serious.

"Explain, and make it good."

"Think of all the things you could do without Karen Sue deciding what's best for you." Fowler gave a sly smile. "You could fix that catfish dinner you like and then watch the sexy show your lovely wife wouldn't let you watch if she were home."

"I know, I know, eliminate bullshit. Provide details."

Fowler told Bill all he felt he should without going into too much detail. At the end of his account of the murder and the plan he wanted to carry out, he looked carefully at Bill in order to see how he was taking it.

"Okay by me," said Bill. "It's up to Karen Sue. Besides, she's been bugging me to take her to that show at the Kit Kat. Reel Foot Henry is one of her favorites. Did you say dinner was included? How about taking the both of us? I could stay in the background."

"Wouldn't work. In the first place, since I don't have any idea of the person I'm after, it's going to be a job for me to keep all my attention on trying to find out who that person is. The fewer people in on a deal the better. I can assure you Karen Sue will not be in any danger, if that's on your mind."

"Like I said, it's all right with me. See what she has to say about it."

Fowler briefed Karen Sue on the plan, and she agreed to go along with it. They were to meet at the club at eight o'clock. He left with trepidation. There was more danger to his plan than he described to Bill. Could he pull it off? The next thing he had to do was to call O'Donovan.

17

Clang Goes the Trap

Fowler, outwardly cool and collected, left Edward's Cleaners, suit slung over his shoulder. He paused and glanced up and down the street. Nothing. That was it, that was what was causing goose pimples to play tag up and down his spine. He knew there was someone watching his every move. Shaking the tension out of his shoulders, he opened the car door, placed his suit on the passenger seat.

He had an hour to nose around the club before his meeting with Karen Sue. Deep in thought, he listened to the purr of the engine for a few minutes before pulling into traffic. Excitement began to build inside him. The rumbling in the pit of his stomach had subsided. It was almost as if he had become the hunter instead of the hunted. He chuckled as he reviewed each aspect of how he planned to capture this elusive, invisible foe. Yet, he instinctively knew it would do well not to underestimate his quarry. He needed all his senses on full alert.

Fowler found the Kit Kat Club busy preparing for the evening activities. He meandered around, taking note of everyone present and what they were doing. Reel Foot Henry was tinkling with a few chords on a piano. He entertained the patrons during intermissions when the featured performers took a break.

"Hey, Reel Foot, m'man." Fowler approached and

looked down at Reel Foot who appeared lost in the chords he was coaxing out of the ancient upright piano sitting in a corner of the room. "Some good sounds. Something new?"

"Naw. I've been fooling around with these chords for years but just can't quite put them all together." Turning away from the piano, he said, "What brings you here tonight? I heard about that African buddy of yours. Too bad. Any word on who did it? The news says it was a chick."

"The police suspect it was some broad all right. But that's about all I know at this time."

"That buddy of yours thought he was some kind of ladies' man. I've seen him in here with quite a few gals. It wouldn't surprise me if one of them did do him in. There was one here with him about a couple of weeks ago, and believe me, they really turned the place upside down. They started arguing and fighting, right out on the dining room floor. The chick pulled a knife and would have done him in, some guys grabbed her. I was surprised to see him in here last night. The owner told him to never come back, and if he did, he'd have his ass thrown in jail. I can't—"

See you later," interrupted Fowler, giving Reel Foot a pat on the shoulder. He noticed Jack, the bartender, arranging things at the bar, so he sauntered over there. Jack was the kind of person who listened patiently to the problems of those who frequented his bar. As such, he was a source of information Fowler never failed to tap.

Jack finally edged his way over to where Fowler was seated.

"Howdy, Fowler," he drawled. "I didn't expect to see you here tonight. I thought you would be out hunting down the person who wasted that African dude."

"That's why I'm here tonight. Thought you might have picked up something, a lead I can use."

"Not sure I can help. Nkombo was a playboy of sorts. He was always bringing a new girl to show off to the guys. According to the report I heard on the radio, the police mentioned a jealous girlfriend as a possible suspect. It might have been that West Indian woman he had a fight with in the club a week or so ago. Boy, that was some mean sister. She would have carved him up into little pieces if someone hadn't grabbed her. I was not about to jump into that scuffle. I watched the action here behind the bar. Lion-taming was never one of my long suits." This brought a chuckle from Fowler.

"Do you recall seeing Nkombo last night?"

"Yeah. I saw him several times. As a matter of fact, he came over to the bar to order his drinks."

"Did you see him with anybody, a woman?"

"Come to think of it, I saw him late last night with some woman."

"Can you describe her?" Fowler tried to suppress his excitement about the possibility of getting a solid lead on Nkombo's killer.

"Not much I can tell you. I had never seen her before. They were sitting in that far corner. You know what the lighting is in here. I was pretty busy last night, and Nkombo and his women weren't high on my priority list. I think she was either a white woman or a light-skinned colored woman, a real cutie. I wish I could help you more, but wait . . . Maybe the girls who were serving the tables last night could help. We had to hire a couple of extras for this weekend. Let's see what they could tell us." He called over two young women who were dressed in the usual short cocktail attire.

"Linda, Betty, this is T.J. Fowler, a notorious private

243

investigator. He's on an international murder case and thinks you two might be able to help him out."

"Jack, as usual, is exaggerating, at least to some extent," said Fowler eyeing the two women. "The police are not sure whether there is an international connection. The man who was killed was an African. He was in this club last night. We're trying to trace his movements to find out who he was with during the time that led up to his death." Turning to Jack, Fowler murmured softly, "Let me see that paper you've got over there by the cash register." It was the Saturday late edition of the *Daily Voice*. The women and Jack waited expectantly as he turned the pages, glancing quickly at each page as he turned them. "Ah," he said at last. "You can count on the newspapers to provide you with all the details of anything as sensational as a murder." Pointing to a picture of Nkombo he asked, "Do either of you remember seeing this man in here last night?" Linda and Betty looked carefully at the picture.

"He doesn't look familiar to me," said Linda quickly, "You've got to remember we were very busy last night. I didn't have a chance to look too closely at anybody."

Betty was slower to answer.

"I'm pretty sure I saw this man here last night. He was sitting at one of the tables in the corner."

"Was he with anyone when you saw him?" Fowler's jaw tightened, as he listened for a possible clue.

"When I first saw him, he was sitting by himself. Later on, I noticed a lady sitting with him."

"Can you describe this lady."

"As I said, I just noticed her as I passed by with some drinks for someone else." She closed her eyes as if trying to jog her memory.

"Go on. Go on," pressed Fowler. "What can you tell

me about her. Was she tall, short, dark, light, fat, skinny? Think! It's very important."

"I think she was white. It was so dark in that corner. Now that I remember, this man told me he would get his drinks at the bar and it would not be necessary for me to come by and check on them. I wish I could tell you more, but that's all I can remember."

Fowler spent a few more minutes with the two women to no avail. He still had no definite description of the mystery woman. His eyes followed Betty as she hurried off to complete her tasks. She was tall, shapely, not bad to look at, light-skinned in coloring, with long hair tied up in some kind of knot. An unsettling thought began to form in his mind. He turned to Jack.

"Didn't you tell me these girls were extras, hired just for this weekend?"

"Right."

"How were they hired? Were they hired through some employment agency?"

"I don't think so. The manager put a card in the front window advertising an opening for temporary jobs. As far as I know, they just walked in, applied, and were hired."

"When did this occur?"

"Yesterday. The manager brought them around and introduced them to me about six or seven o'clock last night."

"Another question. What time did they come on duty today?"

"I saw Linda a couple of hours ago. Betty just got here ten or fifteen minutes ago."

A shudder rolled over Fowler. Once again a hunted feeling came over him. Was it possible the one he had been looking for had been standing in front of him? She fit what little description there was of Nkombo's killer.

Besides, she was the one who served the tables in the area where Nkombo was seated. How much of her story could he believe? The more he thought about it, the more plausible his suspicions of Betty being the killer became. He found himself casually following her every move as she went about her tasks.

The patrons were beginning to file into the club. Reel Foot Henry was at the piano, playing his kind of music for the entertainment of the early arrivals. Fowler smiled to himself—Reel Foot was a very harsh critic of the "modern" music favored by the youths of the day. As far as he was concerned, very little of it was music at all, just a steady unmelodious and irritating bunch of sounds.

Fowler sought out the head waiter and arranged to get a table on the outer edge of the room facing the bar. This would allow him to keep an eye on Betty as she passed back and forth among the tables in that area of the club.

Shortly before eight o'clock, Karen Sue entered the club. Many a male eye turned to follow her as she flounced across the room toward Fowler who stood and beckoned to her. When she was abreast of him, he took her by the arm. His eyes roved up and down her.

"Looking real sharp tonight, Karen Sue. The way these guys are eating you up, I'd better keep my eyes open, for Bill's sake."

"Something new I've been wanting to wear for a long time," said Karen Sue with a smile. "Prying Bill away from that TV isn't easy. I'm kind of glad to get a night out on the town. Good to see how the other half lives."

"What about a drink?" Fowler held her by the arm.

She nodded, and he guided her to the bar. They found a couple of seats and waited for Jack to come over and serve them.

"What can I get you?" Jack directed his question to Karen Sue.

"Vodka and water will do for me."

"The usual for you, Fowler?"

"I've got a favor to ask," said Fowler. "It's important for me to know what's going on around me at all times tonight. I'll fill you in on what it's all about later on. I will be drinking gin and tonic the rest of the evening, but I want you to cut it. I don't want anyone else to serve me but you. Got it?"

"Okay. You want me to start now?" asked Jack, who had no trouble with unusual requests from his customers.

"Yep, starting from now."

Jack returned a few minutes later with the drinks. Fowler tasted his and commented, "Just right. I want to smell the gin but barely taste it. You got the right idea." Karen Sue was satisfied with her drink, so Jack left to serve other customers.

Ostensibly, Fowler and Karen Sue were engrossed in conversation, although he would let his eyes roam in Betty's direction. He noticed she would flash a smile at him whenever she passed by with a tray of drinks. A waiter came and told them to follow him, their table was ready and serving had begun.

Karen Sue moved her chair closer to Fowler's chair when the entertainment began. She leaned toward him, his arm around her shoulders.

At the conclusion of the first show, Reel Foot titillated those who remained with his brand of music. Busboys and waiters busied themselves cleaning the dining room and getting ready for the next wave of patrons. Fowler pulled Karen Sue closer to him and whispered something into her ear. All eyes were focused upon them as Karen Sue bounced to her feet, her voice ringing above the sounds of Reel Foot. She exclaimed angrily, "You've got the wrong one this time, big boy. I'm not one of your one-night-stand sluts." She whacked Fowler across the jowls, picked up her drink, and flung it in his face. She snatched her wrap from the back of her chair and strutted to the door and out of the club.

Fowler, apparently stunned, watched Karen Sue's retreating figure. Her drink trickled down his face and drenched his shirt. Finally, evading inquiring eyes, he headed for the rest room. He was within a few steps, when he was stopped by Betty, flashing a sympathetic smile as she handed him a towel. He gave her a grateful nod and entered the rest room.

When Fowler emerged from the rest room, only a few wet spots on his shirt and jacket remained. He ambled off in the direction of Reel Foot, who was meandering in the field of easy listening harmony. Fowler pulled up a chair and sat, right foot keeping time with the rhythms that poured from the piano.

"Fowler," said Reel Foot, swiveling on his piano stool. "What was that fracas about? Did you get your women mixed up? That was no love tap she gave you. I heard that slap all the way over here."

"Nothing much." Fowler winked. "You know how uppity some of your folks can get."

"Staying for the late show? I've put in my day, and I'm getting out of here. This no-melody noise leaves me cold."

"I'm supposed to meet somebody, so I guess I'll hang around for a while. Maybe I'll head for the lounge and have a drink while I'm waiting."

"Another one of your chicks. That one last night was the best looking black gal I've seen in a long time." With a wave of his hand, Reel Foot said, "See you later."

Fowler weaved his way over to the bar and found a seat at a corner where he had the best view of the club.

"That was some kind of embarrassing deal your friend laid on you," said a voice in back of Fowler. He gave a start and turned to see Betty walking by with a tray full of drinks. She paused for a moment to ask, "Are you okay?"

"Yeah, thanks for the towel," he replied warily. "Just one of those things—you win some and lose some."

Betty smiled and continued on her way. Fowler watched her retreating figure, troubling thoughts once again filled his mind. She did not fit his image of a hit person. Still, whoever wasted Nkombo did not fit either. Nkombo was no fool to be taken in by just any pretty face and a good-looking pair of legs. He had to be totally unprepared for what happened to him. Jack, the bartender, came up and interrupted his thoughts.

"What can I get you, Fowler?" said Jack in a voice loud enough to be heard by those sitting nearby.

"The same. You know, gin and tonic."

Jack returned with the drink and sat it on the bar.

"On your tab?"

"Yeah, thanks." Fowler, drink in hand nonchalantly let his eyes rove around the room. No one seemed to be paying any attention to him, except Betty. Could she . . .

Still, he was sure the person who was trailing him was in the club, and watching his every move. He rose from his stool and plodded off in the direction of the rest room. On his way, he lurched into a man leaving the rest room.

"Watch it buddy," snapped the man angrily.

"Sorry," muttered Fowler thickly. Once inside the rest room, he breathed a sigh of relief. The mystery woman would not likely confront him in the men's room.

When he retraced his steps to the bar he found his seat had been taken.

"Couldn't help it," said Jack crisply as he came by with a drink for another customer. "I wasn't sure you were coming back."

"It's okay. I was thinking about finding a seat over there in the corner. Fix me another of those gin and tonics, and I'll take it with me." He waited until Jack came back with his drink, flashed an O.K. sign to him, and weaved his way to a table in a corner. He placed his drink on the table and sat with his back to the wall. Although his view was limited, he was able to take in most of the activities in the cocktail room. He had barely sat down when Betty came by.

"I see you've got your drink," said Betty with a smile.

"Yesh." Fowler gave his best impression of slurred speech. "Mmm, okay."

"Are you sure you're all right? Do you think you need someone to drive you home?"

"Nope, I'm okay." Fowler took a hearty sip from his drink. This was it. This was the opening wedge. He would have to play it carefully, not appear too eager. "I can handle it." He attempted to stand up, only to slide back into his chair. "All I need is another drink, and I'll be all right," he added with a smirk.

"You don't need any more to drink. You're so loaded now, you can't stand up. I'll have to check with the bartender before I can bring you any more to drink."

"I'm not drunk, goddamit," screeched Fowler. Heads turned in his direction. Betty abruptly headed to the bartender. Minutes later, Jack confronted an apparently inebriated Fowler sitting with his head resting on his arms on the table.

"What's the problem m'man?" said Jack.

Fowler, bleary eyed, raised his head and whined.

"I asked this bitch of a waitress of yours to bring me a drink. She said she couldn't bring one without checking with you. She even offered to drive me home, said I was too drunk to drive. Can you imagine that?"

"I doubt that," said Jack quietly.

"What? You doubt what?" Fowler acted subdued.

"I doubt she would offer to drive you home."

"Why not?"

"You see that tall black guy sitting at the bar, near the cash register?"

"Yeah."

"That's her husband, and from what I hear, he's a pretty jealous dude. He's in here just to make sure nobody tries to lay anything on her. You can believe me when I say she won't be driving you home."

Goose pimples once again danced over Fowler's back, along with a fluttery feeling in the pit of his stomach. Her husband? Could Jack be right? Yet, when he asked himself that question, he knew Jack was right. Now, he was back to square one. He wanted to kick himself for being too quick to conclude on the basis of a few bits of behavior that Betty was his mystery woman. His unknown foe was still unknown and somewhere in the club.

"I've got to get back to the bar," said Jack. "You want anything?"

A plan had began to form in Fowler's mind.

"I've got an idea. Have Betty bring me another drink, and tell her to tell me it's the last one I can get. I'm going to raise hell loud enough to cause you to come over to try to settle me down."

"You finally reach the point where you can't stand any more of my shit and call the bouncers and have me thrown out. Let it be known that I'm too drunk to drive and the club is not going to be responsible for anything that might happen after I leave."

Jack agreed to the plan and, without another word, hurried away to the bar. Fowler wrapped his hand around his drink, leaned over with his head on his arms on the table, and waited.

"The bartender told me to bring this drink over to you," said a voice at his elbow. Fowler slowly looked around with bleary eyes to see Betty standing over him with a drink. He reached out with a shaky hand and took the drink from her, spilling a few drops on his jacket and on the table.

"He told me to tell you that you've had enough to drink and that that drink is the last one you'll get in here," added Betty pointing to the drink on the table.

"What the goddamned hell does he mean, saying I'm drunk and can't have another?" howled Fowler, making a poor attempt at springing out of his chair, spilling most of the drink remaining in the glass. "Go back and tell that sonofabitch of a bartender to come over here and tell me to my face I'm drunk, and tell him to bring me another drink." He weaved back and forth in spite of holding on to his chair for support. Looking around Fowler said in a muffled tone to no one in particular, "Can you imagine that, me drunk?" He was about to drift off into another discourse, when Jack appeared at his table.

"Where's my drink?" Fowler apparently failed to read the anger in Jack's face.

"Sit down! I've had about all I can take from you. The waitress told you right. You're drunk and you've had the last drink you're going to get here," snapped Jack, his voice rising. By this time, many faces were turned in their direction.

"Who said I'm drunk?" Fowler tried his best to rise

out of his chair. Finally making it, he looked around to those sitting nearby and pointed out, "See how steady I am." He staggered across the aisle and plopped down in the lap of a lady sitting at a table, knocking over her drink and the drink of her escort.

"That's it! That's it! You're out of here. The Kit Kat Club is not going to be responsible for anything you do because you've had too much to drink." Jack signaled for a busboy to clean the table while he checked to see if patrons were observing the scene.

"I'm not going nowhere. Who's gonna make me?"

"I'll take care of that." Jack motioned to two large, mean-looking men standing nearby, who quickly came over to the table. "Throw his ass out of here," said Jack. "Treat him as gently as you can so he won't be able to come back and sue the club."

The two bouncers, one under each arm, lifted Fowler from his chair and escorted him unceremoniously toward the exit. He wailed loudly all the way. The men blocked the doorway as Fowler gave the attendant the keys to his car.

"If I were you," said one of the bouncers. "I would take a cab or get someone to drive me home. You're in no condition to drive."

"Motherfuckers," blubbered Fowler. "I'm not drunk. I don't need nobody to drive me home or do anything for me." He staggered to the front of the line. "It'll be a cold day in July when this club gets any more of my money. You can count on that. Believe me when I tell you."

"The end of the line is back there, junior," said a portly man in a dark suit. Several other voices joined in to emphasize the point.

Fowler looked around him, seemingly confused. He pursed his lips as if to say something but changed his mind and slowly wobbled to the end of the line, grumbling to himself as he went. The dim outside light cast an eerie glow on the attendants scurrying back and forth, bringing cars to the waiting patrons. Glancing around, Fowler noted there was no one in back of him. He wondered whether his plan would work or not. Then it happened.

"I think it was terrible the way they treated you," a soft, husky voice came out of the gloom.

Fowler gave no indication he was aware that someone was talking to him and continued to grumble to himself. Yet his every sense told him this was the one whose eyes had followed his every move. There was a soft tap on his shoulder and, with open mouth and head bobbing up and down, he turned to face his adversary.

"I saw it all. It was awful the way they treated you," repeated the voice.

Even in the dim light, Fowler saw before him a beautiful, slender, long-haired, light-skinned colored woman. She was dressed in slacks with a plain wrap hanging loosely about her shoulders. In spite of his all-but-certain feeling that standing beside him was Nkombo's killer, it was difficult to reconcile a cold-blooded killer with such loveliness, half hidden by the shadows. He remembered how wrong he was about Betty and resolved to be patient and see how things unfolded. He said something unintelligible and turned back to await his turn in the line. When an attendant finally brought his car, Fowler fumbled in his pocket in a vain attempt to find a tip for the youth, but found none. "Next time," he said, reaching for the keys.

"I think they're right," said the woman who followed closely on Fowler's heels. "You're taking a chance driving in your condition, honey. I don't have anything going for the rest of the night. I wouldn't mind driving you home."

"Don't need nobody to drive me home," Fowler said angrily. He lurched toward his car and, for a moment, lost his balance. As he reached for his car in order to keep from falling, his keys fell to the pavement. The attendant quickly picked them up and offered them to Fowler.

"I'll take those." The unknown woman reached into her purse for a tip and, at the same time, took the keys away from the attendant. Fowler, who appeared to be falling asleep, leaning against the car, said nothing. Moving quickly, the friendly female wrapped her arms around him.

She was good, thought Fowler. In the process of helping him into the car, she searched his upper body in order to determine if he had a weapon on him. Once in the car, he plumped down in his seat, closed his eyes, and seemed oblivious of the world around him. He wondered whether O'Donovan got his message. While she was going around to the driver's side of the car, Fowler shifted his body so he could watch her through half-closed eyes. She drove slowly for several blocks, then stopped. He felt his whole body become alert.

"Wake up. Wake up," said his unknown helpmate gently shaking him. "Where do you live?" Fowler pulled himself together, shook his head and peered through the window.

"Around the block. Turn right at the next light," said Fowler as he settled back into his seat.

She drove for a few minutes before stopping again.

"Okay, I'm around the corner. Now where?"

"Sherman Street. Sherman Street, goddammit!" snapped Fowler peevishly. "Just keep going until you get to Sherman Street then turn right." He slouched back in his seat, and watched as she turned on Sherman and drove slowly past the row of apartment buildings.

"What number? What's the number of your building?"

"Back up, back up. You've just passed it. The building with the row of lights on each side of the sidewalk." She stopped in front of the building. "Whash your name?" asked Fowler.

"Just call me Candy."

"Mine's Fowler."

Candy came around to help Fowler out of the car. He made several attempts to rise out of his seat, only to fall back again. With her help, he was soon standing shakily on his feet. He reached for his keys, took them from her, whispered "thanks," and turned to enter the building.

"Would you like some company?" said Candy in a hesitant voice. "As I said, I'm on loose ends. No reason why we shouldn't enjoy each other."

Fowler stopped and turned to face Candy, pondering the question.

"Come on," he replied after a moment. Candy followed him up the stairs to his apartment. He fumbled with the lock until she took the keys from him and unlocked the door. Fowler followed her into the apartment, making sure the door remained unlocked.

Once the door was closed behind them, Fowler waddled into the living room and sank down on the couch. Candy came over and curled up beside him. Between kisses, she began to peel his upper garments off him. She rubbed the hairs on his chest as she breathed a hot breath of passion into his ear. When he reached out to fondle her, she firmly pushed his hands away. Fowler had his first opportunity to see Candy in a clear light. She was indeed a beauty—light brown skin, green eyes, and long red hair tied up in a coil in the back of her head, probably a wig, he guessed.

"While you're taking off the rest of your things I'm going into the bathroom to make myself presentable," said Candy. "Which way?"

"Right, end of hall." Fowler fixed his eyes upon the graceful figure gliding across the room, purse in hand. How I could such a lovely woman be a hit person? No doubt about it—she was Nkombo's killer. *She fully intended to leave me the same way, dead.* Unlike Nkombo, he was prepared. As soon as Candy disappeared down the hall, Fowler reached down and retrieved the gun he had strapped to his leg. Sitting up with his back braced by the arm of the couch, he waited.

Candy entered the room so silently Fowler was almost caught eyeing the pistol he held in his hand. Swinging the pistol upward he held it in both hands and took careful aim at her. She was partially undressed, carrying her purse in one hand, and in the other hand holding her clothes, letting them dangle down in front of her.

"What is this, honey? What kind of game are you playing with that gun?" Fowler watched cautiously as she approached, a smile beginning to light up her face.

"That's far enough," said Fowler sharply. "One more step and I'm going to blow a hole in that pretty head of yours. Toss that purse over here, on the floor by my feet, and be careful about it. This gun is tricky and I'm a little shaky right now."

A slight noise was heard in the hallway. "That you, Pat?" asked Fowler. O'Donovan stepped into the room, taking in the scene spread out before him in a glance.

"I got your message. I've been with you since you left the club. Seems to me you could have handled this cute broad without any help from me," said O'Donovan with a smirk.

"How long have you been out there?"

"About five minutes."

"How come you didn't wait fifteen or twenty minutes more? Things were just about to get interesting. I guess Karen Sue got in touch with you okay?"

"No. Some guy by the name of Bill Edwards got hold of me."

"Her husband."

"He called the station. I was following up a lead up this way when the station got me."

"Back to business," said Fowler fixing his eyes on Candy. "Get that purse she's holding, and be careful about it. Don't come between me and her."

O'Donovan walked briskly over to Candy and snatched the purse out of her hand.

"Open it up," directed Fowler. "I think you're going to find a .38 and a silencer in there. That's what she used to kill Nkombo and what she was planning to use on me."

O'Donovan opened the purse and brought forth a snub-nosed pistol and a silencer. He gave her a cursory shake-down then told her to dress. As soon as she was dressed, he handcuffed her.

"The squad car is here," said O'Donovan. "I'll take your lovely killer down to the station." He gripped Candy's arm firmly and headed for the door, commenting as he was leaving, "Speaking of interesting, I have an idea you would have had a great time with this prime example of pulchritude. He's got dick a bigger than mine, I'm not sure about yours."

"I'll be damned. A homo, vestite?" Fowler sat for a long time, gun in hand, thinking about the adversary who had dogged his steps throughout the day. Finally, giving in to fatigue that suddenly descended upon him, he got up, trudged to his bedroom, placed his gun on a table, and flung himself on the bed. Sleep, a long time coming, was a troubled one.

Fowler woke about noon the next morning. He dragged himself into the kitchen and plopped heavily into a chair at the table. Moments later, two heaping teaspoons of instant coffee were stirred into a cup of boiling water. The telephone rang, interrupting his thoughts. Reluctantly, he plodded into the living room and picked up the phone.

"Fowler."

"Are you all right? I thought I would hear from you after we talked yesterday," Sheia said.

"There's been a lot going on since I talked to you. But, I can tell you with a great deal of certainty that we've got the killer of Nkombo behind bars."

"That is good news. So quickly. How did you do it?"

"Later. It's a long story. I'll fill you in when I see you. By the way, I'll be out of town for a few days checking up on a clue to your brother's death. Will call you when I get back."

Fowler dressed quickly, packed a few things in a small suitcase, and hurried out of the building. He paused long enough to let his nosy neighbor see him leave. She spent the greater part of the day sitting at the window of her ground floor apartment, watching the comings and goings of her fellow tenants.

A friend, who had a farm in Virginia, had agreed to his plan to spend the weekend. It was a lazy Sunday afternoon with intermittent periods of overcast and sunshine. There was very little traffic to occupy his attention and thoughts as he headed, not toward Mexico, but to Middleburg, Virginia. Forty-five minutes later, he pulled onto a dirt road that led to the farmhouse of Tom and Linda Stewart.

18

Atonement

O'Donovan left Fowler's apartment in the wee hours of Sunday morning, Candy at his side. With a brusque motion, he pushed her in front of him as they walked down the stairs. They stepped outside just as two uniformed officers hastened toward them from a squad car parked at the curb.

"We got your message, O'Donovan," said one of the officers, his eyes fixed upon the handcuffed Candy. "What've you got?"

"Murder suspect." O'Donovan smiled. "Be careful with her, she's dangerous."

"Right," said the officer with a snicker. "I think the two of us are capable of handling this situation. What should we do—"

"Book her and tell the sarge to put her in one of the back cells. I don't want anybody to see Candy, except those who bring something to eat and drink. Got it?"

"Yeah, but what if she hollers for a lawyer? You know, her rights to one call."

"Don't worry, I'll take the blame. Just do as I tell you."

"Okay. Anything else?"

"One more thing." He handed the gun wrapped in his handkerchief to the officer. "I think this is a murder weapon. Have the effects officer take care of it. I'll have ballistics check it out Monday." The officers placed Candy in the squad car and drove away.

O'Donovan had promised Virginia and the children he would take them for a long ride in the country early Sunday morning. When he made the promise, he had no idea he'd be involved with Fowler and Candy. Oh, well, he thought, it wasn't the first time police work interfered with family life. He was lucky—Virginia was understanding.

With the exception of a dim light Virginia left on in the living room, the house was dark when O'Donovan pulled into his driveway. He quietly entered the hallway leading to the living room, turned off the light, and tiptoed down the hall to the bedroom. Pausing for a moment, he listened to the steady breathing of his wife. He crawled into bed beside her, and she turned over, reaching out to him.

"A long day?" she asked quietly.

"Yes," he said wearily. He drew closer and wrapped his arms around her. "I meant to get home earlier, but got involved in a case Fowler is working on. Go back to sleep. I'll tell you about it in the morning." The soft warmth of his wife's body soon relaxed him.

O'Donovan pulled himself out of a sound sleep a few hours later. The smells tickling his nose told him Virginia was in the kitchen fixing breakfast. For a brief moment, he was unsure of the day. Was it Sunday or was it Monday. As he concluded it was Sunday, she entered the room bringing him a cup of coffee.

"I see you woke up." She placed the cup on a small table bedside the bed.

He took a sip and finding it not too hot, emptied the cup before putting it down.

"Thanks. Nothing like a good cup of coffee to start the

261

day. I was dead to the world when I hit the sack last night, is this, that morning."

"You sure were. You kept talking in your sleep, someone by the name of Candy."

"I'm pretty sure she, or he, is a hit person who killed an associate of Fowler by the name of Nkombo. Fowler thinks there was a mistake made and he was the one who was supposed to be the target of the hit person."

"What do you mean he or she? Couldn't you tell?"

"We thought it was a woman at first, and a pretty one too. It turned out there was a man inside a woman's clothing."

"Want another?" asked Virginia pointing to the empty cup.

"I could use another one. What time is it?"

"A little after nine."

"Damn. I promised an early start for a ride in the country. We aren't likely to get many more nice days before winter sets in."

"Couldn't be helped. We'll do something else. What about taking the kids to the Smithsonian? They always seem to enjoy it."

"Sounds good to me. We could have dinner out and take them to a movie later on."

"I'll get the cup of coffee. Breakfast will be ready in about fifteen minutes."

Virginia returned with another cup of coffee and tossed a robe on the foot of the bed. He slipped into the robe and, cup in hand, headed for the kitchen. On the way, he stopped at the family room. His "Morning, Mike, Kathy," brought little more than grunts from his son and daughter lying stretched out in front of the television. Continuing on to the kitchen, he sat and watched Virginia as she prepared the morning meal.

"I mentioned our plans to the kids," she said. "They're all for it." O'Donovan nodded, finished his coffee, and leaned back in his chair. "Mike, Kathy, turn off that TV and come to breakfast," shouted Virginia. "And I mean right now!" The two children straggled into the room and took their respective places at the table. Bowing their heads, they listened demurely as their father blessed the food. The meal was eaten quietly, punctuated now and then with requests to pass one thing or another.

"I want the two of you to get dressed as soon as you're through eating," said Virginia. "I've put the things I want you to wear on your beds." The two children dutifully marched off to their rooms.

O'Donovan watched his wife clean up after the morning meal. He reflected upon how fortunate he was to have a wife like Virginia. She took care of the children, ran the household, and was always understanding of the demands of the job upon him. The wife of a police officer had to face many things other wives did not have to face.

Virginia paused to tenderly stroke her husband's head. "I'll be through in a few minutes," she said softly. "If you need anything, just holler." O'Donovan got up, stretched, and ambled back to the bedroom. On her way to join him, she peeked into the children's rooms and found they were almost dressed. She joined her husband and went straight to the closet. It was necessary to find something for him to wear. His approach to dressing was to go to the back of the closet and choose the oldest things he could find. It was a pleasant game the two of them played whenever they planned to go out. After a few grumbles, he would accede to her judgment. When the children poked their heads into the doorway of the bedroom a little while later, they found their parents dressed and ready for the outing.

When the O'Donovans filed out of the house, they noticed puffy clouds beginning to float in from the south.

"Do you think we should take our raincoats?" he asked.

"It doesn't look too bad to me," said Virginia as she hustled the children into the car. "Besides, we'll be inside most of the day. I heard the weather report this morning, and they're not expecting rain until tomorrow."

When O'Donovan turned the key in the lock of the front door late that evening, everyone was exhausted. Following the museums and a fair amount of bickering during which the parents were overruled, the Sunday meal was consumed at a pizza restaurant. The movie was also decided by the younger O'Donovans. It didn't suit their father's taste. But since he decided the day was for the family, he went along with whatever they wanted. Both children slept soundly on the way home from the movie.

O'Donovan turned the light on in the hall and then returned to the car to carry his sleeping children to their bedrooms. He had been able to push aside thoughts of his work during the day, but now his mind was filled with questions about what the next day would bring. He undressed quickly and was in bed when Virginia came in.

"Another long day," said Virginia with a sigh. "But it was necessary. We don't have too many chances to be together like today. The kids had a good time, and so did I. I don't think they were too disappointed in not going for a ride in the country."

O'Donovan thought, as he watched his wife undress, her figure had changed little over the years. She was conscientious about keeping it that way. Along with diet, she regularly attended an exercise class at a local community college. When she climbed into bed beside him, he snuggled close to her, caressing her breast and

264

signaling a desire to go further.

"Not tonight, honey. It's been a long day, and I'm worn out. You must be pretty tired yourself. Let's take a rain check, okay?"

O'Donovan let his hand slowly slide away from her breast. The warm feeling began to dissipate.

"Another time," he agreed. Giving her an affectionate pat on the backside, he added, "Sleep good."

He woke early in the morning to the soft patter of rain on the roof. The predicted storm was on its way. Somewhat earlier than usual, he dragged himself out of bed and dressed without awakening the rest of the family. He scribbled a note for his wife, put it on a table, and left to join the lines of vehicles crawling toward the city.

The darkness surrounding him when he left home shaded into a dull gray morning by the time he drove into the parking lot in the back of the 77th Precinct. Captain Levine's car was in its usual place, which was unusual since he was not in the habit of getting to the station at such an early hour. Perhaps he had found out about Candy and was curious about the arrest.

There was only a skeleton crew on duty as O'Donovan hurried across the squad room to his desk. He was rummaging through papers on his desk when he saw Sergeant Smith coming out of the captain's office.

"Morning, Smitty," greeted O'Donovan, looking up from his desk as he felt the sergeant hovering over him. "What's up?"

"Nothing much. What's with you?"

"The same."

"By the way, what's with the good-looking broad you've got hidden away in the back corner?" asked the sergeant eyeing O'Donovan closely.

"Just someone I picked up who might have a bearing

on a case I'm working on. Why do you ask?"

"Only because the captain seems to be pretty interested in her. He checked the log book this morning, called me in, and asked me a lot of questions about her."

"What did you tell him?"

"Nothing I could tell him. I have no idea who she is or why she's here. He sent me to tell you he wants to see you in his office. You'd better have some good answers for him."

"By the way," said O'Donovan as he rose to go to the captain's office. "She is no she."

"You mean a queer?"

"Something like it." O'Donovan winked at Smitty and hurried over to Captain Levine's office.

"Morning, Pat." The captain was standing outside his office smoking his pipe. "Come on in and close the door behind you."

Captain Levine edged over to the window. He took several puffs as he gazed out the window at a steady downpour generating a number of streams flowing down the middle of the parking lot on their way to the drains. Finally, he turned and, with a wave of his hand, said quietly, "Sit down, Pat." He stood puffing on his pipe for a few moments before sitting and leaning back in his chair. "Tell me about the person you've got hidden in the back cell," he said gently.

There was something in the captain's manner that troubled O'Donovan. He had the distinct impression Captain Levine knew Candy was a homosexual, and perhaps he knew more. Several thoughts rushed around in his mind. He quickly decided to tell him no more than necessary.

"Well!"

"I was trying to collect my thoughts," mumbled

O'Donovan hastily. "It's about the shooting of the African friend of Fowler's a couple of days ago."

"Keep on."

"I got a tip Candy's the one who did it, even told me where she could be found. I picked her up and had her held incommunicado. Given the sensitive nature of the shooting, a visitor from another country, I felt you would not want the media in on this before we have a chance to investigate. I plan to have the lab check out the gun I found on her." O'Donovan eyed the captain. "I hope my actions meet with your approval."

"Anything else?"

"That's about it.'

Captain Levine swiveled his chair and looked out the window, puffing away on his pipe. Abruptly he swung around and stood.

"Let's go and have a look at this suspect of yours." He dumped the ashes from his pipe in an ashtray, placed the pipe in a rack, and headed for the door, followed by O'Donovan.

The squad room was beginning to buzz with activities as they threaded their way among the desks toward a door at one end of the room. They opened the door and proceeded down a long hallway, passing a number of cells on the way. Captain Levine stopped in front of the last one in the line, took a key, and opened the door. Candy was standing looking out the window and seemingly paid no attention to the two men.

"I am Captain Levine. I think you know Sergeant O'Donovan," he began impatiently. Candy slowly turned and defiantly faced the two officers. "The officers who brought you in Saturday night read you your rights," continued the captain. "You are in big trouble. The man you killed was a high profile individual from Niberia. Our government has been trying to smooth the relationship with that country since the shooting of their ambassador a few weeks ago. We might be able to go easier with you if you tell us who is behind the shooting. We know someone paid you to do it. Why not make it light on yourself by telling us who it is, or, they are?"

Candy listened quietly to the captain until he finished.

"It's a setup, a frame!" she exclaimed. "A sonofabitchin' PI by the name of Fowler set me up. If you want to find out about any shooting, any shooting, you'd better check him out, the black motherfucker. He must have put the gun in my purse when I went to the bathroom."

Captain Levine looked quizzically at O'Donovan for a moment.

"You say you were set up by a PI by the name of Fowler?"

"That's what I said."

"Tell me more about this contact with Fowler. Where did you meet him? What is his connection with this shooting?"

"I've said all I'm going to say. If you two want to stay out of trouble, you'd better let me see my lawyer. I know my rights. You might not have a job after my lawyer gets through with you. I've had enough of this bullshit."

Captain Levine's attempt to get any more information from Candy failed. She stretched out on the bunk and refused to say anything else. Finally, the captain motioned to O'Donovan it was time to leave. After locking the door, he strode a few yards down the corridor followed by O'Donovan and stopped by a window.

"Looks like an all-day rain."

"Looks like it. We might be in for a few days of this according to the weatherman."

Captain Levine, without turning from his contemplation of a rainy day, spoke in a voice so low, O'Donovan was barely able to understand him.

"Tell me about Fowler? You didn't mention anything about him when you briefed me in my office."

O'Donovan was not surprised by the request. He expected it when Candy mentioned Fowler's name.

"Not much to it. Fowler met her at the club where Nkombo was killed. Someone indicated she was seen with Nkombo the night he was shot." O'Donovan paused for a moment. The captain watched him with unblinking eyes. "Fowler had a hunch that Candy was the mystery woman who was seen at the hotel with Nkombo. He told me about his plan to get her to his apartment. He was to leave the door open for me, and we would see what we caught. When I arrived, he had found the gun and silencer in her purse. I called for backup and we brought her in. That's it."

"So, Fowler is still putting his two cents into our affairs. I told him to keep out of police business. I'd better have another talk with him. Let's go back to my office and call him. If he wants to keep that license of his, he had better get in here right away." He turned and walked swiftly down the hall towards his office. O'Donovan at his heels.

Captain Levine sat and motioned O'Donovan to sit. Pushing the telephone toward him, he snapped sharply, "Call Fowler, and tell him to get in here."

It was a short conversation. Henrietta did not know Fowler's whereabouts, only that he would be out of town for a few days.

"Not there," said O'Donovan when he hung up. "If you recall, I told you he was supposed to be out of town this weekend to bring back that cloakroom attendant from Marcel's," he continued, eyes fixed upon the captain's face.

Captain Levine reached across his desk, picked a pipe from the rack, filled it with tobacco, lit it, and puffed away.

"Try him at home." He watched O'Donovan check an address book and place the call.

"Nothing doing," said O'Donovan after a few minutes. "All I got was his recorded message, the usual, leave your name and number, and I'll get back to you."

Captain Levine remained silent for a few minutes, his eyes fixed on circles of smoke breaking apart as they floated toward the ceiling. Without shifting his eyes he went on, calmly.

"Any idea where he might be holed up this time of day?"

"Knowing Fowler, you might find him anywhere. Most of the time, he either calls me and sets up a meeting somewhere, or I just run into him accidentally. Your guess is as good as mine."

Captain Levine swung his chair around and looked out the window at the rain streaming down it. Sensing there was nothing more to be said about the matter, O'Donovan stood up to leave. "Anything else, Captain?" Without turning around, the captain raised his arm to indicate the discussion was at an end. As O'Donovan was leaving, the telephone in the captain's desk began to ring.

On the way back to his desk, O'Donovan made a quick stop at the coffee machine. He was hailed by the officer of the day.

"Well, Patrick, my boy," said the officer with a smile. "You really got mixed up with some top-drawer folks this time."

"Meaning what?" said O'Donovan as he searched his

mind for a clue to what the other was talking about.

"That cutie you brought in Saturday night sure must know some pretty powerful people. The lawyer who came in to spring her is from one of the most expensive law firms in the city. From all the hell he raised, I doubt you will be able to hold her without some real firm charges."

"Well, well, well. I'll have to look into it right away. Thanks." Cup in hand, O'Donovan walked slowly to his desk. He wondered where Fowler was, as the captain said, holed up. Shaking himself, he returned to the mound of paperwork to be handled and resolved.

It was clear to O'Donovan, Ambassador Msomi had nothing to do with the drug trade. He was set up, plain and simple, but by whom. The issue of a back-up man implicated in Linsky's shooting was pretty well blown by the capture of the rapist, who could be tied to the shooting by the murder weapon found in his possession. Then, there was the matter of the captain. It just did not fit the man he had worked under for many years. There had never been a hint he was anything other than a dedicated, highly professional police officer and leader.

Yet, Fowler had to be given some credit. If he was right about Candy being a hit man out to get him, somebody must think he was getting close to the facts of the case. The murder of Nkombo could very well have been mistaken identity as Fowler maintains. His notion that the threat to bring back the cloakroom attendant would force the ones behind the Msomi shooting out in the open remains to be seen. O'Donovan's thoughts were interrupted by a hand on his shoulder and a voice at his elbow.

"Wake up, Pat," said Jules warmly. "I've been watching you for some time. You're like the guy who is here in body but not in mind. What's happening?"

"This Msomi case has got me going. There's so many

271

angles to it. I'm not sure we're any closer to who is behind it than we were when I first got involved in it."

"Did you hear the latest?"

"What?"

"Well, the captain and the commissioner are going to make a public apology to the Msomi family. The captain has framed a written apology. They're hoping it might help smooth things out, but I don't know."

"When is this supposed to take place?"

"Today, or tomorrow—you know the department. They want to get as much publicity out of it as possible. It'll probably be arranged with one of the local TV stations."

The weekend passed slowly for Fowler. When he arrived at the farm Sunday afternoon, he found Tom and Linda sitting around the flickering flames in a fireplace in the family room. He was welcome to spend the weekend at the farm. However, they planned to go into the city to a concert and would spend the night with friends and go to work from their friend's home. Shortly after the Sunday meal, Tom and Linda donned their rain gear, told Fowler to make himself at home, and left for the city.

Time passed slowly that afternoon. Switching on the television, he found a football game in progress. With a can of beer in his hand, he pulled off his shoes, stretched out, and let himself be entertained by the images that came across the screen. Although his eyes seemed fixed upon the TV, his thoughts could not long escape his musing about the Msomi case. There was the persistent feeling he was coming close to solving the shooting of Ambassador Msomi. He was convinced, more than ever, that Captain Levine was the key to the shooting, and something, he knew not what, was going to happen when he returned to the city, supposedly with the cloakroom attendant. The rest of the evening was spent plodding back and forth to the kitchen for a beer, putting another log on the fire, and watching whatever came up on the TV. It was late when he finally tossed his last empty can of beer into the wastebasket, turned off the TV, and went to bed. He spent a restless night, waiting for the start of a new day.

19

Daniel Msomi's Dream

Fowler lay in bed well into the morning, listening to the patter of rain on the roof. He was in no hurry to return to the city. Dragging himself out of bed, he dressed leisurely, fixed a cup of coffee, and sat at the kitchen table listening to the news before deciding it was time to leave.

The all-night rain had left the dirt driveway a river of mud. He hurried to his car, picked up a stick, and scraped mud off his shoes before entering the car.

Fowler drove in the slow lane of traffic on his way into the city, his thoughts keeping pace with the flip-flop of the windshield wipers. He considered going to his apartment or to his office, but quickly discarded both choices. Until he could get in touch with O'Donovan, it was probably safer to stay away from familiar places. He stopped at a small café in Rosslyn for breakfast. Before entering, he called Sheia and arranged a meeting for eight o'clock that evening. A quick call to O'Donovan resulted in setting a meeting at the Old Post Office that afternoon.

He sat at the table, sipping coffee long after the waitress had removed his used dishes. Finally, deciding he could no longer sit and drink coffee, he paid his bill and left to join others who had a need to brave the elements. He drove slowly around the Lincoln Memorial and stopped briefly to watch the visitors hurry up the steps to face the figure of an earlier president looking down upon them. Fowler did not expect to see any of his contacts out on such a day. Most of them would manage to find some place dry and warm. With a shrug, he continued along the south end of Potomac Park and around the Washington Monument. Deciding there was no point in driving around in the rain, he turned in the direction of the Old Post Office.

Although it was still early for his meeting with O'Donovan, Fowler parked, placed a press card on the dash board and joined the steady stream of office workers and others filing into the building. Tired of coffee, he got a soft drink. Cup in hand, he circled the room until he found a table in one of the corners away from the main flow of traffic, with a view of the entrance. On most days, there would be few empty tables at that time of day. However, the weather had put a damper on many who had their lunch in the Old Post Office. There were plenty of empty tables. Fowler took off his raincoat, spread it on a chair, and waited for O'Donovan. In the meantime, he resorted to one of his favorite pastimes, people watching. Shortly after three o'clock, the familiar figure of O'Donovan entered the building. He saw Fowler's raised hand and made his way to the table.

"Been here long?" greeted O'Donovan.

"Not too long. Grab a seat."

"How about a cup of coffee?"

"No, thanks. I've had enough coffee for the day. I'll do well to finish this Coke. Go ahead and get one for yourself if you want to."

When O'Donovan came back, he brought a cup of coffee and a sandwich.

"Thought I'd better get something to eat as well as drink," he said as he set cup and plate on the table. "It's been a busy day and this is my first time to relax."

O'Donovan munched his sandwich slowly, with an occasional sip of coffee. Finished, he pushed the cup and plate aside and leaned back in his chair.

"Anything new at the precinct?" asked Fowler.

"You mean about the Msomi case?"

"Yep."

"The captain and I went to see what we could get out of Candy. Briefly, very little. As a matter of fact, she, he, take your pick, accused you of setting her up. Claims you planted the gun in her purse when she went to the bathroom."

"I'm sure you and the captain didn't go for that bullshit!"

"I'm not sure about the captain. He was pretty pissed off when he found out you were involved in the arrest. I don't think I've ever seen him so mad. He threatened to have your license, since he told you to stay out of police business."

"What about Candy? What else did she say?"

"Just what I've told you. She clammed up and wouldn't answer any more questions without her lawyer. I found out later the guy representing her comes from one of the fanciest and most expensive law firms in the city. I don't think we'll be able hold her much longer."

"How did Captain Levine act?"

"What do you mean?"

"Did he seem to you to act unusual in any way?"

O'Donovan reflected for a few moments before answering.

"I can't say I noticed anything unusual about him. We went back to his office, and he had me put in a couple of calls, trying to reach you."

"Was he still under the impression I was out of town

picking up a witness?"

"As far as I know, yes. He never mentioned anything about it one way or another."

"Where is the captain now?"

"Hard to tell. He left the station before I did. When I went to get into my car, I noticed his car was gone. He must have had some personal business to take care of. If it had been official police business, he would have taken a squad car. He's a stickler for keeping personal and official business separate."

"He must have had a meeting with someone pretty big. I wonder who it might be."

"Recently, the captain has been seen with a well-known senator. I wouldn't make much of that. He's also been seen with other politicians."

"Who knows? Joseph Msomi must have stepped on some pretty big toes."

Other than some general comments, there was little more of consequence discussed by the two men.

With a "see you later," O'Donovan was the first to leave.

It was still several hours before Fowler was to meet with the Msomis. He sauntered around the lower floors of the Old Post Office his thoughts upon Captain Levine. Where was he? What was the personal business so important that he had to go out on such a rainy day when he could have found plenty to do in his office? An image of Homer's Creole Cookery flashed into his mind. Slinging his raincoat over his shoulder, he trudged toward the exit of the building.

Fowler drove methodically to Homer's place There were only a few cars in the restaurant parking lot. A slow night, he thought, but given the weather, it wasn't the best of nights to be outside.

His thoughts about the Msomi case prevented enjoying the food placed before him. He did not know what to expect. He was sure that the captain, knowing he was going to Mexico to bring back an important witness, had to make some kind of move. Yet, O'Donovan hadn't noticed anything suspicious about Captain Levine. It didn't add up. Could it be he was wrong about the captain all along? Even as this thought entered his mind, he rejected it.

Fowler finished all be was going to eat and was waiting for the waitress to bring his check, when his senses became fully alert. A young white man, he judged to be in his late twenties, entered the restaurant wearing a trench coat and folding an umbrella. Fowler watched him carefully as he peeled back the collar of his coat, but did not remove it. That seemed strange, since it was quite warm in the restaurant. When the waitress came over to Fowler's table, he spoke in a low voice.

"Ever see that guy in here before, the white dude who just came in and is sitting at the counter?"

The waitress turned and gave the young man a close look.

"He doesn't look familiar to me. I don't think I've ever seen him in here before."

"What did he order?"

"Some ribs and baked beans, to go."

At that moment, the youth turned and scanned the room, his eyes quickly moving from one person to another. When he had taken in all the room, he slowly swiveled his stool around as he waited for his order to be prepared.

The thought struck Fowler that he should leave before the fellow sitting at the counter did, just to play it safe. He called for his check and waited for the waitress to follow through on his request. Out of the corner of his eye, he checked to see if the youth was watching him. It did not appear so. He paid for his meal and headed for the exit and his car.

Fowler quickly started the engine and drove out of the parking lot. He made a U-turn and parked across the street from the restaurant where he had a good view of the entrance and waited. A few minutes later, the object of his attention emerged from the restaurant and hurried to his car. He drove out of the parking lot, turned south and soon disappeared from view. Fowler breathed a sigh of relief, made another U-turn and was on his way to the Msomis. As he drove, he kept a sharp watch out for anyone possibly following him. After a few blocks, he relaxed and listened to the sound of the windshield wipers as he drove leisurely to Sheia's apartment.

"T.J. Fowler, here to see the Msomis." The security officer silently perused a daily log sitting on desk.

"Oh, yeah, here it is. Fowler did you say?" This elicited a nod from the other. "Go on in," said security as he pushed a button opening the locked door leading toward the elevators.

Fowler entered an opened elevator and, moments later, walked down the hallway on the twelfth floor to the Msomi apartment. When he got to the door of the Msomi apartment, he found it open.

"Come on in," called Sheia from somewhere in the back of the apartment. Fowler closed the door and stood quietly in the small hallway. Shortly, she came out dressed in a colorful African robe.

"Security let us know you were on your way up. My father is in the living room. You may go in while I fix you a drink. Gin and tonic, right?"

"Right," replied Fowler as he proceeded to the living

279

room. Daniel Msomi was sitting in his favorite chair, a newspaper folded across his lap. A drink of some kind was sitting on the table near him. He turned from looking out the window to face Fowler.

"Come in, Mr. Fowler. Come in," said Msomi in a pleasant voice. "Have a seat. I have some good news for you."

Sheia came into the room with a drink for Fowler and one for herself. She placed his drink on a table next to the sofa, indicating where he was to sit. Fowler wondered what news caused Daniel Msomi to be in such a good mood. He did not have long to wait for an answer.

"Truly a marvelous country, a marvelous country," began Msomi. "I had the most wonderful dream last night." He paused and looked away briefly, as if collecting his thoughts, or savoring his recollections. Fowler took a sip of his drink and waited. Sheia sat across the room where she could view both men.

"It was a very special dream," continued Msomi, looking beyond Fowler and seemingly wrapped up with reliving, what to him was a rewarding experience. "All the animals of the forest were assembled in a large clearing under a cloudless sky. A soft breeze floated over the gathering. It was a very solemn occasion, and many were crowding around trying to find space where they could get a good look at the proceedings. The meeting was conducted by a mature lion dressed in a magnificent robe He was surrounded by older lions as well as some young ones playing at the feet of their elders." Msomi paused to take sip from the drink at his side. "Unlike that stormy night Joseph's birth, when Mbondu made such dire predictions, the ancestral bones were laid out on a bark cloth in an orderly manner. The ancient ones looked upon the bones with pleasure."

"How is your drink?" asked Sheia, pointing to the glass Fowler was holding.

"Fine, I'm okay.

"Young and old became silent and turned as one to see a door open in the side of the hill," continued Msomi, hardly noticing Fowler or his daughter, as he narrated his dream. "A procession of lions streamed out of the hill and into the sunlight. First came the very old lions with their white manes dragging the ground and leaning heavily on their canes. In front of those who followed was a majestic looking young lion with a beautiful black-maned who seemed out of place among the ancient ones. They all took seats in the center of the throng, the black-maned one given a place of honor."

Msomi turned in his chair and looked out the window for several minutes. Fowler noticed tears slowly pick up speed as they flowed down the side of Msomi's black face. Sheia came over and put her hand on his shoulder. He raised his hand and covered hers, neither finding words to say. After a moment or two Msomi turned back to Fowler.

"It was an inspiring occasion," murmured Msomi, nodding his head up and down. "The love and respect given to that young black-maned lion was a sight to behold. The gifts piled up in front of him were too numerous to count. Even the ancient ones paid homage to him. The elders spoke of the many accomplishments of this young lion and how he was respected in lands far removed from his native village. At the conclusion of the meeting, the ancient ones got up and slowly made their way back into the hill, followed by those who came with them. The last one to leave was the honored lion. Before going in and closing the door behind him, he gave one last look at the throng gathered there. The applause was deafening and lasted long after the door to the hill was shut tight."

Msomi picked up his drink and gave every indication the dream was over. Sheia retraced her steps to her chair. For the next few minutes, there was complete silence in the room. Fowler tried to connect dreams and lions to a marvelous country. Failing to do so left him no choice but to wait for an explanation from his host.

"As you can see from the dream, Mr. Fowler, all our problems are over. Your investigation is finished. It was all foretold in the dream I had last night," declared Msomi.

"But I'm not quite sure I under—" began Fowler.

"It could not be any clearer, my good man," snapped Msomi, his voice rising at the opacity of the younger man. "All of those lions. The eldest ones were my ancestors. The young one was my son Joseph. His good name has been restored to him. That is what the dream tells us. He is now welcomed into the land of his ancestors. Did you not see the respect and honor given him by all present? One does not honor and respect those whose name is besmirched with sordid and nefarious activities."

"My father has not told you all that has happened," broke in Sheia. She nodded to her father to continue, which he did.

"Early this morning, the commissioner of police called me and set up a meeting later in the day at one of the local television stations, where a public apology would be given in the name of my son. In addition, the postman delivered a written apology from the commissioner's office early this afternoon."

"But what about the one, or ones, who are behind the murder of your son?" asked Fowler.

"That is of no concern to me. My only concern was

that my son's good name be restored."

"You mean you don't care about bringing the ones who did this to you to justice?"

"No! Nothing anyone can do now can bring my son back to me. His good name will live on as will his good deeds. Finding out who is behind this matter is something for the police department to handle."

Fowler changed the subject.

"What happened to that meeting you mentioned with the commissioner at one of the TV stations?"

Sheia answered, "It was canceled. Captain Levine was to be there with the commissioner. Apparently, the captain was not available. The meeting has been rescheduled for some time tomorrow night."

There was little of consequence relating to the Msomi case discussed during the rest of the evening. Fowler left shortly after ten o'clock, feeling frustrated and facing what he viewed as an incomplete job. *These Africans are strange,* he thought as he rode down the elevator. *They just don't think like most people.*

On his way to his car, his thoughts came back to Captain Levine. Where was he and what kept him from a meeting with the commissioner? It wasn't like the captain to miss a meeting, especially one with the commissioner. He had a hunch the captain was somewhere out there looking for him. Cold shivers started to zigzag up his spine. The first thing he did, once he got into his car, was to reach in the glove compartment and pull his gun out of its holster and place it upon the seat beside him.

Fowler sped across the city, his eyes constantly on the move between the street ahead and his rearview mirror. As far as he could determine he was not followed. Still, to play it safe, he drove past his apartment and parked a few doors away. He scanned the street in both directions and waited for anything unusual to happen. Five minutes or so later, he got out of the car and walked briskly to his apartment building, his hand on his gun in his raincoat. With one last glance up and down the street, he entered the building and hurried up the stairs to his apartment.

It was a long night, and what sleep Fowler got was fleeting and interspersed with periods of sitting up wide-awake trying to pinpoint a particular sound. Morning did not come soon enough for him. A call to his office failed to get his secretary. Still too early for her, he thought. Henrietta's arrival at the office coincided with the amount of work needed to be accomplished. Neither O'Donovan nor Captain Levine could be located when he called the 77th Precinct.

He gulped down a cup of coffee, dressed, and left his apartment, not without checking the street before hurrying to his car. There was little purpose to his driving, and he parked and shut off the engine at the Washington Monument without really knowing how he got there. He sat there, contemplating his situation, oblivious to his surroundings.

Just as he was about to start the engine and go somewhere else, he noticed a familiar figure. Hurrying across the parking lot under a nondescript umbrella that had seen better days was Rat.

Fowler rolled down the window.

"Rat, Rat," he shouted, "over here."

Rat quickly came over to the car, lowered the umbrella, and got into the passenger side.

"Rat, you skinny little motherfucker, what the fuck are you doing out in a day like this?" said Fowler. "I would think you'd be holed up in some dry, warm place with some cute broad to keep you company."

"No time for foolishness, m'man," was the quick retort from Rat. "As you know, communication is my business, and I'm on my way to the museum where I'm to meet a buyer." Giving a sidelong glance at Fowler, he remarked softly, "Since you stopped me and might make me late, maybe you could drive me over there?"

Fowler forgot his usual caution when dealing with Rat.

"Anything I might be interested in?" he asked.

"It's hot stuff, and I'm not sure you would be willing to pay the price. I've got a buyer for twenty-five bucks."

"Twenty-five dollars! What in hell kind of news have you got hold of that would be worth that kind of money? Besides, it probably wouldn't be anything that would be of interest to me."

"Yes, it would, m'man. Seeing it's you and a good friend of mine, I might be willing to let you in on it for less than the going price, say fifteen."

"Fifteen! No news you could ever get hold of would be worth that much." After a few minutes of haggling, Fowler agreed to a price of ten dollars. "Okay, okay, so what's the good news?" he said, handing the money to Rat.

Pocketing the money, Rat replied in a matter-of-fact voice.

"Someone wasted that captain of the 77th precinct. Levine, you know. You used to work there."

"What!" Fowler could not prevent from escaping his lips.

"Yep. They found him done in in his car on a road over in Maryland." Rat opened the car door to leave.

"Wait a minute, wait a minute," said Fowler sharply. "Where did you pick up this information?"

"It just came in on the radio," answered Rat as he

closed the door and hurried away.

At first, anger flushed Fowler's face as he thought how he had been taken in. But this was soon erased by a smile as he mused about how Rat had guessed he had not heard the news and saw this as a way to make a few dollars. He turned the radio on, but it was too early for any news. No luck on another call to O'Donovan.

Fowler reflected upon the questions raised by the captain's death. What was clear was that his only link to the higher-ups who pulled the strings was gone. Finally, deciding nothing could be gained by sitting in the rain at the monument, he slowly drove out into the traffic.

Fowler filled his day with a number of activities carried out in a mechanical manner. He went by his office to arrange to begin work on another case that had been placed on hold until he finished the Msomi case. Sheia left a message for him to call her as soon as he could. He called her and found out she wanted him to come by her apartment that evening around seven o'clock.

He arrived at the Msomis just as the evening news was about to begin. Daniel Msomi motioned for him to sit down, his attention fixed upon the television and the news announcer. Sheia came into the room with a tray of drinks. She sat, drink in hand, and followed the lead of her father in watching the news. The first part of the news was, as usual, given to the local crime wave, followed by the weather. The next picture on the screen was the one Msomi was waiting for. It was the commissioner of police and several dignitaries, and Daniel Msomi. The commissioner was speaking in his bombastic voice.

" . . . and the people of this fair city of ours are deeply apologetic for the dreadful wrong that has been fostered on one of our good friends from across the sea. The good name of his son, Ambassador Joseph Msomi, was blackened by allegations that he was somehow connected with the drug trade. Through the painstaking and diligent efforts of our police department, these base allegations have been disproved. A written apology has already been forwarded to Mr. Msomi on behalf of the department. We feel that no less than a public apology is required." The commissioner had a few more comments before the television station switched to another part of the news.

Fowler quietly watched his host slowly turn away from the screen. For a few minutes all three drank in silence as the news rolled on. Fowler wondered why nothing was being said about Captain Levine. He was sure the news of the captain's death was on the desk of all the news media. Suddenly, a special report came over the screen. Once again the commissioner of police appeared.

"My fellow citizens," he began in a solemn voice. "I have the sad duty to inform you that one of the most dedicated police officers I have had the pleasure to work with in my long years of service to this city, has been found shot to death on a lonely road in Maryland. The initial investigation points to foul play. Captain Levine was a professional, and that could be said without dissent from anyone who has ever worked with or under him. It is surmised he was getting close to resolving a particularly odious case that has been vexing the department for some time." The commissioner held forth for several more minutes before being replaced by other news.

Later that evening, Fowler said good night to Sheia and her father. He stood outside on the steps of the building and gazed at a moon that ducked in and out of the fleeting clouds. For him, the Msomi case was a closed episode, but he was left feeling empty. Once again, someone higher up had managed to escape the tentacles of justice, and there was nothing he could do about it.